THE VEILS OF VENICE

The Urbino Macintyre series from Edward Sklepowich

THE VEILS OF VENICE

An Urbino Macintyre Mystery

Edward Sklepowich

severn
House

This first world edition published 2009
in Great Britain and in the USA by
SEVERN HOUSE PUBLISHERS LTD of
9–15 High Street, Sutton, Surrey, England, SM1 1DF.
Trade paperback edition published
in Great Britain and the USA 2009 by
SEVERN HOUSE PUBLISHERS LTD

British Library Cataloguing in Publication Data

Sklepowich, Edward
  The veils of Venice
  1. Macintyre, Urbino (Fictitious character) - Fiction
  2. Americans - Italy - Venice - Fiction 3. Murder -
  Investigation - Fiction 4. Venice (Italy) - Intellectual
  life - Fiction 5. Detective and mystery stories
  I. Title
  813.5'4[F]

ISBN-13: 978-0-7278-6778-0   (cased)

All Severn House titles are printed on acid-free paper.

Typeset by Palimpsest Book Production Ltd.,
Grangemouth, Stirlingshire, Scotland.
Printed and bound in Great Britain by
MPG Books Ltd., Bodmin, Cornwall.

For Pamela Kinnunen, dedicated animal rights activist, who is greatly missed by her family and friends

The murderer is right in this room. Sitting at this table. You may serve the fish.

The Thin Man

Prologue
Blessedly Dead

Urbino Macintyre gazed from the windows of Florian's at the Piazza San Marco, beautifully bereft on this late afternoon in January.

Snow, a somewhat rare and treasured event in Venice, was falling on the large sociable space.

It was laying a white carpet in the great square for the shivering pigeons, cushioning the steps of the arcades, powdering the face of the zodiac clock, and quickening the rosy brick of the Campanile as the flakes swirled around like confetti.

However, nothing was more transformed than the square's most impressive resident. The Basilica, with a sifting of fresh snow over its domes, horses, and Gothic carvings, resembled nothing less than some strange and improbable oriental confection – and one that only the privileged few were savoring.

'Dead, dead, blessedly dead,' murmured Urbino's companion, the Contessa da Capo-Zendrini.

Soon enough, however, the madness of the carnival season would descend on the city.

Urbino and his good friend were cozily ensconced in the Chinese Salon, surrounded by its paintings, bronze *amorini* lamps, maroon divans, marble tables, gilded strips of wood and burnished parquet floor that had become so familiar to them. To make the experience even more pleasant, they were the only occupants of the room – that is, if one did not count the contessa's white cocker spaniel Zouzou, who lay asleep at her feet on a small blanket.

'Eufrosina is late,' the contessa said. She was referring to her cousin, Eufrosina Valle. The contessa was organizing an exhibition of clothing and accessories designed by Mariano Fortuny, which would be held at her palazzo in May. She had commissioned Eufrosina, her distant cousin, to take photographs for the catalogue. The contessa was basing her faith in Eufrosina's ability to make an important contribution to the exhibition primarily on the woman's photographs of hands, which had received praise a few years before.

The contessa had spent the past six months contacting friends, the friends of friends, dress designers, museum curators, and anyone appropriate in her wide circle to lend her their Fortuny gowns, scarves, and purses. It was one of the most ambitious projects she had yet been involved in, even though she was confining her search for Fortuny items to the Venice area, since the Spanish textile designer had made the city his home. The contessa planned the exhibition as a celebration of the designer and his beloved, adopted city.

What had encouraged the idea was that Urbino's new biographical project in his 'Venetian Lives' series was devoted to Fortuny. He had helped design the catalogue, which was only waiting for Eufrosina's photographs, and had written an introduction.

'The weather must have slowed her down,' Urbino said.

'I suppose so. Or any number of crises at home.'

Eufrosina, a widow, lived with her mother, her younger brother, and three cousins in a once elegant but now run-down building in the Santa Croce area.

'Yes, it's a strange household,' Urbino said. Over the years the inhabitants of the Palazzo Pindar, all of them related to the contessa through her English side, had seldom failed to surprise and even, on occasion, shock him with their eccentricities, and Urbino, it must be said, had a high, proud tolerance as well as a self-indulgence himself in the eccentric.

'And it may be even stranger than we think.' The contessa gave a slight frown and seemed about to add something. She placed a dollop of clotted cream on a morsel of scone and handed it to Urbino.

Urbino knew the contessa too well not to notice that she was nervous and preoccupied. It was not only the way she had been searching the Piazza for any sign of Eufrosina but also the troubled look in her eyes. It had already been fixed there when he had seated himself beside her in her motorboat, and on the ride to the Molo he had noted lapses of attention. She had stared at him blankly while he described the water damage done to the Palazzo Uccello by a recent storm, and he had repeated a question about the Fortuny exhibition two times.

She fidgeted with the blue and green silk scarf that was draped around the shoulders of her black dress. The large rectangular Knossos scarf, printed with Cycladian shapes, was one of Fortuny's most famous creations. It shimmered and caught the light from the lamps, and seemed to have a vibrant, undulating life of its own.

'The scarf is in excellent condition, Barbara, given its years – like you and me,' he added with a playful smile.

The contessa was far from her first youth, and by no stretch of the kindest imagination could she be said to be still in her second. However, in compensation she had made that transition into the rarefied realm of the 'forever young'.

Although she had never divulged her age, and Urbino had never used his biographical skills to uncover it, she had to be twenty years older than his own middle forties. Nevertheless, with her slimness, excellent bone structure, and almond-shaped eyes that radiated warmth, intelligence, and good humor, she could easily pass for someone only a few years older than he was.

One must not ignore, in the interests of complete honesty, however, the role played by the application of art, which managed to leave few traces of great effort, at least insofar as Urbino could detect.

'In good condition? Well preserved, you mean,' the forever young contessa clarified, still fingering her scarf. 'Like us.'

Her faint smile had a trace of sadness.

'You seem distracted today, Barbara. Is something the matter? What do you mean that the Palazzo Pindar may be even stranger than we think?'

The contessa sighed. 'There *is* something the matter, *caro*. It's Gaby. She has the idea in her head that she's in danger, that someone is trying to kill her. Can you believe such a thing?' She gave a high, nervous laugh.

Gabriella Pindar, Eufrosina's first cousin, was the custodian of a small museum in the Pindar family palazzo.

'Someone is trying to kill her?' Urbino repeated. 'Surely she's imagining it. She isn't the most stable person, poor woman.'

Gaby had been suffering from agoraphobia for as long as Urbino had known her. And how many years was that now? At least twenty. She would not go within six feet of the building entrance, for fear that something would happen to her. It was always a vague, unspecified fear. The thought of leaving the house made her tremble. She had refused all attempts to get her to seek professional help.

'True, far from the most stable person,' the contessa agreed, 'but nonetheless, we shouldn't dismiss it. I know she has closer relatives than me, but I feel a responsibility. You'll be spending time at the Palazzo Pindar.'

Urbino would soon start going through letters that Fortuny had written to Gaby's great aunt – who was also Eufrosina's great aunt. They now belonged to Eufrosina's widowed mother, who insisted that no one take them out of the Palazzo Pindar, at least not while she remained alive. Urbino needed to read the letters before he left for America in February to tend to some long neglected family business that involved property in New Orleans. He would be going right before the start of carnival.

'You can keep your sharp eye on things while you're there,' the contessa suggested. 'Maybe you can determine if it's just Gaby's condition speaking or if there is something more serious to it. I certainly don't think she's in any danger,' she added quickly, although her eyes remained troubled. 'But you will have the opportunity for soothing her. She's a gentle, vulnerable soul. By the way, I didn't learn about Gaby's fears directly from her. But I can't go into detail now. Here comes Eufrosina.'

Muffled in a checkered scarf and with snowflakes glistening in her auburn hair, the contessa's cousin was hurrying past the Chinese Salon. Her head was turned toward the square and the opposite row of arcades.

'I'm not sure if Eufrosina knows,' the contessa said. 'I don't think she does. And it is not my place to tell her. You know how that family is.' Her tone – part affectionate, part bemused – was the one she often used when referring to the Pindars. 'I'll explain everything to you tomorrow.'

Urbino agreed to come to the Ca' da Capo-Zendrini at ten in the morning.

Eufrosina walked over to their table in long strides. She was an attractive, willowy woman of forty-five. Much of the joy and grace and beauty of her Greek namesake had left her decades ago, though her light blue eyes still had some of the sparkle of her earlier years.

'Excuse me for being late.' She was flushed and slightly out of breath.

'Who counts the time on such a lovely day as this?' the contessa said, as if straw-colored sunshine flooded the Piazza. 'It might seem strange, my dear Eufrosina, but snow makes me feel more reborn than the spring.'

'I can't say the same for myself. Mother and I can't shake our bronchitis.' Eufrosina's English was British-accented and flawless, like that of all the members of her family. She put down her satchel and took out a lace handkerchief from the pocket of her brown swirl coat. She produced a raspy cough. 'Remember that your place is warmer and snugger than ours.' She loosened her scarf and unbuttoned her coat, but she kept on her gloves of beige kid.

'I hope that you and your mother will recover soon,' the contessa said. 'How is Alessandro?' Alessandro was Eufrosina's brother.

'Oh, he hasn't succumbed yet. I doubt if he will. He never seems to get ill. He lives a charmed life.'

'Good for him.' The contessa patted the space beside her on the divan, where Eufrosina seated herself. Zouzou awakened, looked up at Eufrosina, and returned to sleep.

The waiter came over. Eufrosina and Urbino ordered sherry and the contessa got a fresh pot of the first flush jasmine tea that Florian's stocked for her.

They spoke about the snow and the recent boat races for the Epiphany, which Eufrosina said she had photographed from San Tomà. She kept darting glances across the square toward Caffè Quadri. The conversation had just turned to the Fortuny exhibition, when Eufrosina exclaimed, 'Oh, there's Mother and Alessandro.'

She had gone very white.

Her mother Apollonia and brother were walking across the square from the direction of the Campanile. Apollonia Ballarin made a striking figure against the snow in her almost six feet of height and her uniform sweep of black clothes. The wind blew her black veil behind her and pelted her with snow, but she strode on with determination. It seemed as if she were guiding her son.

'Mother shouldn't be out, but today is Father's birthday. She always celebrates it with a Mass, a visit to the cemetery, and a Fernet Branca at Quadri's.'

Caffè Quadri was less fashionable than Florian's, which was the main reason why Eufrosina's mother preferred it. Urbino suspected that she also associated Florian's with the contessa, who, in her opinion, was too worldly for her own good.

Eufrosina grabbed her satchel and took out photographs of Fortuny's studio in the San Beneto area of the city. She dropped one of them in her haste. The photographs would appear in the catalogue along with Urbino's descriptions of the studio and Fortuny's working methods.

She handed each photograph to the contessa. She seemed unable to keep her eyes away from her mother and brother, who were approaching the opposite arcade.

The contessa passed each photograph to Urbino as soon as Eufrosina started to hand her another. There were photographs of the main façade of the palazzo, its courtyard, and various views of the studio and the library.

Urbino became increasingly disappointed as he looked at one after another. The photographs were mediocre. In most of them, the lighting was poor. Some of Eufrosina's photographs of hands, which had once been exhibited at the family museum at the Palazzo Pindar, had been accomplished, but Urbino feared that she was not up to her new project.

It was evident that the contessa, her lips pursed slightly and avoiding Urbino's eyes, had the same impression. She tried to handle the situation diplomatically, but she ended up damning the photographs with faint praise. Eufrosina had a stricken look. She saw the contessa's generous sum slipping away from her. She gathered the photographs together and put them back in her satchel.

'Do you mind, Barbara?' she said. 'I promised Mother that I'd meet her at Quadri's.'

She was afraid of offending the contessa, who was writing the checks and who was obviously not pleased with the recent specimens of her work. But she was also afraid of offending her mother, who demanded that her two children be at her beck and call and who held a large future inheritance over them. Apollonia dominated every aspect of her children's lives, even disapproving of Eufrosina marrying again, believing that marriage was forever, even beyond the death of one's mate.

'Please go to her, Eufrosina. Perhaps they'd like to join us,' the contessa added politely. 'It would – '

The entrance of a short man in his late thirties, his blond hair neatly barbered, interrupted her. It was Alessandro, Eufrosina's brother. His belted tweed coat, which reminded Urbino of one his grandfather had worn, reached below his knees and gave off a musty smell as if it had been kept in a damp, airless closet. He had a smug look on his good-looking, spoiled face and cold amusement in his blue eyes – eyes that were almost the same pale blue as his sister's.

'Still here, Eufrosina!' he said after bestowing little more than a cursory greeting on the contessa and Urbino. 'Mother is getting impatient. She asked me to come fetch you. You understand, I hope, Barbara?'

'Perfectly, Alessandro. Today is a special day for your mother. I would not want anything to be any different from the way she always likes it to be. Eufrosina and I are finished for now, aren't we, dear?'

The contessa gave her a warm smile, which Eufrosina returned with a look of gratitude as she got up from the divan, clutching her satchel close to her side.

'I'm ready, Alessandro. Let's not keep her waiting any longer.'

'*Now* you're thinking of that. Thank God that you have me to remind you of time and schedules, or else Mother wouldn't speak to you for weeks. Be more aware!'

Eufrosina had become ashen under her brother's criticism.

'It's all my fault for having distracted Eufrosina,' the contessa said. 'Please give our regards to your mother. And tell her that we hope she'll be completely well soon.'

Eufrosina nodded and followed Alessandro out of the room.

'Yes, the photographs were mediocre,' the contessa said as they watched the brother and sister walk across the square. 'I don't know what I'm going to do if the new ones aren't much better.'

'It might be a good idea to see if another photographer would be interested in doing the work.'

'There's a thought.' The contessa's face was clouded.

'I have someone in mind.' He named a photographer who had his studio in Dorsoduro. 'I can contact him if you want. I'll make it clear that it's only a possibility.'

'Let's hope we won't need him.' There was little conviction on the contessa's voice, however. 'It would be such a disappointment for Eufrosina. And it would put a strain on our relationship. But at least there's a kill fee in the contract.'

Now that the two of them were alone again, Urbino was eager to return to the subject of Gaby. But before he had a chance to mention it, one of the contessa's friends from her days at the Venice music conservatory joined them. She was a soprano who had long since retired and who was lending a Fortuny purse to the exhibition.

The two women slipped into reminiscences, doing their best to include Urbino, but he allowed his mind to drift in the direction of Gaby and the occupants of the Palazzo Pindar as he looked out at the snow falling silently, softly down on the Piazza.

And what fell over him, just as silently and softly as the snow, was the conviction that he was on the verge of another one of his cases. He accepted it with a sense of inevitability and with a familiar frisson of apprehension and pleasure.

Part One
Death and Fortuny

One

Despite a gray astrakhan hat, a Moroccan blanket with geometrical designs, and a heavy black wool cape, Urbino was feeling the cold in every part of his body as he sat inside the *felze* of his gondola. Yet he loved every minute of it.

His heart went out to Gildo, however. The young gondolier, who had added only one layer to his usual outfit, was exposed to the buffets of the icy wind as he guided the craft down the small, quiet canal in Santa Croce.

Yesterday's snowfall decorated the tarpaulins of the moored boats, the edges and steps of the canal, the window ledges and eaves, and the bare branches of a tree that overhung a garden wall. Urbino was glad that the snow was lingering. He hoped that the city would see at least one more snowfall, bigger than this one, before the winter was over. When it snowed, the child came out in him, bringing memories of winter visits to his mother's cousins in Vermont.

On their way across the Grand Canal from the Cannaregio, he had noted with pleasure the relative absence of tourists. Urbino hated crowds, and the crowds he hated the most were the ones that flooded the city during the summer, armed with cameras, knapsacks, and plastic bottles of mineral water. He felt a kinship with the few tourists he saw today. He liked to think of them as travelers rather than tourists. They stood on the bridges and at the rails of the waterbuses, gazing around them with what seemed a pure sense of appreciation.

'Are you sure you're all right, Gildo?' he called up to the gondolier, the vapor of his breath making a cloud in the small shuttered cabin.

Gildo's laughter floated down to him from the poop.

'I am more than all right, Signor Urbino.' Gildo's English had greatly improved during the past two years. He always insisted that Urbino speak English with him. 'I am warm, not cold. Remember that I was the one to ask to take out the gondola today. And you know that it is my sport.'

Last September Gildo had participated in the Historical Regatta on the Grand Canal. He and his teammate had come in fifth, just missing the green ribbon. It had been an amazing victory for two rowers competing for the first time in the event.

Urbino never felt really at ease when he was out in his gondola, and not only because of Gildo's labor. The contessa's gift, given on the twentieth anniversary of their friendship, drew too much attention to him. In fact, this morning, shortly after the gondola had slipped out of the Grand Canal and into Santa Croce, a Venetian woman had called out from the parapet of the bridge, '*L'americano!*'

It was a familiar cry. Although the woman could not see him inside the cabin, she knew who it was. Urbino's gondola was the last private one in the city, and his was even more conspicuous because of the *felze*. Gondolas no longer attached them in inclement weather or in any kind of weather at all. They had become a thing of the past. And by now, the handsome, vigorous Gildo with his curly, reddish blond hair was well known as the eccentric American's gondolier.

What pleased Urbino about the gondola, however, even though he disliked the scrutiny and jokes, was the mood it invariably induced. Reflective, calm, and, yes, he had to admit it – with another twinge of conscience to accompany his guilt about exposing Gildo to the weather – privileged. He especially enjoyed the gondola when he was in the *felze* and could observe without being observed. He was particularly grateful for this advantage as the gondola approached a building that loured above him.

'Stop here a few moments, Gildo.'

It was the Palazzo Pindar. Since yesterday at Florian's when the contessa had told him about Gaby Pindar's fears for her life, the building had taken on a different dimension. Urbino still had no doubt that the Palazzo Pindar was a house of whimsy and eccentricity, but could it be one of danger as well? In his two lines of work, Urbino had been in many strange buildings and households in the city, but the Palazzo Pindar was certainly one of the strangest. And now it was about to be a place of work in both his lines.

He had visited the Pindars with the contessa, and on a few occasions he had made solitary tours of its little museum. He had also accompanied the contessa's maid Mina when she went to collect dresses from Olimpia Pindar, Gaby's older sister, who had a dressmaking atelier in the attic.

The Palazzo Pindar was located in the part of the Santa Croce district embraced by a long curve of the Grand Canal. The baroque building had an almost abandoned air. Thick chains secured two large rusted metal doors in front of the broad water steps. The shutters on the windows had long since passed the time when they needed to be repaired or – in most cases – replaced. Patches of stucco had detached themselves, exposing the bricks beneath. The glass in one of the bull's-eye windows was cracked. The buildings on either side of the huge tumbledown palazzo were in good condition and only served to make their neighbor look more dilapidated.

But the Palazzo Pindar was magnificent in its neglect, and its shimmering reflection in the greenish-gray waters of the small canal deceptively restored much of its former beauty.

A tall woman emerged from the mouth of the *sottoportico* beside which the gondola had come to a halt, and walked briskly along the embankment toward the palazzo. At first Urbino thought that it was Eufrosina, because of the figure's height. But it was Olimpia, her cousin. She was wearing a knee-length ocelot coat and a red-and-black cloche hat.

She had her eyes cast down. When she reached the small wooden door that the Palazzo Pindar now used as its entrance, a voice called out her name loudly from the direction of the bridge at the other end of the canal. A middle-aged woman in an alpaca poncho with purple and lilac stripes stood on the parapet of the bridge. Urbino recognized Nedda Bari, who did local charity work.

Olimpia had started slightly at the sound of her name, but she didn't acknowledge the greeting. She went inside the building, without having to ring or use a key, for the door, as was the custom of the Palazzo Pindar, wasn't locked.

With an irritated expression on her face, Nedda Bari stared at the building for a few moments before leaving the bridge and disappearing from view down a nearby *calle*.

'All right, Gildo,' Urbino said. 'The Danieli.'

Before seeing the contessa at the Ca' da Capo-Zendrini as they had agreed, Urbino needed to make arrangements at the Hotel Danieli for a visitor. It was his ex-brother-in-law, Eugene Hennepin, with whom he would leave for America next month. Eugene preferred to stay in a hotel and wanted to return to the Danieli, which he had been pleased with during his first visit to Venice ten years ago.

Gildo started to manoeuvre the boat in the direction that would take them back into the Grand Canal.

Two

The contessa checked the clock on the mantle of the morning room. Urbino should be coming in less than an hour. A strong fire crackled in the fireplace with wood from Asolo where the contessa had a villa.

'Tell me again, Mina,' the contessa insisted. 'Exactly what did Signorina Gaby say to you?'

The contessa wanted to be sure of what Mina had told her. Urbino would want every detail.

A look of impatience, touched with irritation, passed over the pretty features of the contessa's personal maid, but they were quickly banished. Mina, slim and dark-haired, with delicate, porcelain features, had just celebrated her twenty-fifth birthday. The contessa always tried to be careful of Mina's feelings, knowing how high-strung she was. The palazzo staff thought that she favored Mina. She supposed she did. It was a weakness she usually succumbed to with her personal maid, whoever she was. In the case of Mina, the habit was more pronounced. The girl was as endearing as she was efficient, and she had a quick intelligence and a light sense of humor, although none of the latter was in evidence on this occasion or, for that matter, the contessa realized, had been for the past few months.

'She said that someone was trying to kill her.' Mina, whose Italian was marked by a Sicilian accent, lowered her voice when she said 'kill'. She stared at a small table with a collection of ceramic animals as if she were studying them. 'I didn't believe her. But she seemed frightened.'

So did Mina. When she turned her eyes to the contessa, they were wide and unblinking.

'When did she tell you this?'

'Last week when I brought Signorina Olimpia the dress material from you.'

Whenever Mina spoke with the contessa about Olimpia Pindar she was always formal even though the relationship between the two women was intimate. The contessa pretended she did not know the particular nature of the relationship even though Olimpia had confided in her and even though it was evident to most people who had even limited contact with the two of them. It had begun about seven months ago. The contessa feigned ignorance for Mina's sake, and not because she disapproved of the relationship although, in her mind and in conversations with Urbino, she called it a 'romantic friendship'. Mina had never given the slightest indication that it was something she would like to have directly acknowledged.

'Did you mention it to her?'

Mina did not respond right away. When she did, it was in a rush of words.

'I told her the same day. She wasn't surprised. She said that I shouldn't worry about it, that her sister was strange, and that she imagined things. Signorina Gaby *is* strange, contessa. She never leaves the house. I don't think she even looks out the window. And she sometimes just stands at the door of the museum with a sad expression on her face, staring at nothing. She frightens me.'

'Many unfortunate people have her kind of problem. There's no harm in it to you or to anyone else. But why did you decide to tell me what she said?'

'Because I'm afraid that Signorina Olimpia is wrong! Sometimes when we are close to someone, living in the same house day after day, we can't see what other people can see. Do you understand?'

The contessa did, and she knew why Mina said this. From what the contessa had learned about her from the young woman's cousin in Venice, she had suffered from emotional problems when she was an adolescent, and her large family in Palermo had neglected her. The cousin, now dead, had agreed to take Mina in nine years ago.

'She is very upset,' Mina went on. 'I felt it even before she said anything to me.'

Mina touched the region of her heart. In the year that she had been working at the Ca' da Capo-Zendrini, she had given the contessa several examples of her sensitivity to the feelings of others. She could easily identify delicate shades in the contessa's moods and would respond accordingly.

'Has she spoken to you again?'

'No, but when I see her she looks at me in a pitiful way, as if she wants me to help her. I don't know why she told me! I'm afraid she will give me the evil eye. You are relatives, contessa. Relatives must help each other. You are a kind lady. Maybe you can do something. But please do not tell Signorina Olimpia that I told you. She might be upset with me.'

'I'm sure she wouldn't be, Mina. She would understand that you've told me because you're worried for her sister. But I won't say anything to her.'

The contessa considered this to be promise enough. It did not include Urbino. Mina showed a reluctance to pursue the topic and asked to leave shortly afterward. She said that she would take Zouzou out for a walk although she had walked the cocker earlier that morning.

When the contessa was alone, she sat on the sofa staring at the painting on the opposite wall, going over what Mina had just told her. In substance, it was exactly what Mina had told her before. The contessa went over to a lacquered cabinet. She took out an old photograph album that was piled with others on the bottom shelf. She returned to the sofa and paged through the album until she reached a section devoted to the Pindar family.

She looked at a photograph of Gaby. It was one of the few photographs of her cousin in the album, and it had been taken more than twenty-five years ago. It showed a pretty, bright-eyed young woman standing in front of the Basilica arm in arm with her older brother Ercule. She seemed so happy, but this had been before her illness descended on her. She had little joy in life these days. But beneath all her fears and confusions must lie the Gaby that used to be. If only she could be released from the prison of her dark thoughts and emotions.

'You obviously don't want to believe she's in danger,' Urbino said half an hour later as he stood in front of the fireplace warming himself. 'And I know why.'

'Why?'

But the contessa did not need to ask. She knew what he was going to say but dreaded hearing it put into words.

She cast her eyes down at one arm of her chair, as if she were intent on examining the spot where Zouzou had ripped the Fortuny fabric.

'Because if there's any basis to Gaby's fears,' Urbino responded, 'it means that the danger will come while she's in the house. She hasn't left it in years, and she's unlikely to do it now, not unless she seeks help. If she's afraid, she's afraid of someone in the house. And *that* means,' he emphasized as he seated himself in the armchair across from the contessa, 'that she's in danger from someone in her own family, someone in *your* family.'

The contessa was caught out. Urbino had quickly seized upon the main reason for her reluctance to believe Gaby was in danger. The probability was that harm would come to her from someone in the family. And it had become clear to the contessa, after many years of Urbino's sleuthing, that people were most often in danger from those closest to them.

'You're right,' she admitted. 'My family.'

The contessa felt a sharp, familiar ache as she said the word. She and the conte had not been able to have any children, something they both had greatly hoped for. It made her value what family she did have, even family as remotely related – and uncongenial as they sometimes could be – as the Pindars.

'But there's a big flaw in your reasoning, *caro*.' She turned to him with an air of triumph. She had been caught and now she was catching him out, and enjoying it. 'You know how ridiculous they are in that house – or should I say how foolish – the way they leave the front door unlocked during the day. They are so infuriating, so perverse! She could be afraid of someone from outside harming her. It would be all too easy to get inside, at least during the day.'

The contessa had little patience with the Pindar custom. It went back to one of the earliest Pindars who had been a monk and insisted that the building be kept open for anyone who needed food or shelter. However did Gaby put up with the arrangement? But perhaps she was out-voted by her sister and brother.

Urbino nodded. 'True. But logic may be of little help in trying to figure Gaby out – or any others among your distant relatives. And without logic I'm almost at a loss. Actually, I have never been able to fix the Pindars clearly in my mind – their history, I mean. I suppose I've had no need to before now. I know things in bits and pieces, and I certainly have my impressions, but it would be helpful to have the whole picture, or as much of it as you can give.' He played a few random notes on the *fin de siècle* Viennese piano. 'Why not tell me what you know and not leave anything out because you assume I know it? Even with that, there will be holes that we'll probably have to fill in later, but we don't know what those holes are now or where they are.'

'That's the problem with holes much of the time, isn't it? You don't know where they are until you fall into them. Oriana might be able to help us with some of them.' She was referring to her friend Oriana Borelli, who seemed to know more about the private lives of others than anyone else in the contessa's or Urbino's circle. Oriana's knowledge, in which romantic and sexual intrigues played a prominent role, had come to their aid before. 'But she won't be back from Cortina for about two weeks.'

'Is she there with Filippo?'

The contessa smiled. Oriana had a well-earned reputation – as did her husband Filippo – for an ongoing series of affairs that did not weaken their marriage but somehow strengthened it. 'Let's say that the two of them went there together. Whether they went their separate ways once they got there, I have no idea.'

Urbino reseated himself. 'So what do you know from your own chaste perspective?'

'There is a lot of territory between the chaste and Oriana,' the contessa observed. 'I can speak to the family relationships involved. They are always important when you want to understand people. It's a longish story. Well, as you know, the Pindars and I are related through my mother's side of the family. Her mother – *my* grandmother – had a sister named Isabel. She came to visit American friends who had rented a palazzo by the Accademia Bridge. Like you and me, Isabel never left. She met Federico Pindar, the only son of a family that had made a fortune from shipping in the eighteenth century. They had their own shipping company, Pindar Lines. It doesn't exist anymore. Like much of what the Pindar family had back then, it's disappeared. Federico swept her off her feet. He was almost twenty years older than she was, and everyone thought he was never going to marry. When I met Alvise, my mother said that I was following in the footsteps of her aunt, since Alvise was twenty years older than I was. Alvise –' The contessa broke off. Her mood, which had been vivid and gay with the story she was telling, darkened. Tears welled in her eyes. 'Listen to me! This is not about Alvise, but the Pindars.'

'I understand. Your wedding anniversary is coming up. He's on your mind.'

'I wish you had known him, *caro*.'

Alvise had died three years before she had met Urbino.

'I feel as if I know him well. Through you. And everyone who speaks of him has a high regard for him and his memory.'

She gave Urbino a smile of gratitude. 'Alvise knew the Pindars before we married. He called them the "merchant family with the soul of poets." Because of their name. The family has always claimed they are related to the Greek poet, but I doubt that. Their name used to be Pindaro but the "o" got lost somewhere back in the eighteenth century.'

She took a deep breath and continued with her story. 'Their fortunes started to decline right after the First World War. About ten years after Isabel married Federico. The shipping company expanded to Turkey, and had offices in Istanbul and Izmir. Once Federico's father died, he made bad business decisions. Federico and Isabel had three children – two sons, Socrate and Platone, and Apollonia, the youngest of them. You know how the Pindars are with their old Greek names! The eldest, Socrate, had more business sense than his father did, but he died of some disease he picked up in Turkey. He wasn't even thirty. By the time the Second World War was over, all that the Pindars had left was their palazzo in Santa Croce.'

The contessa sipped her caffelatte. 'That's the family that Olimpia, Gaby, and Ercule were born into. Their father was Platone. They had another brother, the eldest, Achille. He was more practical than they were, a throwback to his dead uncle Socrate. And he died young like him, too. Only in his thirties, and when he was starting to turn the family's financial situation around. Olimpia, Gaby, and Ercule inherited the house and the collection – and whatever other assets their parents had. Each got an equal portion. From what I understand, if one of them predeceases the others, his or her portion is divided equally between the survivors. That's the way their wills are made out, according to what Gaby once told me.'

Urbino's face was screwed up in concentration.

'I know there's quite a bit to absorb in all this,' the contessa said. 'Especially for the only child of only children. Sharing inheritances, siblings, cousins, nephews, and aunts. Poor boy! You've got no family to speak of.'

'Don't sell me short, Barbara dear.' A smile replaced the concentration on Urbino's face as he said, 'Let me see if I have this right. Apollonia is the daughter of your great aunt Isabel. Your grandmother was *her* great aunt, which I think makes her your second cousin. And Achille would have been your great aunt Isabel's grandson and Apollonia's nephew, not to mention your third cousin – or would he be between a third cousin and a fourth? Your grandmother was his great aunt.'

Urbino's genealogical skills impressed the contessa, but even though she had thought she was rather clear about the relations in the family, she felt more than a little confused by his nimble negotiation of the branches of the family tree. '*Bravo!* And much simpler to say that the Pindars and I are distant cousins.'

'And this same Achille, distant in his cousinship,' Urbino went on, 'died in a boating accident with his parents. That's something I know. It was a few years before I settled here.'

'Yes. He was engaged to be married. He went out in a sailboat with his father Platone and his mother – Regina was her name. They sailed away from the Lido. A storm blew up. Their bodies weren't found for several days. Everyone was devastated. And not just Olimpia, Gaby, and Ercule, but Apollonia, too. She had lost her brother as well as her nephew. And Eufrosina had a hard time. She seemed to think of Achille more as a brother than a cousin. Much closer to him than she was to her own brother, but Alessandro was a hard person to warm to even back then.

'After the drownings, things got even worse financially for Olimpia, Gaby, and Ercule – and of course Gaby slipped into her terrible condition. Their money has just kept dwindling over the years. Olimpia might make enough to keep her going, and Gaby has hardly any expenses. As for Ercule, I don't know if he has ever had a steady job. He's indulged himself, dreaming of faraway places. They could sell the building. The upkeep alone must be a strain on them. It would bring in a lot of money, but the three of them aren't in agreement about it. I assume that Gaby doesn't want to sell and have to leave. Either Ercule or Olimpia must disagree with her – or possibly both of them.'

'I assume they're bringing in something from the rent they get from Apollonia.'

'Not much, I don't think. And not as much by far as Apollonia is saving by living there, from what I have heard. She is getting a great deal of money from renting out her building. She's a clever woman, Apollonia. The family should put her in charge of finances.'

Apollonia, who was in her late seventies, had managed to put away a large fortune. Her reputation for miserliness, at least at this point in her life, was legendary in the family.

'And I doubt if the museum takes in much,' Urbino observed.

The family had accumulated a small collection of objects and paintings over the years. There were some fine pieces, which could fetch a good price if the family could agree about selling them. So far they hadn't been able to agree.

'In all the times I've been there, the most visitors I've seen are two or three,' the contessa said.

'That's been my experience. But Gaby doesn't seem to mind. She's as proud of it as if it's the Accademia.'

'Sometimes I think it's what keeps her going. I don't know what would become of her without it, although maybe if she were cured, she wouldn't need it anymore. They each have something to occupy themselves, even if they don't make much money from it. Gaby has her collection, Olimpia has her atelier, and Ercule has his dreams. Gaby, Olimpia, Ercule, Apollonia, Alessandro, and Eufrosina. A strange group.' The rip in the Fortuny fabric drew the contessa's eyes. 'All under the same roof these days.' She got up and went over to the sofa. 'Come sit next to me. I'll show you some photographs.'

For the next fifteen minutes they looked through the album.

'She was such a pretty young woman,' she said, indicating a photograph of Gaby in the Piazza San Marco. 'And filled with joy. Look at her expression! Who would have thought she would come to be imprisoned in the house the way she is?'

'Did something trigger it?'

'I don't know. It began not long after her parents and Achille died. That could have been what did it. And there was the usual talk of a failed romance, a man who jilted her. Her condition wasn't severe at first. She just started to become more and more withdrawn, preferred to be by herself. By the way, she wasn't always called Gaby. When she was much younger, up until after Achille died, she was called Ella. Gabriella, Ella, you see. Then she became Gaby. Why she changed her name, I don't know. I could have asked. But there's something about the Pindars that makes you feel uncomfortable asking personal questions. They're all very closed in on themselves.' She turned to the next page of the album. 'These are of Ercule.'

Urbino smiled as he looked at them. He was fond of Ercule, and the contessa knew why. It was because of Ercule's particular brand of eccentricity. He had said a few weeks ago that one of the things he was looking forward to when he would be going through Apollonia's Fortuny letters was the opportunity it would provide to spend some time with Ercule.

'Look at this one.'

It was a black-and-white photograph of a pale, moon-faced young man dressed in the robes and turban of a Turkish pasha. Ercule still affected these outfits. In the photograph he sat on a cushioned divan in a café and smoked a nargileh. Men in flowing moustaches were seated at a nearby table playing cards. It had been taken in Istanbul many years before. Ercule had been in his early twenties.

'Ercule and his Turkey!' the contessa exclaimed. 'He sent that photograph to everyone he knew. He spent several months there. He's never returned. I think he looks a lot like Alessandro here, don't you? The same round face. Well, most of the Pindars resemble each other, more or less. I took the photograph below it,' the contessa went on. The same pale man, though now dressed in a suit and tie and looking a littler older, stood on Westminster Bridge with Big Ben in the background. 'The classic tourist photograph. He insisted. The three of them – Ercule, Gaby, and Olimpia – all came to London one summer when I was there.'

It all seemed far away now. It belonged to the time when she was recuperating from Alvise's death. It seemed that there were so many reminders of Alvise these January days. But were these days very different from any others? She realized she had given a sigh when Urbino turned to look up at her.

'Are you all right?'

'Nothing wrong with a little melancholy, as you well know,' she teased him.

Urbino's melancholy was one of his most appealing traits. And he would never have decided to live in Venice if he hadn't been its chronic victim.

'Here's Olimpia and Gaby in Trafalgar Square.'

The two sisters stood by the fountain with the National Gallery behind them. Olimpia was a few inches taller and a few years older, but the family resemblance was unmistakable. Both young women had narrow faces, the Pindar blue eyes, and an abundance of reddish blond hair that seemed on fire in the sunshine.

'They look so English,' Urbino said.

'Ercule as well. And look at this one of Achille.'

She turned the pages of the album until she found the one she was looking for. The photograph had been taken in front of the Palazzo Pindar.

Achille was in his late twenties. Dressed in flannel trousers and a tweed jacket, he stared into the camera with a smile in his blue eyes. His sandy-colored hair was tousled by the wind.

'He was very good-looking, as you can see,' the contessa said. 'And he was one of the few tall Pindar men. Most of the others have been on the short side, like Ercule.'

Urbino examined the photograph closely. 'You're right, he does look English.'

'It must be the combination of the Venetian and English blood. The two strains reinforced each other.'

'And they're so English in other ways. Your great aunt Isabel seems to have put a strong stamp on the family.'

'And each generation has cultivated it. But sometimes I wonder if there's going to be a next generation for the people in that house. If Achille hadn't died, he would have married, but that wasn't meant to be. Eufrosina never had any children.' The contessa quickly got this out of the way and hurried to say, 'It doesn't look like Olimpia is going to go down the marriage aisle. Ercule is a confirmed bachelor if I ever saw one. And Gaby? No, not unless a great deal changes in her life. Maybe Alessandro. He's the youngest of them. But he'll have to get out from under his mother's influence. She would have to approve, and she's hard to please. The girl would have to be the next best thing to a nun.'

'Do you know who Achille was engaged to?'

'Someone named Nedda Ferro – I should say Nedda Bari now. You know her.'

'Nedda Bari?' Urbino told her that he had seen her earlier near the Palazzo Pindar. 'She seemed to want to talk to Olimpia, but Olimpia ignored her. Is there bad blood between them?'

'I don't know.'

'Isn't Bari renting Apollonia's building?'

'Yes. Maybe it had something to do with that, though what Olimpia's concern in it might be, I have no idea.' The contessa turned a page of the album and pointed to three photographs of Apollonia.

In one of them Apollonia stood in the Campo San Giacomo dell'Orio in front of the church, where she went to Mass every morning and evening. After many decades of throwing herself into the world, Apollonia had become religious twenty years ago – religious to a fault, in the contessa's opinion. It was as if, almost overnight, her cousin's milk of human kindness and waters of gladness had been pumped out of her. Urbino only knew this new Apollonia, who still struck the contessa as peculiar, even like an imposter. She sometimes thought that her cousin's conversion was a compensation for something she had done in her younger years, something she was deeply ashamed of, but what this might be, the contessa had no idea.

The photograph of Apollonia showed a tall, thin, aged figure, with snow-white hair, wearing a long black dress. She clutched a black Spanish shawl around her shoulders. She was not more than a decade older in the photograph than the contessa was now but she looked considerably older than that, or so the contessa liked to think.

Another photograph of Apollonia was the kind of close-up that made the contessa cringe, but Apollonia looked bravely into the camera. A piece of old black lace wrapped her head, showing no hair. The last time the contessa had seen Apollonia with her hair exposed had been more than a decade ago. The photograph had been taken at a restaurant in Dorsoduro during the Feast of the Redeemer seven years ago. Urbino had been with them at the time. As he had remarked on several occasions, Apollonia was one of the few people he knew who treated the festival as the religious celebration it was.

Urbino was examining the photograph now, and the contessa could tell that he was comparing it to the third photograph. This one showed Apollonia when she was about the age of Eufrosina. It had been taken at a ball at the Ca' da Capo-Zendrini. Apollonia was smiling almost mischievously into the camera, her head tilted back. She was elegant in a Fortuny gown in red with gold details, colors she would not be caught dead wearing these days. The Fortuny had belonged to her aunt, Efigenia, her father's sister, who had died at an advanced age after a long illness a few months before her brother and his wife had drowned. Like the letters, the Fortuny had passed to Apollonia. Efigenia and her husband hadn't had any children. It was Fortuny's letters to Efigenia that Urbino would soon be reading. The dress was one of the items that Eufrosina would be photographing, a thought that made the contessa feel a surge of renewed anxiety about Eufrosina's ability to do a good job.

'She was truly exquisite,' Urbino said. 'A real beauty. You can see the traces of it in the photographs from the Feast of the Redeemer.'

'Traces, yes.' The contessa remembered something that Greta Garbo supposedly once said: 'The hand moves over the face every ten years . . .'

A discreet knock sounded at the door. It was Vitale, her major-domo. In his deep voice he announced, 'Signorina Olimpia Pindar is downstairs, contessa. She expressed the wish to speak with you.'

The contessa and Urbino exchanged a quick glance.

'Please have her join us.'

*   *   *

The contessa had last seen Olimpia the month before at her atelier in the Palazzo Pindar, when Olimpia had put one of her prized possessions – a Fortuny purse – directly into her hands. It had belonged to her grandmother, the contessa's relative, Isabel. On that occasion, Olimpia had seemed buoyant and filled with quiet assurance. She had recently received a commission from a theater group in Venice to design costumes for a Goldoni production.

This morning, however, the older Pindar sister's face was tense and drawn although her face lit up, it seemed, when she saw Urbino. Her eyes, which were a deeper blue than those of her cousins Eufrosina and Alessandro, had dark smudges beneath them.

She was an attractive, vivacious woman in her early fifties with a narrow face, a large mouth, and the impressive height of almost all the Pindar women. Her chin-length reddish blond hair, showing few traces of gray, was in disarray. She was wearing black trousers and a long, ocelot coat.

Vitale must have asked her if she wanted to take off her coat and she had obviously declined.

'What a pleasant surprise, Olimpia. You don't stop by at all as much as I would like you to. Please sit down.'

'No, thank you. I'll only be staying a few minutes. I'm happy to see you both together. I won't beat around the bush.' Her English, like that of all the Pindars, showed no trace of an accent and every facility in the negotiation of idioms. 'I know that Mina told you what Gaby said to her, Barbara. And I know' – she turned to Urbino – 'that Barbara told you.'

Because Olimpia was so sure and so correct, the contessa did not attempt to protest.

'Mina promised that she wouldn't say anything to you, Barbara, but it came over me as I was making a sketch an hour ago that she had.'

'Mina is –'

Olimpia broke her off. 'I know,' she said. 'Mina is kind. Considerate. A gentle soul. She has a sensitive heart. That is how I realized that she had said something. She wouldn't be Mina if she hadn't.'

'Exactly,' the contessa agreed. She glanced at Urbino, who was still standing and was looking at the two of them with an unreadable expression on his face.

As Olimpia continued, she paced the room, putting the contessa, understandably influenced by the ocelot coat, in mind of a large cat.

'Gaby likes to get attention. I love her, but it isn't a good idea to humor her. She has to face reality. I worry about her. Ercule does, too.' There seemed to be true concern in Olimpia's voice. 'Poor Gaby is in no danger from anyone but herself. No, I don't mean she'd do anything to harm herself, but the way she's afraid of everything and doesn't try to change no matter what I say to her – no matter what anyone says to her – it's self-destructive, isn't it?'

'From what I understand,' Urbino said, following Olimpia with his eyes as she moved around the room, 'Gaby has an emotional condition that – '

'I realize that, and I sympathize with her.' Olimpia came to a stop in front of a collection of watercolors. 'She's my little sister, don't forget! I wish we could have the old Gaby back. But we know her better than anyone else does. And I know her better than Ercule. It would do more harm to her to take seriously this – this nonsense she is spreading around. If we all just ignore it, it will go away and some other strange idea will take its place. No one means her any harm. She knows that. Gaby doesn't have an enemy in the world. You won't help her, either of you' – she swept them both with her eyes – 'if you give any credence to what she said.'

The contessa wondered if Gaby had been saying things to anyone else in addition to Mina. Olimpia had just said that Gaby was 'spreading around' her fears of being in danger.

'What you say could be true, Olimpia, but it's all the more reason why you should try to get her some professional help.'

'Ercule and I know that, and you've tried yourself. You see how resistant she is. Ercule and I have hopes that we will eventually be able to persuade her. But we are not about to cart her off against her will. We know our sister well. So when you come to our house, Urbino, please don't think that you have to put on your stalker's cap.'

She gave a laugh that was more like a whinny, in which the contessa heard the release of a great deal of tension. But Olimpia's face remained as tense as before, and the smile that spread across it now drew even more attention to her agitated state.

'Whatever time I spend in your house,' Urbino said, 'is going to be spent reading the letters Fortuny wrote to your great aunt Efigenia.'

Once again, Urbino's command of the relationships in the Pindar family impressed the contessa.

'And I assure you,' the contessa said, 'that I only have Gaby's best interests at heart. We are all cousins, aren't we? And you can consider Urbino family, too. We have all adopted him, haven't we, just as he's adopted Venice? Everyone means well, and that is what is important. Mina cares a great deal about you, and because she cares about you, she cares about Gaby. That is why she told me. You shouldn't be upset with her.'

'Did I say that I was upset with her? I think I said the opposite. I under-stand her very well. Better than anyone. I don't fault the dear girl in any way.'

'Most interesting,' the contessa said after Olimpia left. 'Needless to say, she's quickened your interest.'

'Definitely. And I'm not so sure that that wasn't exactly her intention.'

Three

'You can take them downstairs to the museum,' Apollonia Ballarin said to Urbino the next morning in her *salotto* in the Palazzo Pindar. She and her two children lived on the second floor, with Eufrosina and Alessandro, below Olimpia's attic atelier and above the Pindar *piano nobile*. 'There's no place for you to read them here. You'd be in the way.'

Unlike the Pindar siblings, Apollonia Ballarin made a point of speaking in quick Italian with everyone who had any knowledge of it. As she spoke, she looked at him directly and held herself straight and stiff as she always did, conveying a sense of imperial authority.

The once beautiful woman was dressed completely in black and had a black lace veil draped over her shoulders, as if she kept it ready to draw over her head and face at any required moment. Her customary piece of black lace wrapped her head, showing not one strand of her white hair. Gloves of black kid sheathed her hands. They were certainly warranted by the cold of the room, which had only a small space heater. But perhaps they were one of the woman's last vanities, intended to conceal her age-spotted, wrinkled hands.

Apollonia was tall and thin to the point of emaciation, and today she looked more gaunt than usual, probably the result of her bronchitis. Urbino sometimes thought that she took most of her nourishment from her daily morning communion. If it were not a sin to have communion twice in one day, she would surely have indulged herself.

But the elderly Apollonia, whose skin was as white and dry as parchment, would be unlikely to deviate from the straight and narrow path that she believed was bringing her to her heavenly home — even if someone had held a pistol to her head. She would have considered dying as a martyr a wonderful end to a life that had been one of great excess until her donning the equivalent of sackcloth and ashes fifteen years ago.

A faint ammoniac odor hung on the air of the large room. Faded frescoes adorned the walls, and it was over-furnished, even cluttered, with a preponderance of religious objects — small wooden statues and portraits of saints, rosary beads, prayer books, and missals. Two corners were devoted to plants — pots of twisted cacti, sickly looking aspidistra, sharp-leaved mother-in-law tongue, and, high on the wall, a huge spider plant whose browned tips dangled and groped a few feet above the floor.

Apollonia's lawyer, Italo Bianchi, was standing across from his client, who occupied a sofa upholstered in heavy damask fabric with a pattern of *fleur-de-lis*. Did Bianchi's presence mean that Apollonia was going to ask Urbino to sign a statement that he had the letters in his possession for a few hours? A briefcase, unclasped, lay on the floor beside the sofa. Bianchi, as short and round and pink a contrast to his client as there could possibly be, was also the lawyer for the Pindar siblings and the contessa.

Apollonia did not ask Urbino to sit down. When she gave a curt nod to Bianchi, he went over to an armoire and removed a white lace covering from a little shagreen box. He handed the box to Urbino.

'I'll take good care of them,' Urbino assured Apollonia. 'This isn't the first time I've dealt with valuable documents.' Even more valuable than these, he didn't add.

'But it is the first time you are dealing with Signora Ballarin's documents,' Bianchi said in the excruciatingly slow Italian he affected whenever he spoke to someone who was not native to the language. 'They are as precious as relics.'

'Don't be sacrilegious!' Apollonia's voice was firm and disapproving. There was cold fire in her blue eyes. 'Mariano Fortuny was no saint. I would have burned the letters if my aunt had not cherished them. I'm letting him look at them in her memory.'

And for a generous sum, Urbino said to himself. He was not in the habit of paying for access to important papers but Apollonia had refused to share them with him unless he agreed to a non-negotiable fee. She might have put her soul on the path to heaven but she hadn't taken her eye off her bank account.

'And don't take them from the building and have them photocopied,' Apollonia warned.

'I have no intention of doing either. I'll treat them with all due respect.' Urbino got up. 'Let me get started. Excuse me.'

Urbino descended the marble staircase to the ground floor, which had once been a warehouse for the Pindar shipping company. The walls of the vestibule exuded an atmosphere of damp. Gaby was at the far end of the room by the heavily secured entrance to a small, rear courtyard. The Pindars were just as diligent about keeping the courtyard entrance barred as they were lax about keeping the front door open. Gaby's back was turned, and she was sweeping the floor with brisk, energetic movements.

She had greeted him when he had arrived, but she did not raise her head now from her work.

Two connecting rooms to the right of the embankment entrance were given over to the Pindar collection, which was accessible only through one door. The other door had been plastered over.

Two other rooms were directly across from the collection on the other side of the vestibule. Their doors had been painted blue once upon a time, but the color had long since faded. The contessa had told him that, as far as she knew, the rooms were usually locked.

Urbino entered the first room of the museum and came to a halt a few feet from the door.

The room, like the one beyond it, was crammed. The museum had a motley collection of objects. Among them were old carved chests with gilt ornamentation, heavy wooden armchairs, Turkish tiles, shells and fossils, carnival masks, a Doge's baton, antique cooking utensils, an array of pens that the Pindar family had used to sign various business agreements, ledgers, musical instruments including an exquisite mandolin, a large seventeenth-century globe, a lamp from one of the ships of the Pindar line, small daggers, navigation charts, a small tapestry, a suit of armor, an Egyptian cat mummy partly wrapped in its winding cloth, and two oil paintings.

One of the paintings hung on the left-hand side of the door into the second room. It was a large portrait, by a Bolognese painter of no renown, of the ancestor who had started the family on its upward climb in the seventeenth century, Creonte Pindar. His severe, pinched ascetic look and the sharp blue eyes staring at the viewer in a superior manner, along with a monkish fringe of black hair, gave him more the appearance of a member of the clergy than a merchant.

The other painting, which occupied most of the space on the right side of the door, was a Gabriele Bella. It depicted a procession in the Piazza San Marco following the election of a Doge. It was similar to one at the Querini-Stampalia Gallery near the Campo Santa Maria Formosa. It was probably the most valuable item in the collection.

In no way had the Pindar family been astute collectors, and a large number of the objects were the gifts of business partners and clients in Italy, Greece, and Turkey. Many of the objects were little more than curiosities.

The collection was displayed in cases and cabinets, affixed to the walls or propped against them, hanging from the ceiling, and standing on the floor. The arrangement was haphazard. Descriptions for the objects were written on small slips of white paper in a spidery hand.

The black ink had become gray and the description was often indecipherable.

Urbino passed through the first room into the second, where a large carved wooden table with four chairs was set up in a corner. He placed the box of letters on the table and seated himself in one of the uncomfortable chairs. The room was chilly, as was the other one. The lack of proper heating in the winter and of air-conditioning in the hot weather must be slowly doing its damage to the objects.

Against one wall was a carved and gilded chaise longue, upholstered in a worn and faded pink floral pattern, which looked like something Marie Antoinette or the Marquise de Pompadour might have reclined in. A red woollen blanket was rumpled at one end of the sofa. Gaby took her naps in the chaise longue during the long and many hours of silence when no one rang the museum bell. He also suspected that she often slept in it at night, finding comfort surrounded by all her treasured things.

Urbino took out a pencil, a sharpener, and a pile of white blank note cards from his satchel and laid them in front of him on the table. He opened the box. The letters, all on the same white paper, now faded, were neatly folded and stacked on top of each other. The envelopes were no longer with them. Had they been lost? Destroyed?

'You've come back down quickly,' Gaby said. She was standing beside the doorway at an angle that gave her a view of both rooms and the door into the vestibule.

Gaby, with her long face, large mouth, and reddish blond hair, closely resembled her sister, but she was heavier by about twenty pounds and her blue eyes were slightly hooded. Almost as tall as Olimpia, she habitually kept her shoulders hunched and her head slightly pulled down. She had once been as attractive as her sister, but her emotional problems had taken their toll on her face, which was heavily lined. She had a death-like pallor, as a consequence of having stayed inside the house for the past two decades.

He did notice, as he had on other occasions, that Gaby never had her back turned to the entrance of a room for longer than necessary. Her eyes had a habit of surveying doorways and she never went closer than five or six feet to the main entrance out to the *calle*, even when admitting visitors.

She wore a gray smock-like dress that almost reached her ankles. An indigo-colored scarf was wrapped around her throat, and pulled down on her long, unkempt hair was a small red woollen cap that vaguely gave her the look of a female cardinal. A damp, musty smell wafted from her that reminded Urbino of the scent that her cousin Alessandro's clothes had given off at Florian's the other day.

She screwed up her face and managed to get a handkerchief to her nose a second before the sneeze came, followed in rapid succession by two others.

'God bless you,' he said. 'I hope you don't mind that I'll be spending some time in the museum. I will try to keep out of your way and out of the way of visitors. I think you know that I'm reading letters that were written to your relative Efigenia. They were written by – '

'Fortuny!' she shouted, cutting Urbino off and startling him.

The name echoed off the walls.

He was about to say that the letters were indeed from Mariano Fortuny when Gaby showed that her enthusiasm wasn't limited to identifying the Spaniard so vociferously, but that it had been the prelude for one of her favorite games. It was a word game.

'Fort! Rot! Turn! Urn! Nut! Your! Our! For! Or! Nor! Toy! Run! To! On! No! Not! Fun!' The words rushed out of her. Gaby was in one of her excessively energetic phases, which alternated with periods of almost complete lethargy. This particular word game probably gave her a needed feeling of control.

When she recaptured her breath, she said, 'Fortuny's a good one! Who would think that there are so many words in only those seven letters? Oh, I forgot two. Tour! Runt! I think that's the end.'

She was filled with energy today, but she would fall, unfortunately and inescapably, into her other state tomorrow or next week, maybe later today. Whenever it would be, it was as inevitable as were these excited, light-hearted states. Probably she had confided in Mina in one of her dark and down moods.

'Give me another word. Please!'

'Gabriella,' he said.

She frowned. 'That's too easy. I've done it many times.'

'What about Mina Longo?'

She stared back at him. Her face broke into a smile.

'A very good name! *Two* names. How clever of you.'

She took a deep breath, but before she could utter one word concealed within the names, a man's hearty voice called out, 'It's you, Urbino! I heard voices. I thought that we had a visitor at our little museum. It has been a long time, hasn't it, Gaby dear?'

It was Ercule Pindar. His moon-shaped face was open and candid, with the Pindar blue eyes almost always twinkling behind his round, gold-rimmed glasses.

Gaby ignored him, took an orange-colored rag from her pocket, and started to rub the freestanding globe in quick movements.

Ercule, who was portly and short, wore an oversized dark brown wool coat. A thick black scarf was wound round his throat. His large coat pockets bulged. If Urbino had been forced to bet money on what was inside them, he would have said that they were books – and not only books, but exotic travel volumes and most probably about Turkey. The Pindar family's connection with that country and the Venetian Republic's long relationship with Constantinople had ignited his interest years ago. It was still burning strong and bright.

'Yes, it's me. I have some work to do here.' Urbino indicated the box of letters. 'I'll be working so silently everyone will think I'm one of the exhibits.'

'If anyone comes by to notice. Gaby wanders around all by herself most of the time. Just her and the things, and not one solitary soul putting down any money. These things are not doing anybody any good. There are better ways to make money from them.'

Gaby stiffened. He smiled with unmistakable affection. It was possible that both Olimpia and Ercule were engaged on a program of not coddling their sister, as Olimpia had warned Urbino and the contessa against doing. But Ercule's comment struck Urbino's ears as cruel. The museum meant everything to Gaby. Being parted from it would be a calamity.

'Those are Apollonia's letters,' Ercule said, turning back to Urbino.

'Great aunt Efigenia's letters,' Gaby corrected him sharply.

Gaby's respect for provenance amused Urbino. It was what you would expect of the curator of a museum, although Urbino doubted that she could provide the origin for even half of the objects in the Pindar collection, no matter how much she treasured and needed them.

'Right, Gaby,' her brother agreed. 'Great aunt Efigenia's letters. And that's great great grandfather Oreste's globe, dear sister. But it is ours now. Yours, Olimpia's, and mine, like everything else in our little museum. Oreste was before our illustrious association with Barbara's family, Urbino.'

The Pindar clan's fondness for the Italian versions of classical Greek forenames was one of their idiosyncrasies, but it was not consistently applied. It was like some uncontrollable impulse that struck Pindar parents in unpredictable attacks and could end up with comical results, as in the case of Ercule, who could not have been more different from his namesake.

Gaby put the cloth back into her pocket. She stood looking at Urbino and Ercule.

'Ask me where I am today, Urbino.' A mischievous smile played on Ercule's round face.

If Gaby had her word game, Ercule had his own little game. He frequently asked the same question, 'Where am I today?'

Urbino, who knew the answer because it was invariable, decided to give the appearance of mulling it over. He cast his eyes in the direction of Oreste Pindar's globe.

'Could it be . . . Istanbul?'

'Good! But to be more exact, let us say Constantinople *and* Istanbul.' He reached into one of his coat pockets and pulled out a book with the title *Imperial Istanbul*.

'Exquisite,' Ercule said. 'You see how I prefer the stones of Istanbul to the stones of Venice!' He slipped the book back into his pocket. 'Come by and visit me one of these days. We'll have a nice chat.'

'I'll leave you to your work,' Gaby said when Ercule's footsteps faded away up the stairwell. 'If you need anything, just let me know. I shall be in either the next room or the vestibule. I – '

The buzzing of the doorbell interrupted her. Her face brightened. 'Oh, my! The bell for the museum! A visitor! You've brought it good luck.' She hurried into the vestibule. '*Avanti, per favore!*'

Gaby was going through her usual procedure for admitting people to the building. She would cry out for them to enter through the unlocked door after they rang the bell. She never went to the door and opened it for anyone.

Low voices came from the vestibule. Gaby guided two middle-aged women, who spoke English with a German accent, into the first room. She described the objects in a voice that thrilled with notes of happiness. After the women had expended their curiosity over the cat mummy, they admired the Gabriele Bella before passing into the second room. Urbino picked up the first letter and did his best to create an air of industriousness. Perhaps their opinion of the museum would be higher if they thought that it held important documents.

Urbino suddenly felt protective toward the Pindar collection. It was a way of expressing his desire to protect Gaby from disappointment or something much worse.

When Urbino was alone, he started to give the letters his attention in earnest. Even given his methodical way of working, he should have no difficulty getting through them all before leaving for America.

The first letter, written in November 1925 from the Palazzo Fortuny in Venice, was a thank you for a dinner Efigenia had given Fortuny and his

Edward Sklepowich

wife Henriette. The occasion was a staging of *Saint Joan* at the Goldoni Theater. Fortuny's printed silk velvet had been used for the costumes and stage sets. Another letter from Venice, dated September 1928, had a pen and ink drawing of the Jemaa el Fna in Marrakech and referred to a Biennale exhibition of his sketches of Morocco and Spain.

The third letter had been written in January 1930 from Paris after Fortuny had been obliged to close his factory on the Giudecca because of the stock market crash. The factory produced cotton prints made on the innovative machines he had installed. Efigenia had offered him a sum of money to help reopen the factory.

Urbino made some notes. His handwriting was cramped due to the cold in the room. He found these details about Fortuny's formerly unknown relationship with Efigenia fascinating. They would help flesh out his portrait of a man he not only admired but also, in the humblest of ways, identified with. For there were some pale parallels to Urbino's own life.

Fortuny, like Urbino, had been born elsewhere, in Spain, but had fallen under the spell of Venice and had made it his home and the center of his work. He had bought a Venetian palazzo and renovated it to suit his special needs — although in Urbino's case the palazzo had been inherited. He had been a man of great curiosity, with a love of things Venetian and Arabic. But Fortuny, unlike Urbino who feared that he was something of a dilettante, had excelled in various domains. He had defied categories, being not only a textile designer and couturier, but also a painter, inventor, sculptor, set designer, theater director, costume designer, and photographer.

And he had been an eccentric — for example, dressing in summer clothes in the depths of winter and sporting a black Inverness cape — which only endeared him to Urbino's heart more, as the Pindars did.

Urbino unfolded the next letter, written in October 1931 in London, where Fortuny was working on a lighting project for the Royal Academy, but, chilled as he was, he had lost his concentration and returned all the letters to the box.

As he sat at the table, his eyes started to bring into focus an object in the collection that he had been staring at without actually seeing. As he took in its details, he realized that it was something he had not noticed in the collection on previous visits.

It was an oblong wooden box the size of a small vegetable crate. It was designed as a miniature stage. Constructed of dark wood and lacquered, it rested on its longer side on a shelf. On one side of the box, a piece of Fortuny fabric, pleated in the way that Fortuny had devised, simulated a theater curtain. It must have been cut from a much larger swath of material. Across the top of the box was a carved ornamental panel with 'Melponeme' and 'Thalia' painted in cursive gold letters. On the stage of this miniature theater were small carved and painted wooden figures. Urbino went over to examine them.

There were four figures, none higher than nine inches. It did not take Urbino long to identify them as caricatures of some of the house's residents: Olimpia, Gaby, Ercule, and Apollonia. They were lined up as if receiving an audience's applause after a performance. A delicately carved bouquet of white roses was at the feet of the Apollonia figure, painted flat black and holding a string of purple rosary beads. The black lace head covering that Apollonia wore all the time looked more like a snood and revealed a fringe of white hair.

Urbino picked up the figure representing Olimpia. It wore a yellow coat spotted with black: an ocelot coat.

Gaby's voice startled him. 'Alessandro!' He almost dropped the figure. He put Olimpia back on the stage. He waited for Gaby to start spouting the words lurking within her cousin's name, but instead she asked, 'Do you like the theater?'

'It's very well done.' He turned back to look at the figures. The whole effect was weird, but amusing. 'Yes, I do like it.'

'Alessandro is very talented. I told him he could put it down here. The museum hasn't had a new addition since my grandfather was alive.'

'Alessandro did it?' Urbino had not been aware that Apollonia's son was interested in woodcarving or carpentry. He had not been aware he was very much interested in anything. He was well past the age when he should have applied himself and found a job, but his main and only job seemed to be looking after his mother – and living off her.

'Yes, our Alessandro.' Warmth filled her voice. 'He's working on statues of Eufrosina and him. He wants to do the whole family of us under the same roof. He was so excited about the idea that I told him he shouldn't wait until he finished the others to put these on display.'

'How clever to have the names of the muses of both tragedy and comedy on the stage.'

'That was my idea! Neither one alone suits us. Our family has had both comedy and tragedy. Often at the same time.'

Gaby went over to the stage and picked up the figure of Olimpia. She rubbed it against her sleeve and replaced it, taking care that it was exactly aligned with the others as it had been before Urbino had examined it. She moved the figure of Ercule, whose roundness and spectacles had been exaggerated and who was wearing a long white robe, fractionally closer to Olimpia and away from the figure representing her. The Gaby figure wore a small red cap and a red scarf, and a gray, uniform-like outfit with pants.

Gaby started to dust Alessandro's theater with the orange cloth. Urbino bid her goodbye and brought the box upstairs to Apollonia. Bianchi was still there, sitting with her in front of scattered papers that looked like legal documents. She hardly said a word, took the box, counted the letters inside, and gave him a curt nod. It was his dismissal.

It seemed warmer outside the Palazzo Pindar than inside. Sunshine fell from a pale blue sky, and even though a cold wind was blowing from the Dolomites, it had an invigorating effect. Most of the snow had melted, but wherever it lingered, it maintained a purity that provided refreshing accents to the scene.

Urbino set out for the Campo San Giacomo dell'Orio. The *calli* were lively with local residents. Tourists seldom found their way into this area, even in the height of summer. In a few minutes, he was walking past the round-apsed church with its square brick campanile that dominated the large, but somehow secretive, square. Children, bundled up against the cold, ran across the stones and rode their tricycles.

He went into a restaurant beside the canal and ordered a plate of *tramezzini* sandwiches and half a liter of red wine. As he ate, he picked up a copy of that day's *Gazzettino* that someone had left on the table. He read the headlines, but nothing caught his interest. His mind was a jumble of many things, and they all centered on the Palazzo Pindar.

The contessa had asked him to keep his ears and eyes open. Olimpia's visit to the contessa, although apparently intended to quench any worries, had had just the opposite effect on him. His curiosity was fired even more.

The time he had spent in the Palazzo Pindar had brought a few revelations. Ercule had showed something other than his usually genial side by mocking Gaby's devotion to the collection and the absence of visitors. He had also made a point of emphasizing that the collection belonged to him and Olimpia as well, and not only Gaby.

As for Gaby, she was as troubled as ever, and her attachment to the family collection was one of the symptoms of her illness. Olimpia and Ercule seemed concerned about her, as well they might be, and they seemed to have genuine feeling for her. But Olimpia's dismissals of her fears of being in danger and Ercule's barbs suggested that their concern and feeling might be compromised by more selfish elements.

Gaby had confided her fears in Mina. Would she be inclined to confide them in him? He had known her for a much longer time, and there was his relationship with Barbara to recommend him further. By telling Mina, she might have hoped that Urbino and Barbara would become aware of her fears. There might be reasons she did not want to speak with either of them directly. Or maybe she had told Mina in the hope that she would say something to Olimpia, and not necessarily to Urbino or the contessa.

Urbino's thoughts returned to the collection, unusual in its inclusion of many disparate objects whose only reason for being together was that they were related to the Pindar clan.

The latest edition to the collection was one of the strangest of all: Alessandro's theater with the carved wooden figures of four living family members, and with those of him and his sister Eufrosina waiting in the wings to make their appearance. Was affection behind the curious effort? Or was it his intention to poke fun at his relatives by turning them into caricatures? Urbino was curious to see what Alessandro did with the figures of Eufrosina and himself.

Urbino finished his wine. Fifteen minutes later he was crossing the Grand Canal in the *traghetto* that ferried passengers between Cannaregio and Santa Croce. The cold wind whipped against his Austrian cape and his eyes smarted.

When the *traghetto* reached the landing at the Campo San Marcuola, he headed toward the Palazzo Uccello, which was in a quiet area of the Cannaregio between the Grand Canal and the lagoon. He kept going over Olimpia's visit to the contessa. She had seemed determined that Gaby's fears should be discounted. It had been the purpose of her trip, hadn't it?

But then Urbino, as he often did, considered the situation from the opposite point of view. This way of thinking often rewarded him with insights that might never have come to him otherwise.

Suppose Olimpia's whole purpose in coming to the Ca' da Capo-Zendrini had not been to influence the contessa to discount Gaby's comments but instead to take them more seriously? She had seemed pleased to find Urbino with the contessa. Perhaps she knew that her visit would have its devious effect more surely and more quickly because of his presence. She must know that she could count on his skepticism, given his experience as a sleuth.

Were Urbino and the contessa playing into her hands? What could her motive be? The Pindar family was fond of games, and this could be one of Olimpia's, and a very serious one indeed.

As Urbino crossed the hump-backed bridge by the Palazzo Uccello, another possibility, closer to his original one, occurred to him.

Maybe Olimpia was not so much clever in making the visit as she was desperate to put them off a scent.

Desperation or a game? Which of the two might it have been?

Four

The next day, after the contessa had taken lunch in the conservatory with only Zouzou as her companion, she waited for Mina.

Earlier, she had told Mina that there were two pots of orchids that she could have for her room. Mina had said she would collect them after the contessa had her lunch.

After the dishes were cleared away, the contessa walked around the conservatory, examining the plants. It was one of her favorite spots, especially in the winter. It looked very much the way it had when she had married the conte. An incongruous scattering of old sofas, chairs, footstools, small tables, and bookcases were set amidst the plants and flowers. Ivy twined in and out of the back of the cane sofa.

Zouzou, from her position beneath the cages of parakeets, kept looking toward the door to the hallway. The contessa felt that she was waiting for Mina, too. It was one of the times of the day when Mina walked her. Zouzou was solid white — or as solid white as a cocker spaniel could be bred. Unfortunately, whatever genetic manipulation had made her white had also made her partly deaf — a disability that endeared her even more to the contessa and Mina.

The contessa sat down in an upholstered chair between two potted palms and paged through magazines. When almost an hour had passed, the contessa went in search of Mina. On the staircase to the staff's quarters, she met Vitale.

'Have you seen Mina?'

'Earlier, contessa. But she hasn't come back yet.'

'Hasn't come back yet? Where has she gone?'

The major-domo raised his eyebrows ever so slightly. 'I have no idea. But she left an hour ago. I assumed she was going on an errand for you.'

The contessa, who was protective of all her staff and especially Mina, nodded her head. 'I'm sure she's doing something that she knows needs to be done.'

'Yes, contessa. Mina is a good worker, a good girl. None of us likes to see her upset.'

The contessa's heart started to beat more quickly. 'Did she seem upset?'

Vitale took a special pleasure in having everything run smoothly in the house. The contessa detected some uneasiness in him.

'She did. It was when she asked me if Signorina Pindar had been here recently. I told her that she had paid a visit the day before yesterday when Signor Urbino was here.'

'Thank you, Vitale. Would you please tell Pasquale that I'd like to go out in ten minutes?'

The contessa continued down the staircase with what she hoped was the appearance of a calm she did not feel. She felt a sense of urgency and anxiety. She needed to get to the Palazzo Pindar as soon as she could.

The wind insisted itself against the cabin of the motorboat as Pasquale manoeuvred it to the water steps beside the Palazzo Pindar. A few people hurried along the *fondamenta*. The attic windows of the building reflected the gray sky.

Pasquale guided the contessa to the pavement and watched her as she went up to the door of the building.

She was about to press the bell even though she knew the door was probably on the latch as usual. But even in the contessa's present state of mind, her sense of propriety was strong.

Before she pressed the bell, she noticed that the door had not been closed. Her immediate thought was that Mina had been in too much of a hurry to close it, for the contessa had no doubt that this was where the young woman had come after rushing from the house.

The contessa pushed open the door, slipped into the vestibule, and closed the door behind her.

The vestibule was chilly and silent.

'Gaby?' The contessa's voice echoed in the large space.

There was no sign of Gaby. The door to the museum was open and the lights were on. Perhaps she was taking one of her naps on the chaise longue.

On the other side of the vestibule, the blue doors were closed on whatever was inside.

The contessa ascended the staircase to the landing of the *piano nobile*. She didn't pause outside the Pindar *portego* though she threw a quick glance inside the large room with its high-backed, square chairs, broken chandelier, and flaking plaster.

She continued up the staircase to the story occupied by Apollonia, Eufrosina, and Alessandro. The door to their apartments was closed.

A low cry, like a cat in distress, broke the silence. The cry became louder. As the contessa hurried up the staircase, which was narrower here than below, the cry had turned into a howl. The door to Olimpia's atelier was open. She stepped inside.

Winter light poured through windows on the large open space.

Magazines, sheets of paper, a mannequin, tape measures, pins, ribbons, books, a lampshade, and fabric of various kinds, including a piece of Fortuny material in a floral design, littered the floor.

Olimpia lay on her back on the floor, surrounded by scattered Euro notes. Her eyes were open wide, staring sightlessly up at the ceiling. Blood seeped from her chest, staining her dove-gray dress.

Kneeling beside her was Mina. Her blue coat was still on. She turned a tormented face to the contessa. Tears ran down her cheeks. Her hair was disheveled.

'I killed her! I killed her!' She started the keening again.

In her right hand was a pair of scissors, with long blades, blades that were covered in blood.

The contessa moved forward a few feet, but stopped. The scissors remained in Mina's hand. The contessa felt ashamed, now and later, of her hesitation, but she remained rooted to the spot.

Footsteps sounded behind her.

Gaby stood in the doorway, her clothing rumpled. A few seconds behind her came Ercule, carrying a thick book, and then Eufrosina, with her coat thrown over her dress and held clasped at the throat by a pale hand. None of them ventured any closer than the doorway, taking in the bloody scene as Mina continued to scream, the scissors still in her hand.

A few moments later Apollonia, helped by Alessandro, joined them. As soon as Apollonia took in the scene, her lips started moving, but the contessa could not catch her words.

She hoped it was a prayer. The dead woman needed it. And so, the contessa feared, did both Mina and herself.

Part Two

Moving in Mysterious Ways

Five

Olimpia Pindar's funeral was held at San Giacomo dell'Orio, the church Apollonia Ballarin visited more in a month than Olimpia had probably visited in her whole life.

There were only a few mourners. Not even the funeral of her sister had been able to induce Gaby to leave the Palazzo Pindar. Among the family members it was only Apollonia, white-faced and peaked-looking and still suffering from her bronchitis, who seemed at ease – and not just at ease but as if she were entertaining in her own home.

Eufrosina, Alessandro, and Ercule, who sat with her, kept giving her side-glances as if they were following her cues.

Nedda Bari, who presumably would have been a family member if Achille had not died before they could marry, sat with two pews between her and the others. The heavy-set woman wore her alpaca poncho with purple and lilac stripes over burgundy-colored slacks.

Next to Bari was a thin blond woman in her thirties, whom Urbino had never seen before. Dark circles pocketed her eyes. She was wearing a worn cloth coat and a drab brown kerchief. When he asked the contessa whether she knew the young woman, she said that she didn't.

Also in attendance were Italo Bianchi, Savio Santo the family physician, two middle-aged women who had worked as seamstresses for Olimpia, and Natalia, Urbino's cook and housekeeper.

From the time Olimpia's body arrived in a plain wooden coffin, with four church workers as pallbearers, until it was brought out again and put into the motorboat that took it to the cemetery island, the whole service struck Urbino as rushed, although he could not say that the priest had omitted any of the customary prayers.

The air of Olimpia being rushed to her burial remained with him during the time of her interment on San Michele. Even her rest would be far short of eternal, Urbino thought as he stood with the contessa beside the gaping grave. For she had been put into one of the burial fields whose occupants would be dug up after a mere twelve years, at which time her remains would be put in a common grave. It was not always lack of money that dictated this fate, but often the shortness of memory and the waning of grief. Olimpia had left no instructions for a different kind of burial, having been taken from life abruptly and at a relatively young age. Neither Gaby nor

Ercule had made any effort to give their sister anything but the cheapest burial.

Although the contessa often assumed the burden of perpetual graves for family, friends, and staff, who would have been consigned to oblivion without her generous intervention, she had not yet made any arrangements for Olimpia.

Some delicacy and calculation influenced this decision because of the contessa's close relationship with Mina, who had been arrested for Olimpia's murder. If the contessa had rushed to assume all the burial experiences, it might seem as if she believed in Mina's guilt and were trying to compensate for her personal maid's brutal act.

Making things worse was that in Mina's statement to the police, she had insisted that she had killed Olimpia. But when Mina had been calmer and after she had consulted with the attorney the contessa had engaged for her, she had explained what she had meant. She had found Olimpia lying on the floor with the scissors in her chest. She had been alive then, grabbing at the scissors. Mina, in panic and confusion, had pulled them out. A few moments later Olimpia had died without uttering a single syllable but only a long sigh. Ercule, Gaby, Apollonia, Eufrosina, and Alessandro – all of whom said they had been in the house all day – claimed they had heard no arguments or any unusual sounds coming from Olimpia's atelier until Mina's screams had drawn their attention.

Despite Mina's revision of her confession, she had been charged with murder. Mina's fingerprints were the only ones on the scissors that could be positively identified. The motive was believed to be either jealousy, given the nature of the relationship between the two women, or robbery, considering the money found around and beneath Olimpia's body.

'I wish I could have done something for Olimpia now,' the contessa said half an hour after the burial. The two friends had parted from the other mourners and were on the path that would take them to another area of the cemetery island. The destination had become a ritual. It was the Russian and Greek Orthodox compound, where Serge Diaghilev was buried. The ballet impresario had been a friend of the contessa's mother.

'I feel so guilty,' the contessa said as they neared the brick wall of the compound. 'But I had to tell the police what Mina said.'

'The others told them the same thing, remember.'

'I still feel guilty. Maybe if I had told Mina that Olimpia had come to see me, this would not have happened. What I mean is that she would not have been there at all. Olimpia would still have been murdered, but Mina would have been safe with me in the house.'

Urbino gave her elbow a gentle, comforting squeeze through her gray wool coat.

They walked in silence toward the brick wall at the end of the graveyard. Beyond the wall, boats were making their way to Murano and Burano. Dark clouds moved over the water from the direction of the Dead Lagoon, unwashed by any tides. The Orthodox compound and the Protestant graveyard next to it were filled mainly with foreigners who had died in Venice and been buried there, far from their families.

'What a state Mina must be in! How terrible she must feel!' the contessa broke out, disturbing the quietness of the scene. 'How I wish I could see her.'

So far, the contessa had not been given permission to visit Mina at the women's penitentiary on the Giudecca. Mina's attorney was working on the problem, as was one of the contessa's friends, who had contacts with the Questura.

'Mina is so sensitive,' the contessa went on. 'God only knows how she's coping. Lanzani says that she's doing all right.' Giorgio Lanzani was Mina's attorney. 'But he doesn't know her. He can't read her the way I can.'

When they reached Diaghilev's grave, she said, 'Thank God there are some certainties in this life of ours. There will always be a slipper on his grave.'

A worn, mouldy ballet slipper lay on the simple tombstone. A spider had spun a web across its opening.

Small stones adorned the top of the memorial, placed by visitors in the Russian tradition. On the ground were a vase of red roses, flickering votive lamps, and a sheet of musical notation encased in clear plastic. Urbino picked the sheet up. He read aloud what was handwritten across the top in black ink: '*Le Scarpine di Diaghilev. Diaghilev's Ballet Shoes.*' The musical notation had been done by hand. He hummed several bars.

They went to the nearby grave of Stravinsky and his wife. Small stones, votive lights, and fresh cut flowers, which had been left by admirers, adorned the composer's modern-style marker as they did Diaghilev's grave.

Urbino and the contessa made a circuit of the compound, tracing out the inscriptions, some of them faint, on the markers. Most of the graves bore Russian names, written in both Western and Cyrillic script. Whenever Urbino was in this section of San Michele, he felt as if he were surrounded by the graves of characters out of a Tolstoy novel.

They stopped in front of a stone effigy of a recumbent woman, who had died at twenty-two. A bouquet of fresh red roses lay in her stone arms.

'Someone always remembers Sonia,' the contessa said. 'And many of the other dead, too.' She indicated the ones that had fresh flowers and were well tended.

They passed into the main area of the cemetery.

'Cemeteries used to depress me,' the contessa said. 'Now what soothes me is seeing how so many of the dead are still alive in the hearts of those they've left behind. Even those who have been dead for a century seem to have someone who remembers them.'

Urbino did not point out that many graves in the compound and elsewhere were abandoned and neglected.

Urbino and the contessa fell into a silence until the contessa came to an abrupt halt as they were crossing the cloister. 'Save Mina! Make it possible for her to weep on Olimpia's grave. You have to do it before you leave for America!'

'I'll do my best.'

Urbino could make no stronger promise than this. It would be difficult to establish Mina's innocence between now and his unavoidable trip back to America. He had a solemn but hopefully not impossible charge.

That evening, as Urbino was having his coffee in his library, he re-read the article in *Il Gazzettino* about Olimpia's murder.

MURDER IN SANTA CROCE
Art Collection Unharmed

'I loved her. I killed her.'

These are the words of Mina Longo, 25, formerly of Palermo, who is being held for the murder of Olimpia Pindar, 54.

According to Professor Alberto Lago, the medical examiner, Signorina Pindar, a dressmaker in the Santa Croce area, died in her workshop as a result of trauma to the chest by a pair of scissors.

Longo, a close friend of the murdered woman, was seen entering the residence of the murdered woman in an evidently distressed state half an hour before she was found beside the body of Signorina Pindar.

Longo worked as a maid at the Venice residence of the Contessa Barbara da Capo-Zendrini, the British widow of the deceased Conte Alvise da Capo-Zendrini. It was the Contessa da Capo-Zendrini who summoned the police to the murder scene.

Pindar is survived by a brother Ercule Pindar and a sister Gabriella Pindar, who live in the building where the murder took place. The Palazzo Pindar houses a collection of art objects and curiosities that were acquired over the years by the Pindar family, who were among the most prominent import-exporters of the city from the eighteenth century to the nineteen thirties. No damage was done to the art collection insofar as has been determined up to this point.

The police are making every effort to reconstruct the series of events that led to the tragic event.

The details were simple, stark, and incriminating. Fortunately, the article did not mention that Olimpia was the contessa's cousin, although the police were well aware of the fact.

After finishing his coffee, Urbino went for one of his long walks. It was eight o'clock. It was a clear, chilly night. A cold, damp wind was blowing from the lagoon.

He went to the Piazza San Marco, approaching it through empty squares and alleys. The only sounds were his own solitary footsteps, the lapping of water against stone, muted voices from behind shuttered windows, and at one point, faint and far off, someone whistling a phrase from an aria of Verdi.

He wandered into Florian's, but stayed only long enough for a quickly drained glass of wine before setting out for the Riva degli Schiavoni. He had vaguely in mind the Public Gardens at the eastern end of the city, where he often went, even later at night, to sit on a bench and think as he looked out across the lagoon.

The Danieli, where Eugene would be staying, spilled light on the pavement from a golden but decidedly deserted interior. The staff members had the air of elegant and slightly bored caretakers.

He was about to break into his stride along the wide Riva when, on an impulse, he hurried to the *circolare* that was about to depart from the San Zaccaria landing.

He went out to the unoccupied stern and seated himself beside the door.

Soon, the Basilica, the Doges' Palace, and the broad sweep of the Riva seemed to be floating, brightly illuminated, between the dark waters and the night sky.

For the next hour and a half, as the boat made its circuit through the Giudecca Canal and into the lagoon past the cemetery island to Murano, then back to Venice, Urbino indulged in speculations about Olimpia's murder in which the dynamics of the Palazzo Pindar — or what he knew of them so far — and Gaby's fears played prominent roles.

Only a few days ago Gaby had been the focus of his and the contessa's concern, and she still was, perhaps even more so now that her sister had fallen victim to the fate she seemed to have feared for herself. Whether she was actually in mortal danger or only imagined she was, was something that he needed to find out.

Now it was Mina who needed their immediate help, and in helping her, they might be able to help Gaby – or at least get to the source of her fears. As the contessa said, Mina had to be saved – saved from many years in prison, and he had only a relatively short time to do it in. So much was against the girl. She had been discovered next to Olimpia's dead body by no less a witness than the contessa herself, she had been grasping the murder weapon, and she had initially insisted that she had killed Olimpia.

No, it did not look good for Mina, who also had the history of her emotional disturbance against her.

Another fact, almost as damning as the others, was certain to be exploited. Mina and Olimpia had been involved in what the clever Jesuits had warned Urbino against at boarding school. A particular friendship.

Had Olimpia had any particular friendships before she met Mina? Urbino had little doubt that she had. It was logical to assume that Olimpia – unlike Mina, who was hardly more than a girl – had had an earlier relationship, and even more than one.

A former particular friend might have been seething with jealousy about Mina. It was not hard to imagine those feelings leading to the fatal attack. Nor was it hard to imagine what Apollonia, the upholder of rigid moral values, had thought about her niece. The Palazzo Pindar must have crackled with the tension between the two women. And Apollonia's disapproval would have extended from Olimpia to Mina and to anyone else she had been involved with.

Urbino needed to know more about Olimpia's past. Vital clues to the murderer usually lay in the victim's past, in his relationships with others.

At least this had been Urbino's experience. Although murder could come to those who were in the wrong place at the wrong time or who had been selected randomly, this wasn't the world that Urbino's sleuthing carried him into. His passion for order, a passion that left him unsatisfied until things were set right, was exercised on a smaller, more intimate, but no less dangerous stage.

Urbino warned himself, however. It was premature to be making any assumptions about the murder and the Palazzo Pindar. Yet he had made a huge one.

The answer to Olimpia's murder lay under the roof of the Palazzo Pindar and among its occupants – or, at the very most, not much further afield in some person or persons closely connected to the house and them, some friend or business contact of Olimpia or of another family member.

As Urbino gazed out at the slowly changing scene, he ran through the classic motives for murder, one by one, as a mental exercise, trying to imagine scenarios for each of them, and trying to connect them with the House of Pindar. Motivation was what interested him the most in his investigations. His interest in it was related to his biography writing, where so much was interpretation and where truth was not always directly related to cold facts.

He speculated about each possible motive as far as he could, but there were great gaps that were related to the gaps in his knowledge about Olimpia and the other members of the household.

The motives that seemed to make the most sense, at least at this early stage, were greed, jealousy, and revenge.

Could Olimpia have fallen victim to someone's greed? With her out of the picture, the murderer might have money from an inheritance or an insurance policy.

All three siblings had owned the Palazzo Pindar and its collection, and now, according to what the contessa had told him about the agreement among them, it belonged to Gaby and Ercule. Olimpia's business had not been very lucrative, from what Urbino knew. He needed to put it into the equation. She had recently signed a contract to design costumes for the Goldoni production. Had anyone else been competing for the commission?

As for jealousy, someone could have been furious about her preference for Mina; so jealous that the person had been driven to murder. It was even possible that someone had seen her as a prisoner who had to be freed from what was believed to be Olimpia's malign influence.

The unstoppable flood of questions and speculations continued to surge through Urbino's mind as the boat throbbed past the cemetery island where the cypresses twisted in the wind, and entered the canals of Murano with their deserted embankments and closed glass factories.

Urbino pursued a different tack. Had Olimpia been in possession of a dangerous piece of knowledge, something she could never have imagined would lead to her death? Had her exploitation of someone's dark secret driven her victim to murder?

Or might someone have been blackmailing her? Had all the money scattered on the floor of the atelier been Olimpia's payment to her blackmailer – or someone's payment to her – in a transaction that had gone deadly wrong?

As the boat started its return journey across the dark lagoon, Urbino hoped that he could reestablish himself at the Palazzo Pindar as soon as possible. He also needed to speak with the contessa's staff.

Urbino had no sooner returned to the Palazzo Uccello than the telephone rang. His ex-brother-in-law Eugene's voice boomed over the line from Rome.

'I've been tryin' to get hold of you all this mornin' and ever since eight-thirty tonight. Thought you had slipped out of town to escape me.'

'I'm waiting with open arms.'

'That's what I like to hear. Don't want to think you've lost your Southern hospitality. You've lost plenty else. I have every intention of gettin' you back into Southern shape when you come back with me.'

Anxiety stabbed Urbino when Eugene mentioned their departure. Would he be able to do what he needed to do?

'Everything's on schedule. I'm almost ready for Venice,' Eugene was saying. 'Seen the Vatican, poked around the ruins, and thrown enough coins in the fountains. Nothing much has changed from ten years ago. Guess that's why they call it the Eternal City. Eternally the same! Now it's see Venice and die. Isn't that what they say?'

'See Naples and die.'

'Seems they should say it about Venice. It's a dead old city. That's why you like it, I know that. Say hello to Countess Barbara. Tell her I'm lookin' forward to seein' her again.'

Six

What impressed itself upon Urbino two days later was how normally the Pindars were behaving despite the fact that Olimpia – sister, niece, and cousin – had been brutally murdered the previous week. Of course, what was normal for the Pindar clan was most peculiar for almost anyone else.

Urbino had rung the palazzo bell to announce he was there, half thinking that a buzzer system might have been installed since Olimpia's murder. But Gaby's cry, much fainter than usual, came from within for him to enter. The large door was on the latch. As he passed into the dour building, he had the feeling he usually did. It was as if he were entering a place of strange, impoverished privilege where eccentricity reigned.

This was the first time Urbino had seen Gaby since her sister's death. Her pallor was unrelieved today by any rouge, and her red cap was set on her head at an angle, as if done hurriedly. Her blue eyes had a glazed, feverish look. He offered his condolences.

She received them with a quiet nod and a bowed head. 'It isn't easy to lose a sister – or a brother. It is harder than losing a parent. And Olimpia was taken away so suddenly from us, from everything.' She looked in the direction of the museum and, for one fleeting second, the closed blue doors of the rooms opposite the museum. 'What would happen to my things if something happened to me, if I was taken away from them without any warning? They are my children – even the poor little cat mummy all wrapped away from the world. Mothers never want to leave their children.'

As she had been speaking, she had started to breathe harshly. She seemed on the point of tears. She took deep breaths. When she continued to speak, her voice was weaker. 'Please tell Barbara that I don't have any bad feeling toward her. I mean because Mina took away our sister.'

'I'll tell her. And when you see her, you can tell her yourself.' Urbino wondered what the contessa's response would be. To accept assurances of this kind from Gaby, without qualifying them, would be like acknowledging that she believed in Mina's guilt. 'I understand how you feel about your things, how you feel about leaving behind something you care about.' He paused. Gaby had mentioned only her fear of being parted from the collection, but Urbino thought it appropriate to add, 'And people you care about. Whenever someone close to us dies, we feel insecure. But you shouldn't worry, Gaby. What happened to Olimpia was something' — he searched for the right way to express it — 'something unusual.'

Wasn't he risking dangerously misleading the woman by stilling her fears in an attempt to draw her out? He felt caught in a bind that he knew he was going to be caught in repeatedly in this case. The bind came from the need to pretend to believe that Mina had murdered Olimpia and that there was no danger to anyone else now. If he gave any strong impression that he believed the murderer was still at large and that Gaby, and the others, needed to be on their guard, he would be alerting the murderer, assuming as he did that the murderer was under the roof of the Palazzo Pindar or closely connected to it.

Gaby had been staring at him as he spoke, her pale face screwed up into a tight expression. He expected her to burst into tears, but instead, she said in a clear, calm voice, 'Before Mina killed Olimpia, I used to wake up early in the morning. I couldn't fall back to sleep. I kept thinking that something terrible was going to happen to me. I told Olimpia. She said to stop thinking such nonsense. But now she's dead. I think that I was afraid for her and for myself at the same time. It was a premonition.'

A few minutes later, Urbino ascended the staircase past the Pindar *portego* to the floor occupied by Apollonia, Alessandro, and Eufrosina. A man's muffled voice came from the other side of the closed door. Urbino could not make out what it was saying, but it continued without interruption until he knocked.

Alessandro admitted Urbino into the *salotto*. His attractive face was unshaved. He was dressed in a dark-blue turtleneck sweater, a maroon scarf, and brown corduroy trousers whose kneecaps were bagged and shiny with age. He held a worn leather-covered book, but his hand concealed the title.

Apollonia, black-draped and with her head tightly wrapped in black lace, was in imperious possession of the sofa. Her face looked much more gaunt than it had at the funeral. A small electric space heater was positioned in front of the sofa. The odor of camphor was strong on the closed air in the room.

Apollonia gave Urbino a stern nod. Eufrosina, sitting across from Apollonia in a mahogany armchair with a high back, acknowledged him with the ghost of a smile. Alessandro stood behind his mother.

Eufrosina was wearing a brown wool trouser suit. A green knit hat was pulled down low over her auburn hair.

If Urbino were to apply Eufrosina's theory about hands to her own, he would have said, from the way one was grasped tightly in the other, that she was nervous and trying her best to conceal it. Her hands were gloved, not in the beige leather gloves she had been wearing at Florian's, but black cotton ones. Eufrosina's preference for gloves was unusual, considering her series of photographs of bare hands, but perhaps she found pleasure in emulating her mother, who was wearing her habitual gloves of black kid.

Apollonia had not asked Urbino to sit down.

A low table held an old brass samovar with teacups, a camera, a wood-carving knife and a gouge, a missal, a labeled pharmacy flask containing bright green liquid, and three small round lidded containers covered in Venetian paper. One of them was unlidded. Bright red pills nested inside.

'Get the box for Urbino.' Apollonia's voice was weak.

Eufrosina started to get up.

'I meant Alessandro.'

Alessandro went to the sideboard, which was thick with triptychs, icons, and wooden statues of saints. One of the statues was of the Blessed Virgin Mary, treading on a serpent. The other was of St Anthony. The statues had an unfinished, yet appealing quality to them precisely because of their roughness. They were most likely Alessandro's handiwork.

Alessandro took the shagreen box from beneath its white lace covering.

'I appreciate that you're letting me see them again despite your troubles,' Urbino said.

'We have an agreement,' Apollonia said. 'And the sooner you finish, the sooner my aunt's letters can be at rest again.'

Eufrosina, whose nervousness had only increased during the past few minutes, picked up the camera from the table. It was a traditional camera, not a digital one.

Apollonia stared at the camera. 'Don't go pointing that thing at me!'

'I wasn't, mamma. I thought I'd take some photographs of Urbino's hands carrying great aunt Efigenia's box.'

Eufrosina withdrew a handkerchief from her pocket and gently brushed it over the camera. 'I wish you'd be more careful with your shavings, Alessandro. They get everywhere. You should do your carving in your room.'

'He can do it where he likes. St Joseph was a carpenter. Poor devoted St Joseph. Hardly anyone thinks about him. A sadly neglected saint. And Christ was a carpenter. Our Alessandro is following their example with his woodcarving, are you not, my dear?'

Eufrosina positioned the camera above Urbino's hands, to one side, and then – to his surprise – kneeled on the Turkey carpet for some shots from below.

'Would you like another cushion, mamma?' Alessandro took one from a pile in a corner of the room, plumped it, and placed it behind his mother's back. 'Some more tea?'

'No, thank you, dear.'

'What you should have is another spoonful of the syrup.'

'An excellent idea. I'm glad that one of my children has good sense.'

Alessandro poured green liquid from the bottle into a teaspoon and administered the medicine to his mother, careful not to get even a droplet on the voluminous lace veil that covered her shoulders and chest. He patted her mouth with a napkin.

Apollonia leaned her head back and closed her eyes.

Eufrosina had been observing her brother's attentions with an impassive face. She now stared at her mother, who was breathing smoothly. In a hoarse whisper, moving closer to Urbino, she said, 'Please tell Barbara that the new photographs will be better. I'll begin to take them soon.'

Apollonia snapped to attention. 'What's that?' A rattle came from her chest. 'What are you whispering to Urbino? That is rude. Have I brought you up to be like that? If you think he is going to lend you any money, you are sadly mistaken.'

Alessandro, who was sticking to his mother like a limpet, said, 'Neither a borrower nor a lender be.'

'Exactly.' Apollonia reached up to pat her son's hand. 'You probably told him you'd pay him back with your inheritance! Don't hold your breath, my devoted daughter. Just because you've thrown away your dead husband's money is no concern of mine. Money slips through your fingers like water.'

'She was talking about her photographs,' Urbino said.

Eufrosina gave him a grateful look as she returned to her armchair.

'Her photographs!' Apollonia said scornfully. 'Photographs and hands! Hands and photographs! Hands reveal everything, she says. Yours are always grabbing money!'

Eufrosina's long face, which had turned paler, wore the weary, resigned look of someone who had become accustomed to verbal abuse.

Apollonia started to cough. Red patches appeared on her cheeks. Alessandro brought her a glass of water, but she waved it away. She leaned back farther against the cushions. When she had recovered, she said, 'Faces reveal everything, not hands.' Apollonia turned her own face to Urbino, with traces of beauty lingering in it despite the ravages of age. 'And letters. They reveal a lot about the writer and the recipient.'

'That's always been my belief,' Urbino agreed. 'I rely on them for my books.'

'And they can be inspirational.' Apollonia stared at Urbino. 'St Paul's Epistles. Very inspirational.'

'They are indeed,' Urbino agreed. 'And so are Peter's, John's, James', and Jude's.' Urbino managed to drag the other Epistle writers from the dark lumber-room of his Jesuit education.

Eufrosina started to recite the recipients of Paul's Epistles. She rolled off the names of the Corinthians and Ephesians and Galatians and Thessalonians with an enthusiasm that left her almost breathless.

'The Philippians, the Colossians, and the Romans, too,' Alessandro said. 'You forgot them.'

Alessandro went on to name Paul's other Epistles. Urbino was beginning to wish for a cup of tea. Eufrosina stared down at the floor.

It was time for Urbino to take his leave.

'Once again accept my condolences for Olimpia's death,' he said.

Apollonia fingered the black lace veil. 'We see what a life without God at its head can come to. May God have mercy on her soul. And may God forgive Barbara's wretched maid for having done His will.'

Urbino, still wearing his cape and with his scarf wound tightly around his throat against the chill, had been in the museum for almost an hour. He had been reading the same letter all that time, or rather the first sentence, over and over again. His concentration for the letters was completely broken. He needed to save Mina. He hoped he would eventually recapture his original enthusiasm for the letters. But these days they were mainly valuable to him as an excuse to nose around the Palazzo Pindar and to try to get to the bottom of things before he had to leave with Eugene.

Gaby, in respect for his work, was keeping to the vestibule and the other room of the museum. He caught her staring at him a few times when he looked up.

Silence reigned from the apartments above.

'Is everything going all right?' Gaby asked from the doorway. 'You keep frowning.'

Her face was more animated than before, and her voice had lost its earlier dull and troubled notes. She had passed through one of her mood shifts in the short time he had been upstairs.

'I think I always frown when I'm concentrating.'

'Take your mind off work for a little while. Go look at the statue of Eufrosina.' Gaby's voice held a faint trace of laughter.

'The statue of Eufrosina?'

Urbino went over to Alessandro's little theater. A new figure had been added. He picked it up. It was a woman with black hair and ungloved hands that were disproportionately large. The arms were positioned away from the body, palms outward, with the fingers widely splayed, as if she were a saint displaying her stigmata.

'Eufrosina hasn't seen it yet. She won't like it.' Gaby was now standing behind him.

'I'm not sure about that. She might see it as an advertisement. She uses her hands to photograph hands. Do you like the one of you?'

'Yes. But it makes no difference if I like it or if Eufrosina likes hers. Alessandro is an artist.' Her eyes radiated warmth. 'Artists can do as they wish. They see things we don't see.'

'But Eufrosina is an artist, too. She sees things in people's hands and then helps others see them.' Urbino replaced the Eufrosina figure. 'And don't forget Olimpia.'

Both of them turned their attention to the figure of her dead sister.

'What do you mean?' Gaby readjusted the Eufrosina figure.

'She was an artist, like Alessandro, like Eufrosina, although she didn't use wood or photography. She designed clothes. As an artist of her own kind, she saw things that other people don't see, just as you said about Alessandro.'

Gaby gave the appearance of considering this for a few moments. 'That may be true. But there were many things that Olimpia didn't see.'

'Like what?'

'She couldn't see that Mina was a danger to her, could she?' Gaby lamented. She gazed with what seemed distaste at the figure of Olimpia. 'She couldn't see that Mina would kill her! And she couldn't see that I was right when I told her that something bad was going to happen to me! It happened to her instead. But she was my sister, and so something bad *did* happen to me, too! It came right into the house, like a thief, and changed everything.'

Urbino saw his opportunity to bring up the topic of the unlocked front door. 'You know, Gaby, it would be a good idea for you and Ercule to keep the front door locked all the time.' Urbino felt almost ridiculous stating the obvious. 'And a security system would be an excellent idea. I can give you the name of a reliable company. Then you wouldn't have to worry about anyone coming in and stealing your things.'

'I'm not afraid of anyone stealing things. In all these years, nothing has been taken. And didn't our ancestor, Fra Angelo, say, "When the door of the palace is locked against the needy, the family behind the door will become the needy." And locks and a security system wouldn't have kept Mina from slaughtering Olimpia.'

Urbino was considering a satisfactory response, when Gaby said, 'Give me Eufrosina.'

'Eufrosina?' He started to reach for the Eufrosina figure but then understood what she meant. 'Eufrosina,' he repeated, enunciating each syllable clearly.

'In, fin, rose, nose, fuse, sin, as, fur, fun. And there are some words that sound the same, but are different. It's the "a" and the "e" that makes the difference. "For" the preposition and "fore" the noun and the adjective. And there's "or" the conjunction and "ore" like in gold and silver and "sore" like in pain and "soar" like a bird.' Gaby was most definitely in her element. She had not finished yet. 'There's "surf." Let me think . . . What other ones? Did I say sin?'

'I believe you did.'

'There's fear and ear.'

Gaby chuckled. Yes, she was most definitely in a different mood from her earlier one. 'That's funny, don't you think so? Eufrosina has ear and nose but she has no hand! Yes, very funny!' She looked at Alessandro's carved figure of Eufrosina with the big hands, and laughed with such candor, and so lightly, that Urbino smiled back. Gaby watched him with wide eyes. 'Promise me something. Don't tell Apollonia that Eufrosina has sin in her!'

Her eyes shining with amusement, she held her right index finger up to her lips.

Half an hour later, after staring at the same letter and making random scribbles on a notecard just in case Gaby was observing him from the other room, he returned the letters to Alessandro, who opened the door barely a crack.

As Urbino was leaving the landing outside the Pindar *grand portego*, a man's voice said behind him, 'You've been trying to sneak past.' It was Ercule. 'Do you have time to join me?'

'With pleasure.'

Ercule gave him a bright smile. Two kaftans were pulled over his short, plump body. One was in red cotton with gold ogival designs and had wrist-length sleeves. Over it was a short-sleeved green kaftan in velvet brocade, spotted with a design of red tulips. Perched on his head was a red and orange *corno* hat of the style that the Doges used to wear. It was tall and conical with a peak rising from the back. It was not an original Doge's bonnet, but a modern version. Beneath it was a white cotton cap, a *camauro*, which covered his ears and tied under his chin. On his feet were brown kid slippers with appliquéd arabesques.

The entire effect might have seemed more humorous to someone other than Urbino, who sometimes wore, while at home, pointed *babouche* slippers and a skullcap that he had acquired during his long stay in Morocco.

Urbino offered his condolences for Olimpia's death.

'We're managing, me and Gaby. Now we are only two. Many people believe that no one dies before his time, but it is difficult to accept. She died too young.' Ercule was about three or four years younger than Olimpia had been. He moved into the *portego*. 'This way.'

He led Urbino across the draughty room. Its two long walls were flanked with dark wood chairs and covered with classical frescoes and heavy mythological tapestries. The cold seeped up through the worn carpets through the soles of Urbino's shoes. A large Murano chandelier, missing many of its pieces, dominated the room and cast strange, flickering shadows on the walls and the ceiling. Maroon velvet drapes were drawn across four tall French doors opposite the staircase. The doors gave access to a small courtyard below them.

The room had a somber air of happy, prosperous lives once lived in it but now gone forever.

'Right through here.' Ercule opened a door at the end of the *portego*.

Ercule stepped aside. Urbino entered a large room where a fire crackled in a bronze fireplace. The air held a musty odor mixed with the aroma of sandalwood and sweet, acrid smoke. From the ceiling hung a cylindrical ottoman-style mosque lamp that shed a dusky light over colored tiles, tortoiseshell, and mother-of-pearl.

'*Hos geldiniz!*' Ercule said. '"Welcome" in Turkish!'

Pillow-strewn divans, ottomans, carved Rococo armchairs, antique wooden screens, a tall freestanding candelabra, a backgammon table, and a single-stem nargileh created intimate areas. Turkish rugs were layered on the floor. One wall, in front of which a tall brass incense burner emitted a plume of smoke, was inlaid with worm-eaten dark woodwork. A mandolin, similar to the one in the collection, lay against the cushions of a divan.

In his eclectic outfit, Ercule looked completely suited to the room's furnishings. Together, they seemed to compose the personality of their owner.

'You've created quite an environment for yourself.'

Ercule's round face beneath the Doge's bonnet glowed like a bright, full moon. 'I raided the collection years ago. Gaby would never let me near any of the things now, though you never know! I have my eye on a few of them.'

'If you can't get to Istanbul, this is certainly an excellent second-best.'

'I'll get there, by hook or by crook, and I won't care what happens to this place, love it though I do.'

By 'this place,' Urbino was not sure whether Ercule meant the Turkish room or the whole Palazzo Pindar.

'All I need is money. I'll say goodbye to Venice. I'll sail away in a boat. A boat it must be.' Ercule closed his eyes behind their round, gold-rimmed glasses. He smiled as if he were contemplating a vision of Istanbul's domes and minarets seen from a boat.

'Dreams are important to have,' Urbino said.

'Not just important to have.' Ercule's blue eyes opened wide. 'But also to get rid of! I want the reality. And I'll get it!' He gave Urbino a sharp, assessing look. 'You might be able to help me. But please sit down.'

After removing his cape and his scarf, Urbino seated himself in an armchair by the fire. Beside him was a divan that was awash with a sea of books, brochures, and catalogues. From what Urbino could see, most of them dealt with Turkey, Istanbul, the Ottoman Empire, and Islamic culture. As Urbino was placing his briefcase down on the floor, his eye was caught by a large book with a worn leather cover. He picked it up. It was one of the volumes of Sir Richard Burton's translation of *The Arabian Nights*.

'A first edition,' Ercule said. 'But I have only one other volume. Let me make us some coffee.'

Ercule went to a cupboard and took out a small metal pot with a long handle. He measured coffee into it and poured in water, and then placed the pot over some of the lower flames of the fireplace. Soon the aroma of coffee filled the air.

'Here we are.' Ercule put a tray down on a small table beside Urbino's armchair. It held two small cups with thick, midnight black coffee.

Urbino took a sip of his coffee. It was delicious. 'How might I be able to help you?'

'A silly idea of mine. You're spending time in the museum. You can't help but be with Gaby. Gaby *is* the museum and the museum *is* Gaby. You might put in a good word for me.'

'A good word?'

'About the collection. The house. If we sell them, we'll make enough money to do what we want to do.'

To do what *you* want to do, Urbino thought, but he did not say it. What he did say was, 'But what would become of Gaby? She hasn't been out of the house for years.'

A far lesser consideration – but one, nonetheless – was the disruption it would mean in the lives of Apollonia, Eufrosina, and Alessandro. But Ercule could point out that they had their own house to return to.

'It would be good for Gaby!' Ercule said with more enthusiasm than sympathy for his sister's condition. 'It would be the push she needs.'

This had been Olimpia's opinion, as she had expressed it to him and the contessa. It appeared that Olimpia and Ercule had been of the same mind when it came to Gaby's condition and the best way to remedy it. Had Olimpia also shared her brother's desire that the house and the collection be sold? If she had wanted to sell, it would have aligned her with Ercule against Gaby – and possibly also Apollonia and her children. If she had been against selling, then Ercule would have been farther away from realizing his dream.

'I'm not so sure about that,' Urbino said. 'We should encourage her to get treatment. If things go well for her, she might be open to change. Did Olimpia want to sell?'

'It depended on the day of the week. I could have brought her around to it. Now it's only Gaby – unfortunately.' He gave Urbino an embarrassed look. 'Olimpia and I tried to get her to agree to sell some pieces, but the collection is like a family, she says. Everything should stay together. Olimpia didn't have any problem with parting with a few things for a good price. She was having financial troubles, but she had seemed less worried about money lately.'

'So both you and Gaby need to agree on selling anything.'

'Yes, since each of us owns one-half share of everything.' Ercule scratched the side of his head. 'If any of us were to predecease the other and had no children, his – or her – share goes to the others, equally. That's how we got Olimpia's share.' A cold, congested expression had been settling on his face. 'Poor Olimpia! Being murdered like that. And by Mina, of all people! I thought she was so gentle.' He touched the Doge's hat. 'Olimpia made this for me.'

Ercule stood up. He placed his empty cup on the tray next to Urbino's. 'Do you think you could help?'

'I doubt if I have much influence with Gaby. And as I said, the best approach is to persuade her to get treatment. Then, with time, she may be able to see things differently. You'd have a healthier sister *and* your dream.'

Ercule turned his face away but not before Urbino saw the annoyed look.

'I have two things to take us away from upsetting topics,' Ercule said with forced cheerfulness. He went over to the cupboard and reached behind a pile of books. 'The first is this.' He lifted up a bottle. '*Raki*. The best grade. It's Turkish.'

He went through a small door partly concealed by one of the screens and returned a few minutes later with two glasses with ice in them. He poured generous portions of the *raki* in the glasses.

The *raki*, which Urbino was drinking for the first time, was not to his liking, any more than *grappa* or *ouzo* was. Ercule downed his and poured himself more.

'The second thing is this. Let me find it.' Ercule fished around in the pile of books before finding the one he was looking for. 'It's Pierre Loti's *Aziyadé*. An English translation.'

Loti's book, which Urbino had read years ago, was a nineteenth-century French novel about Ottoman Istanbul. It told the story of a romance between a Frenchman and a beautiful woman from the sultan's harem.

'Listen to this,' Ercule said.

He reseated himself on the divan, and started to read long passages. He skipped around in the book, but whatever he read was about love and assignations, and rich with exotic descriptions of the old city.

After fifteen minutes, Ercule's voice started to fade away. His head, in its ridiculous but affecting ducal hat, drooped toward his chest. He looked vulnerable as he sat on the sofa, the Loti book ready to drop from his hands, his breathing slow and steady.

Urbino got up quietly, collected his briefcase, cape, and scarf, and left Ercule to whatever dreams he was having.

Late that afternoon, after returning to the Palazzo Uccello for lunch and a nap, Urbino went to a small pastry shop on the Via Garibaldi in the Castello area. The front window was filled with a tantalizing display of *baicoli*, *zaleti*, *bussolai*, *pignoleti*, and other traditional Venetian sweets. The aroma in the shop was delicious.

The shop was owned by an elderly couple. Urbino was a regular customer. The reason he had come this afternoon, however, was not to get his usual selection of pastries – although this was what Nicoletta started to tend to after they had exchanged greetings – but to ask her and her husband Marco about Mina.

The couple owned the building and lived above the shop. The apartment above theirs had been rented out to the cousin Mina had come to live with when she had left Palermo, where she had gone through a rebellious phase in her early teenage years.

Nicoletta and Marco, who were childless, were fond of Mina and had helped her in many small ways. In fact, it had been through them that the contessa had connected with Mina when she had accompanied Urbino to the shop. Mina had been behind the counter, helping the couple.

It was to be expected that the conversation this afternoon would turn to Mina.

'Something is wrong with our system when a good girl like that is accused of murder!' Nicoletta said, shaking her head slowly as she placed *zaleti* biscuits in a small carton. 'Mina wouldn't hurt a fly.'

'It must be a mistake,' Marco said. 'We've read what was in the paper and we hear what people are saying, but we don't believe it.'

'Neither do the contessa or I. Mina has a very good lawyer.'

'And she has you,' Nicoletta said. She started to arrange *baicoli* in another carton.

'Yes . . . Well, I was wondering if Mina ever stopped by here with anyone in the time she has been working for the contessa. I know she visits you often.'

'At least once a week,' Marco said. 'She doesn't forget us. But no, she comes alone. She never even came with her friend, the one who was murdered.'

'She came once with the contessa,' his wife corrected. 'As for her friend the dressmaker, Mina always had good things to say about her. She would never have done anything to hurt her.'

'Has she seemed troubled in any way recently?'

'Always as bright as sunshine. She grew out of whatever emotional problems she was having in Sicily. We never saw her depressed. These days, though, being on the Giudecca, I suppose it would be only normal for her to be depressed, wouldn't it? It's a good thing her cousin Anna isn't alive to see what the poor girl is going through. She gave Mina the love she needed. All she needs is someone to care about her.'

Seven

That evening, the contessa retired to her boudoir early, after having tried to calm herself with a game of patience, which, unfortunately, had belied its name. The pastels burning in the blue Fes urn scented the boudoir with roses. Surrounded by her well-worn books, her small Longhi paintings, and other objects dear to her heart, and with Zouzou pressed against her side on the pink brocade sofa, she sipped her chocolate as she read the memoirs of Lorenzo da Ponte, Mozart's librettist. A box of marrons glacés were within easy reach.

She had prepared the chocolate herself. This was usually something that Mina had done. The contessa did not need Mina to do it for her or to do much else. She was a self-sufficient woman, although the largeness of her staff might have indicated otherwise. But the Ca' da Capo-Zendrini needed tending after in ways that were far beyond her, even if the building had been a third or a fourth of its size.

No, she did not need Mina for all the little ministrations the young woman performed. The contessa felt this more this evening than she ever had, because what she was feeling was how much she missed Mina's company. For Mina was her companion, and now the poor girl was locked away and the contessa could not even pay her a visit.

The contessa ran her hands through Zouzou's silky fur and tugged affectionately at her long ears. The cocker spaniel gave the contessa a look from her dark brown eyes that the contessa interpreted as nothing short of the depths of devotion.

The contessa had spent the whole day at home, not even taking Zouzou out for her evening walk as she usually did, but assigning the task to one of the housemaids.

A little earlier, she had stepped out on the balcony to get some air and take in the view of the Grand Canal, washed by the white light of a frosty moon. A few dimly lit boats, with wakes like strings of pearls, gently broke the silence. Reluctantly, she had abandoned the scene and gone back into her boudoir, where a strong blaze burned in the fireplace.

She was now doing her best to absorb herself in da Ponte's account of a gambling episode at the Ridotto during carnival. But she kept feeling

Mina's absence, even though the girl would have been in her own room at this time.

How was Mina doing? Was she being well treated? Did she think the contessa had abandoned her? Did she still believe that Olimpia would not have died if she had not taken the scissors out of her chest? Had she —

The ringing of the telephone interrupted her thoughts and awakened Zouzou, who had fallen asleep with her head in the contessa's lap.

It was Urbino.

'No, I wasn't asleep,' she said. 'I've been thinking about Mina. I still haven't heard from Corrado Scarpa about when and if I'll be able to see her. He's doing his best.'

'*Coraggio*, Barbara. He'll work something out.'

'Are we any closer to getting the poor girl out? I have faith in your abilities. Even if you were only at the Palazzo Pindar for a few hours, you must have learned something. You must have impressions.'

'Plenty of impressions. I'm not as ignorant as I was when I went there, but what it all amounts to it's much too early to say.'

Urbino gave her details of the conversations he had had with Gaby, Apollonia, Eufrosina, Alessandro, and Ercule, interweaving them with his suspicions and puzzlements.

When he finished, the contessa said, 'Am I wrong, *caro*, or did I detect a trace of amusement in your voice? Is it appropriate?'

'Most inappropriate, but they can be a rather amusing group. Even poor Gaby can be amusing with her word game. But I'm under no illusions, and I won't be distracted or misled if I can help it. Maybe amused is not the right word, though. Maybe it's that I feel as if I'm looking at a performance. They are almost like actors in a play. Each of them has his or her role. It usually develops that way in families. But with the Pindars it's almost as if, in some strange way, they're all acting, but whether they might be acting in concert is something else entirely. When someone has something to hide, he becomes an actor. That's obvious enough. But it forces everyone around him to act as well.'

'Alessandro's little theater seems to have influenced your thinking.'

'It's very apt, isn't it, his theater? The drama of the extended Pindar family: love, death, and eccentricity.'

'Not too extended, not with only five members. You'll notice that I'm taking myself out of the picture for the moment.'

'Five members alive, one recently dead.'

'Sounds like a game tally.'

'That's apt, too. The Pindars love their games — and their hobby horses, their little obsessions. Even their disputes and disagreements seem scripted.'

'And you say you didn't notice anything different about them?'

'They all seem very much as they have always been. As if they decided to go on as usual, despite Olimpia's death.'

The contessa slowly turned her revolving silver photograph frames with photographs of her dead. Alvise, her mother and father, her grandparents on both sides, a close aunt and uncle, some cousins. 'Isn't that what we're supposed to do? Go on as usual?'

'Not when there's been a murder in the house.'

'Yes, a murder in the house of Pindar, in *my* family. But you shouldn't look only under the Pindar roof.'

'Exactly. We need to know more about everyone's life outside the house. As for Gaby, she might not leave the house, but that doesn't mean she has no contact with the world beyond it. And we need to know more about everyone's financial situation.'

'Everyone in that house has money problems, with the exception of Gaby, who doesn't care about money at all. Eufrosina has borrowed some money from me since her husband died. As for Alessandro, he isn't exactly pulling in the money from wood-carving or anything else.'

'Great expectations,' Urbino said.

'What does Dickens – ? Oh, I see! Their inheritance from Apollonia.'

'Which she was taunting Eufrosina about. Eufrosina and Alessandro seem to be in competition for it, or maybe each just wants to make sure he gets his proper share – or more than that, if possible.'

'Maybe that's the "sin in Eufrosina" that Gaby found so amusing – Eufrosina's greed.'

'Or something else. Or maybe nothing,' Urbino came back with. 'Gaby could be trying to stir up problems for Eufrosina. She doesn't hide her fondness for Alessandro. But it's hard to know how much credence to give to what she says. And if we're talking about money, we shouldn't neglect Apollonia. She doesn't have the problem of not having enough. *Her* problem is being sure to hold on to what she has and wanting more.'

'Ercule came right out and said he needs money. There's some honesty in that.' The contessa sighed. 'Money, the root of all evil.' She had a sharp vision of the money scattered across the floor of the atelier. 'Money and blackmail go together like a hand in a glove. But the question, as you've said, is whether Olimpia was victim or blackmailer. If she were a victim, the obvious reason would be that she was gay, but that doesn't make sense. She didn't keep it a secret. You can only be blackmailed for a secret – for something you want to conceal.'

'But someone might have been blackmailing Mina through Olimpia. She wouldn't want her family, the little that she has, to know about her relationship with Olimpia. Of course, there is no chance she is going to be able to keep any of it a secret now.'

'Poor Mina! But if someone wanted to blackmail Mina through someone, I would have been a more logical target.'

The contessa wondered what she would have done to protect Mina from exposure. She doubted she would have given in to blackmail.

'If blackmail is behind Olimpia's murder,' Urbino said, 'and she was the blackmailer, then whom was she blackmailing? What did she know about the person? And who else might have known the person's secret?'

The contessa would have preferred it if Olimpia had been a victim of blackmail and not a blackmailer. Blackmail was cowardly and despicable, although it did not deserve being murdered for. But she could imagine someone so tormented, so fearful, so desperate that murder seemed the only escape. She focused her attention back on Urbino.

'. . . and you must see what I mean, don't you?' he was saying. 'It's not only the living Pindars and not only Olimpia. We need to know more about Achille.'

'You're not suggesting there was foul play there? He died in an accident.'

'Nonetheless, we need to know more than we already do about him and the accident. Something you've forgotten about the accident or the family might come back. I'm going to need your help. There's no reason why you couldn't gather some impressions yourself, Barbara. Impressions and information.'

'From whom?'

'From the people it would appear most natural for you to speak to, to be around. Think about who they are.'

The contessa did just that, as she sipped her chocolate.

'Apollonia, for one,' she said after a few moments. She reached for a marron glacé. 'I've had more contact with her than the others. And she's closer to me as a relation than any of the others.' And closer in age, as well, she thought, but did not say.

'Who else?'

The contessa thought some more as she bit into the marron glacé. 'Eufrosina. She's doing the photographs. If what you say is true about the way they're all behaving as usual – '

'*Acting* as usual,' he interrupted her.

'If they're all *acting* as usual, then I'll do the same with Eufrosina. I'll tell her that I see no reason why we shouldn't proceed on schedule with the exhibition and the catalogue. And I'll show her that I mean it.'

'Have you been considering postponing?'

'It had occurred to me. But it seems important for me – for us – to carry on as we planned. Maybe Eufrosina and everyone else will think that I'm trying to put Olimpia's murder behind me. That could only be to our advantage. Having Eugene here will be a good thing, too. He'll help give us the appearance of going on as usual, of showing a visitor the sights. When is he coming?'

'The day after tomorrow.'

The thought of Eugene coming didn't please her entirely even though she liked the man. His arrival would bring Urbino's departure with him closer. Her heart quickened as she realized what Urbino needed to accomplish before then.

'You can even bring him by the Palazzo Pindar and show him the museum. It will give you a good excuse for being there – or another good excuse, along with the Fortuny letters. As for me, I'll do my best to behave as I always have with them – allowing for some understandable bouts of nerves, all perfectly controlled, of course. It would not seem normal if I behaved *completely* as usual. After all, my personal maid just murdered Olimpia.' The contessa gave a high laugh that sounded unpleasant to her ears. 'That's what *they* believe.'

'Or what some of them may want to believe.' Urbino paused, and then added, '*And* what one of them wants us to think he or she believes. But you will do fine. You're a consummate actress, my dear, a mistress of social artifice. When you have the desire to please and charm, you do it seamlessly. And you definitely know the value of benevolent deception.'

'It seems you've thought a lot about this.'

'Ever since we first had the sweet, happy fortune to meet.'

'If you're heaping praise on my head – rather questionable praise – to manipulate me, it isn't necessary. You will be proud of me. And so will Mina be proud. By the way, my father used to call me his little Sarah Bernhardt, so you're not the first.'

She turned the revolving holder to her father's photograph. He was dressed in black tie for one of her piano concerts at the Venice Music Conservatory. Tears came into her eyes. It had been so long ago, those first happy days of Alvise, long before she had met Urbino.

'By the way,' Urbino said, 'there's at least one other person you can use your divine skills on. Italo Bianchi.'

'Of course. The Pindars and I have him in common. I'm sure there's some legal counsel that I need, that I can *say* that I need, since I'm so good at – what did you call it? – benevolent deception.'

'You'll work it out.'

'We're a team. We've been called the Anglo-American alliance,' she reminded him. This was how some Venetians used to refer to them. And after many years of their relationship – and living outside their cultures – their speech had even become influenced by each other. 'A team, an alliance, a league of two. Call it what you will, *caro*. But I warn you. I refuse to be called Dr Watson.'

'Understood. Let's call you my Nora, then, and I'll be your Nick.'

'I can live with that!'

'You already have your Asta.'

'Asta was a cocker?'

'A male fox terrier – in the film. A female Schnauzer in the book.'

'Such a wealth of information about the trivial.'

'But haven't you noticed, Barbara, how often the trivial can be the most significant things in our cases?'

The next morning, shortly after getting up, the contessa went to the ground floor of the house, descending the formal staircase from the *piano nobile*. Although the large entrance hall was at water-level, it was well heated. The room, decorated in a sea motif with portraits of sea captains and a frieze of a Venetian ship with the da Capo-Zendrini coat of arms, was very secure. Both of these conditions – its lack of dampness and security – so different from the *androne* of the Palazzo Pindar, were essential for the success of the Fortuny exhibition, which would be held in the largest room that flanked it.

The staff had cleared out the room before Christmas. Centuries ago, the rooms around either side of the *androne* had been warehouses, like the rooms in the Palazzo Pindar's entrance hall, but now all of them were used for storage except for two of them that had been converted into an apartment for the boatman.

Vitale followed her downstairs.

'Is there something you were wanting, contessa? Are you going out in the boat?'

'Not now, Vitale. I just want to look around.'

'If you need anything, please let me know.'

He went over to an armoire carved with dolphins and seashells. He opened the door and made himself busy examining the umbrellas, boots, and waterproofs inside.

Vitale was uneasy. But it was not only Vitale who was on edge. All the staff was. She had gathered them together the morning after Mina had been taken into custody. She had assured them that she believed Mina was innocent and would soon be back in the house. They had shifted nervously and exchanged glances.

She knew what they were thinking. That she was deluding herself because Mina was her favorite. There had been resentment toward Mina among the other staff almost from the time she had come to the house. But this was not because of anything that Mina had done. The contessa was aware that she had not been able to disguise her special fondness for Mina, no matter what Urbino said about her acting abilities. She trusted, however, that when Urbino spoke with them they would have no trouble putting aside whatever petty jealousies they might feel and would help Mina as best they could.

The contessa opened one panel of a double door ornamented with gilded sea horses. It gave her the soothing view she wanted. The waters of the Grand Canal, pearl gray in the morning light, stretched beyond the blue-and-white-striped *pali* of her boat landing to the buildings beyond. Small waves from a passing waterbus slapped the motorboat and rocked it gently. The mooring rope, tightening and slackening, creaked in a pleasant way.

She stood looking out at the scene, despite the cold that crept in from the Canalazzo. She savored the damp air that she always thought, to the amusement of whomever she revealed it to, smelled green. After a few minutes of watching the rhythm of the water traffic and the flinging open of shutters on one of the palaces opposite, she closed the door.

She entered the exhibition room and started to walk around. The first impression one had was of a sea of soft, gentle, but rich colors that shimmered with a vitality that Fortuny had transferred to the silk through his magical way of dyeing it. Glass cases, with white featureless mannequins, had been installed throughout the room. A small platform had been constructed at the far end, where a four-string quartet would perform during the exhibition.

Some of the gowns, jackets, tunics, and cloaks had already been mounted on the mannequins. Scarves, masks, purses, and pillows were displayed on rods and cubes. Tiered silk ceiling lamps, with tassels, glass beads, and Arabic decorative motifs, shed an opalescent light and contributed to the fairy-tale look of the exhibition. The catalogue would be selective, and only some of the items would be photographed and described.

Several of the items were the contessa's, and her favorite among these was one she now lingered in front of. It was a gown that had once belonged

to Eleonora Duse, before the contessa's mother had been fortunate enough
to acquire it through a relative of the great actress.

It was a finely pleated Delphos tea gown in mauve-colored silk velvet
with lavender stencilling and bat-wing sleeves. Its Venetian glass beads
were almost the exact color of the wood violets the contessa remembered from her youth in the English countryside. The colors blended
and shimmered together in the morning light refracted from the Grand
Canal.

The contessa, who found it difficult to admit to being superstitious,
considered the dress talismanic. She wore it usually on only two occasions
– when she was weary and when she was depressed. The gown seemed to
have the power to lift her fatigue and disperse the clouds of her depres-
sion.

Now, feeling both a little weary and dispirited, just the sight of the dress
made her feel better.

Another Delphos dress displayed near the talismanic one was also hers,
but her mother had not passed it on to her. She had bought it at an auction
in London fifteen years ago. It was black silk stenciled with tan Venetian
glass beads. It carried good memories for her, the most recent of which
was when she had worn it at the first performance at the newly restored
La Fenice. In the same case as the Delphos dress was another of her prized
items, a velvet short jacket, stenciled with designs based on Islamic tiles
and seventeenth-century Venetian lace. It had been Urbino's birthday gift
to her a few years ago.

She passed displays of velvet cloaks, Knossos scarves, and silk purses –
one of the handbags, green silk velvet, was the one Olimpia had lent her
– to stand in front of the gown Apollonia had contributed. The contessa
had seen Apollonia wearing it on several occasions. She had looked absolutely
stunning in it, but the last time she had worn it, as far as the contessa
knew, had been more than twenty years ago.

The dress, one of Fortuny's loveliest creations, had belonged to Efigenia,
Apollonia's aunt. It was garnet-colored silk with gold imprinting and had
a silk gauze bodice in a gold-colored floral pattern.

When the contessa had taken it out of its tan cardboard box – its
pleats, through the magic of Fortuny's technique that remained a mystery,
as fresh and tight and crisp as the day the dress had been made – she had
been strongly tempted to try it on. But superstition had deterred her.
Apollonia had told her that no one would wear the dress until after she
was dead. There was certainly no chance Apollonia herself would wear
it again, given her soberness and preference for black. And when the
contessa had collected the gown at the Palazzo Pindar, she remembered

how coldly angry Apollonia had become when Eufrosina had asked her mother if she could try it on.

The contessa would not be surprised if Apollonia planned to sell the gown, along with the letters. The dress alone could bring in several thousand euros for her bank account.

Eufrosina might never get the opportunity to wear it, let alone own it. Its inaccessible beauty and comfort would tantalize her in its case as she photographed it for the catalogue.

Ah, Eufrosina and the photographs! Whatever had the contessa been thinking in giving her the commission? Family feeling and sympathy for Eufrosina had overridden her usual good sense in these matters. Based on the photographs that Eufrosina had shown the contessa and Urbino at Florian's, she doubted that her cousin was going to be able to do proper justice to the wondrous colors, textures, and shapes of the Fortuny items.

She should have listened to Urbino from the beginning when he had expressed his doubts about Eufrosina being up to the job. Now it was too late to rectify the situation without embarrassment for both her and Eufrosina and resentment on Eufrosina's part.

The thought cast a shadow on her circuit of the exhibition. She went upstairs to her morning room, where she sat down at the piano and started to play *The Well-Tempered Clavier*, hoping her mind would clear. After she had played half a dozen of Bach's preludes and fugues, she still had not been able to think of a gracious resolution to the problem.

The contessa's new career as an actress on the larger Pindar stage began later that morning when she visited Apollonia.

She should have rung to see if Apollonia would see her but she didn't want to alert her, nor did she want to be told that she couldn't come. She assumed that once she was there, in the Palazzo Pindar, Apollonia probably would not refuse to see her.

Pasquale took her in the boat across the Grand Canal to Santa Croce. Zouzou, who loved being on the water and, the contessa hoped, being in it as well when the good weather came, accompanied her. It was a gray day that suited the contessa's mood. A solid ceiling of clouds filtered the winter sun, pouring down a strange light that made the buildings and the waters of the Canal seem to glow from within.

When they reached the embankment alongside the Palazzo Pindar, the contessa left Zouzou with Pasquale. She went up to the building, so majestic but so much in need of repair, and rang the museum bell.

'*Avanti!*' came Gaby's muffled cry from within.

The contessa turned the lion-headed doorknob and entered.

Gaby stood by the museum entrance. Disappointment dropped over her long face when she saw that it was the contessa and not a visitor to the museum. The disappointment was replaced by a look of uneasiness that flickered in her blue eyes. She was wearing Olimpia's ocelot coat. The contessa was momentarily struck by how much Gaby's resemblance to her sister was heightened just by wearing it, although the coat, which was in excellent condition and had a rich gleam, made the clothes beneath it look shabbier.

After they greeted each other, Gaby said, running her hands down the front of the coat, 'It's *mine* now.' There was a defiant note in her voice. She stared at the contessa.

'It becomes you.'

'Thank you. How is Mina?'

The contessa hoped that her skills as an actress helped her to show less surprise than she felt at the sudden, unexpected question.

'She's doing well enough under the circumstances, or so I hear.'

'I feel sorry for her. She was carried away. Olimpia could make people angry, even without trying. It was one of the things she couldn't see, the way she upset people. I tried to tell her.' She thrust her hand into the pocket of the coat and pulled out a soiled handkerchief. She applied it to her nose. 'Yes, I always told her that she should be more careful of how she treated people.'

The contessa wondered how much of this criticism of Olimpia was personal to Gaby. Probably much of it, since the two sisters, so different in temperament and other ways, had lived in the same house for so long together.

'Olimpia never showed that side to me,' the contessa said, stretching the truth. The memory of Olimpia's behavior at the Ca' da Capo-Zendrini was still fresh in the contessa's mind.

'People don't show everything to everybody.'

'That's true. Do you know if Apollonia is in?'

'She's at home. I will ask her if she is well enough to see you. She's still ill. If anyone comes to see the museum, just tell them to wait until I return.'

On this hopeful note, Gaby went up the staircase.

Left alone, the contessa peered around the dark, chilly vestibule. It was in a lamentable state. Her gaze became fixed on the two closed blue doors across from her.

Like most people, the contessa was fascinated with locked rooms. But her healthy curiosity was tinged with a fear. It was not only because she had read the fairy tales about the bad things visited upon those who dared to open locked rooms, but also because she had personal experience with the danger. For many decades one room of the Ca' da Capo-Zendrini had been kept locked after a family member had died in it under mysterious circumstances. The contessa had finally agreed to open the room and make it accessible during a house party – only to have its newest occupant murdered in it.

'Apollonia will see you, Barbara.'

The contessa started. Gaby, her hands thrust into the pockets of the ocelot coat, stared at the contessa with the trace of what seemed to be a mocking smile on her lips.

Apollonia was reclining on the sofa in her cluttered *salotto* barely a foot away from an old space heater. A blanket was tucked around her. Her face beneath the black lace covering was gray, and her blue eyes were feverish. The contessa was alarmed. Apollonia looked frightfully ill. The contessa was not prepared for it even though Urbino had said that the woman had visibly declined since the funeral. Her blue eyes looked bruised with fever, and the flesh had sunk down upon her prominent cheekbones.

Alessandro was behind the sofa, standing straight and making the best of his shorter than average height. He was holding a book with worn brown leather covers. His good-looking face was fatigued, and his blond hair was in need of combing. He had recently shaved – small fresh cuts marred his cheeks – but he had left a wispy moustache on his upper lip.

'Here's Barbara, Mamma,' he said in a low voice.

'How are you, Apollonia dear? Excuse me for saying so, but you look very peaked. Have you seen the doctor recently?'

'Santo's been here, yes, yes. I'm well enough.' Her voice was much weaker than the contessa had ever heard it. 'Age gets us all in the end, Barbara. No doctor is going to help you.'

'I – I am glad to hear that Santo is stopping by. He is an excellent doctor. He took wonderful care of my dear Alvise, may God rest his soul. Is Eufrosina here?'

'She left a short while ago.' Alessandro offered. 'Looked like she was going to take photographs. She had some of her equipment with her.' He placed the book on a small table behind him.

'Hands, hands, only hands!' Apollonia cried out.

Alessandro gave a laugh. 'Out, out damn spot! She should take photographs of Lady Macbeth.'

'Hands, hands, hands,' his mother repeated. 'Is it Eufrosina you're looking for? Sit down. There.' She indicated a wooden chair without any arms.

Alessandro helped the contessa out of her coat and draped it over the other armchair.

'No,' the contessa said as she seated herself. 'I came to see you.'

'A visit of charity? Charity is a virtue, but it is a black vice if it makes you feel proud. Proud to be healthy, to be traipsing all around the city when you know I'm lying on my sofa.'

'I knew you weren't feeling well. I thought there might be something I could do for you, something I could get for you.'

'Alessandro takes care of whatever I need.' As if in illustration of this, he brought over a glass of water and held it in front of her while she took a few sips through a straw. When she had finished, she peered at the contessa sharply. Her eyes were bloodshot. Without any preliminary, she broke out with, 'You must feel very upset with Mina Longo. She could have turned against you instead of Olimpia.'

Astonished, the contessa said coolly, 'I doubt that.'

Apollonia nodded her head. 'Say whatever you want to say, but she could have done. Sad for poor Olimpia, but fortunate for you. Alessandro dear, would you pour some tea for our cousin?'

Apollonia spat into a handkerchief that she pulled from her sleeve. She closed her eyes. Her chest rattled loudly.

As the contessa was taking her first sip of tea, Apollonia's eyes opened. 'Don't worry. You will feel better when Mina is properly punished. We all will. And *she* will feel better, too. If, of course, her account with God is good.'

The only part of what Apollonia said that the contessa thought it appropriate to respond to was the last part. 'That is something between her and God. We can't see into another person's soul — nor should we try to invade its privacy.'

'Well said.' Apollonia smoothed the blanket against her sides.

The contessa searched her mind — or Urbino might call it her repertoire — for the right way to continue with the visit.

'I'm concerned about the security of this building,' she began. 'There's no camera and no buzzer system. The front door is unlocked.'

'Not always,' Alessandro said.

'Barbara is right,' Apollonia said. 'It's a bad arrangement. You know we do not like it. You know we were talking about it recently.'

Alessandro looked puzzled, but said nothing in response.

'Perhaps I can do something to help,' the contessa continued. 'I'd like to offer to have a security system installed.'

'After the horse gets out of the barn — or into it.' Apollonia gave a laugh that provoked an even deeper rattle. 'You feel guilty. Because of Mina.'

'I feel concerned, as I said.'

'It's not your business, Barbara. But why mention it to me? Have you spoken with Gaby and Ercule? In my house by San Zanipolo, we always were careful about keeping the front door locked and bolting the windows. But this is *their* house.'

'I haven't mentioned it to either of them yet. I thought that – that' – the contessa searched wildly for something plausible – 'that you could help me convince them.'

'Why do you think they would need convincing? You would be paying for it.'

Apollonia's thoughts were never much farther away from money than they were from religion.

'You think more clearly than they do.' Well-placed flattery was almost always good. 'Gaby thinks they have an obligation to keep the front door open during the day time because of a relative who was a monk. I am sure you know whom she means. With your understanding of religious things, you might be the best person to have her see that the monk didn't mean for the door to be kept unlocked in – in perpetuity.' The contessa was proud of coming up with a word with such religious resonance. 'He lived centuries ago. It was a different world.'

'Are you saying religious advice must bend with the times like a reed in the wind?' Apollonia came back with, marshalling her own appropriately Biblical image.

'Of course not,' the contessa said, even though her opinion was very much the opposite. She fished around in her mind for another suitable approach. After a moment, she said, 'And if Gaby and Ercule aren't concerned about themselves and about their things, certainly they'll be sensitive to your worries. You just said you think it is a bad arrangement. People often take better care of others than they do themselves.'

'Do you think so?'

'I've often found that to be true. By convincing them, you – you would be helping them to do a good deed, to be good Samaritans, so to speak.'

'The good Samaritan helped a stranger. Alessandro and I are family.'

'But the story of the Samaritan is a parable. We have to interpret it. Like the one about Christ feeding thousands of people with hardly any fish and bread.'

'That wasn't a parable! Are you saying you don't believe it?' Apollonia's eyes widened. Another rattle sounded from her chest.

'You're wiser about these things, Apollonia. And in your wisdom you can surely see that not only would you be advancing Ercule and Gaby spiritually when you encourage them to do a good deed for you, but you would be advancing yourself spiritually, too.'

'How is that?'

It was obvious she had quickened Apollonia's curiosity.

'When we make it possible for another person to do good, we – we earn a spiritual profit for ourselves. Yes, a spiritual profit!' The contessa was proud to have stumbled upon – or rather improvised – this irresistible appeal to Apollonia's two most dominant motives.

Apollonia looked at the contessa with what seemed to be a newfound respect.

'I see your point.'

'And there's another reason.' The contessa feared she might be risking what she had accomplished so far but she could not help trying to apply another turn to the screw. 'By being responsible for encouraging them to put in a security system, you would make it impossible – or very, very difficult – for anyone to commit the sin of theft.'

Did Apollonia look at her with more skepticism now? It seemed so.

The contessa was starting to regret having overplayed her role when Apollonia, who had been studying her face, said, 'You make sense. Not like Gaby and Ercule. I have told them a hundred times that they have to take better care of what God has been good enough to bestow on them. It's a slap in God's face to put it in any danger.'

'Exactly.' The contessa marveled at Apollonia's enunciation of a theological principle that was also a neat justification for her miserliness.

Alessandro, who had been following the exchange with a great deal of nervous attention, helped his mother to some more water.

Apollonia applied her handkerchief to her mouth and started to speak in a voice even weaker and fainter than before. Her first words, muffled by the handkerchief, were garbled, but the contessa soon made sense of what she was saying: 'And I've always thought it peculiar how they seem almost happy to have this building vulnerable. As if they want someone to come inside who shouldn't. Someone to steal or do something worse, like your Mina did.'

The contessa bowed her head. It seemed that she had made her point with Apollonia. 'May we all help each other be as good and kind as possible.'

'I now see why you came this morning, Barbara.'

The contessa slowly raised her head. 'Why is that?'

'To show your better side. To allow it to shine. You have been keeping it hidden. Don't forget that it's like a candle that can be easily extinguished.' She wet two fingers and quenched an imaginary candle that was standing on her chest. 'God works in mysterious ways. It was wrong of you to try to resist him.'

Apollonia broke out into a severe spasm of coughing. Alessandro hurried over and sat beside her. The contessa put her cup and saucer down on the table. Guilt and embarrassment consumed her as she looked at Apollonia lying on the sofa, her eyes closed. In pursuing her agenda, she had wearied an already weary and gravely ill woman. When Apollonia had stopped coughing, the contessa said, arising, 'I do hope, dear Apollonia, that you will have Dr Santo stop by again soon. I have stayed too long and taxed your energy. I'm sorry.'

'We shouldn't count time or effort when it's a matter of doing God's work.'

When the contessa was out on the landing, she cast a quick glance up to the attic landing. The door of Olimpia's atelier was closed. The contessa gave an involuntary shiver, remembering the scene she had witnessed, the one she doubted she would ever be able to expunge from her memory.

As she continued to linger on the landing, the sound of Alessandro's baritone from the other side of the door rewarded her. She strained to hear what he was saying:

> *Luogo è in inferno detto Malebolge,*
> *tutto di pietra di color ferrigno,*
> *come la cerchia che dintorno il volge.*
> *Nel dritto mezzo del campo maligno*
> *vaneggia un pozzo assai largo e profondo,*
> *di cui suo loco dicerò l'ordigno.*

It was from one of the cantos of Dante's *Inferno*. Knowing what Apollonia's opinion of Olimpia must have been, the contessa did not find it difficult to imagine the kind of Dantean punishments of her cousin that Apollonia had coldly thrilled herself with. She wondered how much she might have influenced Alessandro and Eufrosina against their cousin. Even if she hadn't influenced them, they might want her to believe that she had, in order to advance their own interests.

When the contessa reached the vestibule, Gaby, still in the ocelot coat, was sweeping the floor near one of the blue rooms. She kept her head down as she said goodbye.

*   *   *

Twenty minutes after leaving the Palazzo Pindar, the contessa ascended a bright, well-swept staircase that would bring her to another stage requiring her talents this morning. It was the offices of Italo Bianchi, located in a building on the Grand Canal near the Rialto Bridge.

Bianchi's secretary, a prim, middle-aged woman, greeted her and ushered her into a large room where reflected light from the Grand Canal played among the dark, solid furniture and old framed oil paintings. Bianchi, who had some of the wealthiest and most prominent clients in the city, believed that it would be in keeping with his conservative skills if he didn't change anything in his offices from the days of his father. The senior Bianchi, whom the contessa had known in his later years, had handled the conte's affairs.

A heavy writing desk crouched against the far wall. The junior Bianchi, plump, pink, and in his fifties, sat behind it. The contessa seated herself in a carved Venetian armchair with faded brown and maroon upholstery. It provided a view of the Rialto Bridge through the wide windows. A small group of tourists stood on the stone bridge, looking at the Grand Canal and taking photographs. Soon enough, with the coming of carnival, the bridge, as well as other popular points in the city, especially the great magnet of the Piazza San Marco, would be crowded with revelers.

'What a surprise, contessa! A surprise and a coincidence! I am happy to see you,' Bianchi said in the slowest and most deliberate Italian possible. 'But what is this that I see? You look very nervous. It is Mina Longo, yes. It has drained you.'

The contessa hoped that his observation meant that she had succeeded in projecting an appearance of stress, nerves, and fatigue, and not that her face was actually etched with them. 'I *am* stressed, Signor Bianchi. That is the reason I have come to see you.'

Bianchi smiled. 'Have you forgotten? I am a lawyer. Not a physician.'

'I need advice. You are correct. It is directly related to Mina Longo.'

'Yes?'

'I'm concerned that I may be held responsible in some way for — for Olimpia Pindar's murder.' She had no need of her histrionic skills to make her voice quaver. 'Because of Mina. I have heard that people have been brought to court and sued for large sums of money because their children had done something illegal. Of course, Mina is not any relationship to me, blood relationship, I mean, whereas Olimpia was. But Mina was my employee, and she's young. I suppose I could be considered — what is the term? — *in loco parentis*. I want to distance myself from her, you see.'

She had spoken her lines. She waited for Bianchi's response.

He raised his eyebrows slightly. 'A wise decision. But do not worry. You have no legal responsibility.' Bianchi paused. 'And no moral responsibility. Put it out of your mind, dear contessa.'

'A great burden has been removed.' The contessa, trying to project a sense of disburdenment, lifted her head, smiled, and straightened her shoulders slightly – slightly but not too much, always being aware of the perils of over-acting. 'But of course I'll never forgive myself. This tragedy came from my own house, from the hands of the very person who turned down my bed at night, who fixed my hair, who brought me my evening chocolate.'

The contessa, fearful of getting too caught up in her performance, restrained herself from going on with any more of Mina's personal attentions, happy that Bianchi had no Marxist sympathies.

'The shock is still new, contessa. The wound is still fresh.'

'Indeed.'

The contessa took in the rows of leather-bound law volumes, the rather grim oil painting of Bianchi Senior, and a neat stack of files on the desk. As casually as she could manage, she said; 'I wonder what will become of that lovely building now that poor Olimpia is gone. The income from her business must have been an indispensable help in keeping it afloat.' The contessa sighed. 'Just one more thing for me to add to my plate of worries.'

'Olimpia's business didn't bring in much, but she had been seeing an improvement. Her bank account received an infusion of fresh sums over the past few months.'

'I understand that she had recently signed a contract to design costumes for a theatrical production.'

Bianchi nodded.

The contessa remembered something Bianchi had said when she had arrived. 'Why is it a coincidence that I've come this morning?'

'Because I was going to telephone you. About Olimpia's will. She made a new one two months ago. You are mentioned in it.'

The contessa was sure that her expression of surprise could not have been greater if she had feigned it.

'Me? Are you sure? I had not the slightest notion. That's most unusual.'

'Not really. One client made a bequest to her grandmother. And your will leaves the Ca' da Capo-Zendrini to someone older than you are.'

The contessa's genuine surprise had to make some brief room for an equally genuine irritation at Bianchi's clarifications. 'I meant that Olimpia and I weren't close.'

'Bequests have been left to strangers.'

'And what did she leave me?' The contessa hoped that her question reflected the curiosity she felt but none of the avidity she didn't.

'Her ocelot coat.'

The image of the ocelot-clad Olimpia walking back and forth in her morning room last week was quickly followed by one of Gaby, wrapped in the fur coat at the Palazzo Pindar.

'But it belonged to her mother. I'll give it to Gaby. She should have it.' She didn't say that Gaby already did have it.

'You are free to do with the coat as you please. No conditions were placed upon the bequest. But Olimpia wanted you to have it.'

'Did she say why?'

'No. And I do not ask such questions. If the client gives me a reason for a bequest, it is of his own free will. Sometimes the reason is mentioned in the will. But it wasn't in your case.' He paused. 'Or in Mina Longo's case.'

'Mina?'

'Olimpia left all her possessions and assets – other than the house, the collection, and her coat – to Longo. Her clothes, her jewelry, the contents of the atelier, and close to ten thousand euros, not much, but good enough for someone in Longo's line of work, I would say. But Longo will never get anything. A murderer cannot inherit anything from his victim – no bequests of any kind, nothing from a life insurance policy. Unless Olimpia is survived by a child or a husband, which does not seem to be the case, the generous legacy she left to Mina goes to her oldest, living sibling. Gaby.'

'Did Olimpia have a life insurance policy?'

'No.'

'Are Gaby and Ercule aware of the provisions in Olimpia's will?'

Ercule had not given any indication to Urbino yesterday that they had been, but Gaby had referred to Mina as clever when she was criticizing her sister for not seeing things clearly. Now the contessa thought she understood why Gaby had said this.

Bianchi gave her a condescending smile. 'My dear contessa, of course they are aware of it! I would not be speaking about any provisions of the will that do not concern you if they were not. I went to the house to read it to them.'

Still in a state of astonishment and perplexity over what she had learned from Bianchi, the contessa made another visit. It was to the theatrical company that had commissioned Olimpia to design costumes. The offices were above a mask maker's shop near the Campo San Tomà.

The outer office was filled with potted plants and plastered with posters and photographs of previous productions.

No one was in the outer office except the assistant, a small, thin girl dressed in black.

'I'd like to see the company director about your upcoming production of *La Locandiera,*' the contessa said.

The assistant knocked on a closed, leather-covered door and went inside for a few moments. 'Signor Walther will see you,' she said when she returned. 'Let me take your coat.'

The director of the company was a short-haired blond man of about thirty-five dressed in a salmon-colored suit and purple tie.

After she sat down, she introduced herself, dispensing with the 'contessa' as she usually did.

'How may I help you?' He spoke Italian with a strong German accent.

'Olimpia Pindar was my cousin.'

A more serious expression passed over Walther's regular features. 'I am very sorry for your bereavement, and especially under such tragic circumstances.'

'Thank you. I know that my cousin was designing costumes for *La Locandiera.*'

'Yes. We engaged her three months ago. She had done some preliminary sketches. We were pleased with them. Your cousin was accomplished.'

'She was. It's about her work for your company that I've come.'

Walther looked puzzled. 'But we don't have any costumes she worked on. Just her sketches. I believe she was close to finishing one costume. And even if we did have the costume, it would be our property, along with the sketches and anything else she had finished. According to the contract, you understand.'

The contessa shifted in her seat and cleared her throat, even though she was seldom a seat-shifter or a throat-clearer, no matter how embarrassed and ill at ease. But she wanted to create the proper effect, since her audience was now a professional one, unlike the ones she had already performed before this morning. Walther seemed to be studying her intently.

'Let me explain why I'm here, Signor Walther. The young woman being held for her murder was in my employ.'

Walther opened his eyes wider. 'I thought I recognized your name. You are the English contessa.'

Walther's three words, '*la contessa inglese,*' made a tight knot form in the stomach of the owner of this title. The contessa realized the implications of his words – to be more exact, the histrionic implications. Her concern for Mina had prevented her from seeing them clearly and fully.

The terrible event that had occurred in Olimpia's atelier was a fascinating drama – even a melodrama – in which she, 'la contessa inglese', had an essential, deliciously ambiguous role. It was an intriguing triangle: the murdered dressmaker; her murderous lover, a simple lady's maid; and the English contessa, the recipient of the domestic attentions of the passion-crazed murderess.

The contessa could only too easily imagine the script that went along with these precisely defined roles, especially hers.

And she had revealed something to Walther that the gossiping masses – the contessa could paint such a vivid picture! – would seize on as a marvellous fillip. *La contessa inglese* was actually the cousin of the brutally murdered woman.

'Yes,' the contessa said, gaining control over herself. 'It is because my cousin's accused murderer was working for me that I have taken it upon myself to come here. One feels a strange responsibility in such matters. I am not speaking morally or legally. Yes, a strange responsibility for having been, however innocently, a link between the two parties.'

Walther continued to regard her closely, his hands clasped.

'Since I am interested in the theater and enjoyed your Gozzi production a few seasons ago,' the contessa continued, 'I thought I would inquire as to whether I could be of help.'

She paused to take a breath.

Walther leaned forward and asked, 'You are an actress, contessa?'

'Oh, no, you misunderstand me.'

'Because you strike me as a woman who might make a very good one.'

The contessa, who was somehow able to feel flattered amidst all her other emotions, bestowed a little smile on the director. 'Thank you, Signor Walther. That is a considerable compliment coming from you. But no, I'm not an actress.'

'A costume designer, then?'

'Not a costume designer either, but it is about a dressmaker, a costume designer that I have come.' The contessa started to speak more quickly than she usually did so that there might be no more misunderstandings. 'It's unfortunate that your company has been deprived of its designer under such circumstances. I would not want to see your schedule disrupted. I can recommend two excellent ones in Venice. Unless you already have someone in mind, someone you were considering along with my cousin? Perhaps my cousin, so unfortunate in her tragic death, was fortunate in having been given preference over another designer?'

Since this was what the contessa mainly wanted to know, she felt as if her question drew a great deal of attention to itself. But if it did so, Walther gave no indication.

'She was fortunate in having no competition. But we have had to move quickly, and have found a possible replacement, if we can convince him to take on the project. He lives in Milan.'

'I hope everything will go on as scheduled.'

The contessa settled back against the chair in the cabin as Pasquale brought the motorboat out into the Grand Canal. She was looking forward to being back at the Ca' da Capo-Zendrini, where she could be off-stage.

The day had turned slightly warmer, and the gray sky had given way to a sky daubed with streaks of bright blue. The *palazzi*, which still had the power to impress her with their beauty and improbable setting, unrolled themselves on both sides of the watery avenue. After a few minutes, they set her mind briefly wondering about the romance and intrigue, beauty and violence that had been enacted behind their colorful façades, maybe not too much different in kind, if not degree, from what had taken place in the Palazzo Pindar in its more humble setting. Despite having passed from one owner to another over the centuries, most of the palaces carried either the name of their original owner or, like her own building and the Palazzo Pindar, that of some subsequent illustrious one who had made a particular mark on the city.

As the boat approached the water entrance of the Ca' da Capo-Zendrini, she drank in the sight of the palazzo almost as if she were seeing it for the first time, a morning that was still fresh in her memory so many decades later. She could still hear the conte's soft voice, saying in his accented English, 'Cominelli designed it. Stone from Istria. Can you see the frieze of lions on the attic, Barbara dear?'

How proud Alvise had been of the building, almost as grand as the Palazzo Labia further up the Grand Canal, another of Cominelli's designs. How Alvise had hoped – how they had both hoped, sadly and vainly – that they would be able to pass it on to a son or a daughter.

The contessa, so preoccupied with thoughts about Olimpia's will and the two remaining owners of the Palazzo Pindar, worried about the future fate of the Ca' da Capo-Zendrini. Her will, made after the conte's death, bequeathed the building to the conte's youngest nephew, but he was a man older than she was, as Bianchi had reminded her. She should remake the will and name one of the conte's younger relatives to inherit in the eventuality that his nephew died and that she was, for whatever reason, unable to change the will. Life could be sadly unpredictable.

As the contessa, feeling weary after her efforts of the morning, was approaching the staircase that would take her up to the *piano nobile*, her steps were diverted by sounds from the room where the Fortuny exhibition was being set up. Two members of her staff — young men who did gardening and minor repairs — were disassembling the glass case with the Eleonora Duse gown. Vitale was supervising them, his arms folded.

Eufrosina was standing beside the display of scarves and purses. The glass case that had enclosed them had been taken apart and placed against a wall. Olimpia's moss green silk velvet purse, one of the contessa's Knossos scarves, and a pleated black purse lent by the conte's grandniece, which had been slightly rearranged on the cubes and rods, were among the items. Eufrosina was taking one photograph after another. A tripod stood against a wall.

Vitale joined the contessa. 'She came shortly after you left, contessa,' he informed her in a low voice. 'She said that she needed to take photographs of some of the clothing but that she couldn't take them while they were still in the cases. I've been here most of the time.'

'It's all right, Vitale.'

Eufrosina stood up. She was dressed in a suit of striped mauve wool, stylish but worn and soiled on one knee. Black cotton gloves covered her hands.

'Good morning, Barbara, or is it good afternoon?' Her voice was constrained. 'I've lost my sense of time. I wanted to take some photographs today. I hope I have not disturbed things by removing the glass cases but — but I don't want to risk any reflections. I want to do my best and show them to you right away so that you will see how good they can be.'

She averted her gaze from the contessa.

This particular display was not one of those that the contessa and Urbino had decided should be photographed for the catalogue. The contessa had given Eufrosina a detailed list of the items that needed to be photographed. The woman must be confused. But the contessa saw no point in drawing her attention to her error. Eufrosina was obviously distracted and anxious about the commission. The contessa did not want to disturb her further and make it even more difficult for her to concentrate on her work.

'I'm sure they will be very good,' the contessa assured her. When the contessa reached out and touched her arm, it was trembling. How could the contessa ever remove her from the project? It would shatter the poor woman. The contessa silently berated herself, yet again, for having decided to have her do the photography. Why hadn't she listened to Urbino!

The contessa's words did not appear to calm Eufrosina, if indeed she had heard them or even felt the contessa's consoling touch. Her eyes darted around the room as she continued to explain to the contessa how she was determined to do a good job. She wouldn't come back to the Ca' da Capo-Zendrini for a few weeks, but she would devote her energies to the Fortuny Museum. Although she spoke loudly, her voice seemed to come from a long way off. When she started to speak even more quickly, the contessa could not follow what she was saying. It flowed and surged with references to lenses and polarizing filters and reflections and incandescent lamps and exposures and flaws and flashes. The contessa continued to listen without understanding anything except that Eufrosina was feeling the effects of severe stress and that whatever photographs she was taking today could hardly be better than the mediocre ones the contessa and Urbino had already seen.

When Eufrosina finished, the contessa asked if she would like to have lunch.

'No, I must go, but thank you.' She hurried over to her tripod and started to fold it.

'I visited your mother this morning.'

'You did?' Eufrosina seemed surprised.

'Yes. I don't think she is well at all. She said that Dr Santo had been there recently. But it would be a good idea to encourage her to have him come again as soon as possible. How is your bronchitis?'

'Much better, thank you.'

Eufrosina was drawing on her coat.

'Pasquale will take you wherever you want to go.'

'Thank you, but there's no need for that.' But a few moments later, after the two workers had helped her collect her things, Eufrosina changed her mind and said she would appreciate Pasquale's services. All of the nervous energy had drained from her. Her face was slack. The contessa stood at the open door of the water landing, watching as Pasquale backed the motorboat into the Grand Canal to take Eufrosina across to Santa Croce.

A few minutes later, the contessa returned to the exhibition room. She told the workers that they need not put the glass case back around the display of purses and scarves. She would have them do it another day.

That evening the contessa and Urbino went to a small restaurant near the Piazza San Marco for dinner. She wanted to get out of the house even though she had been gone all morning.

Being at home in the evening reminded her of how Mina was lying in some cell in God knew what a state. Corrado Scarpa had still not been able to get her permission to see Mina. She had spoken with Mina's attorney,

Giorgio Lanzani, who was able to convey messages back and forth. Mina had told him to assure the contessa that she was fine and that she hoped they would see each other soon.

Shortly after they sat down, the contessa started to provide an account of her day's performances, which continued through dinner.

Having ordered only a salad, she had little to distract her from rendering each scene in detail. Urbino was able to give her his full attention despite his indulgence in a three-course meal that included roasted eel cooked according to an old Venetian recipe. He listened to what she said and how she said it, and scrutinized her face for any additional revelations.

When it came to dessert, the contessa could not resist the ricotta cake, which necessitated a postponement of the rest of her account until she had finished it.

Tonight, as always, Urbino was an excellent listener, and he kept his interruptions to a minimum, usually to have her repeat something he did not quite catch the first time around or to give him more details and impressions.

It was only after they had re-settled themselves in the bar and started sharing a bottle of Montepulciano that they examined the fruits of the contessa's efforts more closely.

'An excellent job, my very dear Nora,' Urbino said.

The contessa felt herself glowing under his praise. 'And also your very dear Sarah Bernhardt?'

'That, too.' Urbino twirled the wine glass in his hand. 'Do you think Mina knew about the will?' As she expected, he seized on what was surely the most relevant thing she had learned. 'If she did, it could change a great deal. No, not about how we feel about her innocence, but she might have said something about it to someone if she did know. Maybe Gaby. After all, Gaby confided in her about her fears.'

'I have no idea if she knew.'

'She might have felt uncomfortable telling you. She kept most of her relationship with Olimpia to herself.'

'And I never pried.' This was not because the contessa had not burned with curiosity, but because she was a keen respecter of others' privacy. But the problem with privacy in a murder investigation, as Urbino had pointed out to her on numerous occasions, was that it could not be respected – and should not be. The private life, the hidden life, was often what had led to the violence. One could only hope that, after a case was solved and the guilty person had been exposed, the uncovered secrets that had had nothing to do with the case could be re-interred.

'It makes it worse for Mina,' Urbino observed. 'I hardly need to tell you that. You can imagine the scenario that the police will have already created. Each piece probably seems to fit perfectly. Moneyless girl from Sicily in the service of an aloof, wealthy woman.'

This was not all that far from the scenario the contessa had tortured herself with in Walther's office but she took umbrage with some of Urbino's description. 'Mina is paid very well, and I'm not aloof! I do not *fare la contessa* with her, you know that. I put little distance between us.'

'Don't defend yourself by saying that to anyone, Barbara! People are going to try to pull you into the picture. Don't give them any more encouragement than they already have.'

'I already am in the picture. *La contessa inglese*,' she murmured.

'Precisely. As you said over dinner, *la contessa inglese* seems to have already been assigned her role in a deadly triangle. And there could be more than a few tongues wagging – in the heads of people who don't know you and never even heard of you until now – that *you* could have murdered Olimpia. Oh, you can be sure they'll be able to work out a very plausible motivation for that.'

Urbino held up his hand as she started to protest. 'But let me continue with the other pieces in the scenario. I'll revise them slightly. A poor young Sicilian woman. A generous, warm, and wealthy mistress of the house – you see, it does not look too much better. Then there is the lonely, unmarried dressmaker, rattling around in an old palazzo with a bunch of other eccentrics. Dressmaker gets smitten, gets manipulated, gets murdered. It's all so damnably neat.'

The contessa's heart sank. 'I'm afraid it is. And I had to get the ocelot coat. I hope that doesn't get around. It could look like a pay-off for having been the go-between, the – what is the name I am thinking of?'

'The Pandarus.'

'Yes, the Pandarus! But why did she leave it to me?'

'It might have been her way of thanking you for being responsible for bringing – quite innocently – Mina to her notice. Olimpia never would have met her if it had not been for you. Or she might have left it to you because you *are* family. And you appreciate beautiful things. You have a respect for tradition, continuity. Leave it to Gaby? A kind sisterly act, certainly. But where would the poor woman wear it?'

'In the house as she's doing now! It's cold enough in there for it. I will give it to her. Or, rather, let her keep it.'

'She must be upset that Olimpia didn't will her anything. Her share in the house and the collection she expected, of course. It appears to be what the three of them agreed to, even maybe what they promised their father if the topic ever came up while he was still alive.'

'I wonder if she took the coat before or after the reading of the will. And it makes one wonder if she took any of Olimpia's other things, from her rooms and from the atelier.'

'Yes, it does make one wonder.' Lines of concentration deepened along his brows and under his eyes. After a few moments he said, 'Olimpia could have been murdered because of something she had or was thought to have had. Someone else wanted it, needed it. I don't mean money.'

'What do you mean?'

'I am just speculating, Barbara. I have no idea what it might have been, but it would have had to have great value of some kind. Gaby and Ercule get her share of the house and the collection, but they are not getting her personal possessions or perhaps not the contents of the atelier, although Bianchi did not mention that. Mina gets all that, but if she is convicted, whatever Olimpia bequeathed her will go to Gaby, wouldn't it? She's the next oldest sibling.'

The contessa nodded.

'In a manner of speaking,' Urbino added, after taking a sip of wine, 'it would be to Gaby's advantage to keep Mina looking as guilty as possible. She would get Olimpia's possessions. And we've seen how eager she was to take over the ocelot coat. She would clearly benefit from Mina's conviction, even if she had nothing to do with Olimpia's murder.'

The contessa could not believe that Urbino — or, to be honest, she as well — had reached the point where they had to consider such things about Gaby or anyone else in the Palazzo Pindar. But she knew that they had set out on a course that they could not turn aside from, no matter where it led.

The contessa, who had thought that she had uncovered some interesting facts and possibilities, was realizing that things were much more complicated and even more disturbing than they had originally seemed to be.

The wine was giving her a pleasant feeling, but it was making her sleepy. She had already had three glasses over dinner. She was not sure she would be able to follow Urbino through many more of his ruminations.

'As always,' Urbino said, 'the problem is figuring out what the facts mean. Like your ocelot coat. Why did Olimpia leave it to you? And what about this business of the door of the Palazzo Pindar not being locked during the daytime? That house, that museum are Gaby's and Ercule's patrimony as they were Olimpia's along with them. They should want to protect what they have from any damage, any theft, as Apollonia says. The loss of some of the objects would be Gaby's main concern, but there is also money involved. Some of those things could be sold for a pretty penny. If the house and the museum had a good security system and anything were to be stolen, they might not be able to recover the objects but they would recover some money. Even if they have insurance now, they wouldn't get a cent if anything were taken.'

The contessa did her best to try to follow each question and each point some distance toward a possible answer and clarification, but it was proving to be a very short distance.

'Do you have any answers, *caro*?' The contessa took another sip of wine.

'Ideas and questions, not answers. The ideas and questions are relatively easy. One seems to generate another. It's the answers that are difficult.'

The waiter came over and poured more wine for them.

'Let's see if Apollonia can help influence Ercule and Gaby to put in a security system. She's the matriarch, in a manner of speaking, and the Pindars have great respect for tradition and the past, even if it's taken some unhealthy forms. And since you've offered to assume the costs, they might agree. They might seize the opportunity to toss aside a family tradition that's become ludicrous – *if* tradition is the real or main reason behind it.'

The contessa's head was throbbing. It had been a long day and several glasses of wine too many. She brought up again, hoping she was not slurring her words, how ill Apollonia had been today. 'I doubt very much if she's up to the task, not now. She was trying to be her usual self, but she's declined considerably since the funeral. She used to know so many people, be the life of the party. Now she is all alone, except for Eufrosina and Alessandro. Most of the people she used to know are dead. The few others don't seem to care.' The contessa felt a strong surge of sympathy for Apollonia. How well she remembered her in her prime, and it did not seem all that long ago.

'It's sad. But sick mothers – even desperately ill ones – often outlive their children,' Urbino observed. 'Or even die before their disease gets them. If you had asked me who, of everyone in the Palazzo Pindar, might end up murdered I wouldn't have said Olimpia or even Gaby – at least not before we learned she's afraid of something bad happening to her. I would have said Apollonia. It is a terrible thing to say when she is so ill, but I keep thinking of that. She's a sacred terror. I wouldn't want to be on her bad side.'

Urbino's glass seemed almost empty again, but perhaps she was mistaken. The contessa suspected that her vision was going the way of her concentration.

What Urbino had been saying for the past few minutes floated in her mind, where it was bumped, jostled, and nudged by almost everything else he had been saying this evening.

She did her best to keep her attention anchored.

Urbino was moving on to Eufrosina and her behavior in the Fortuny exhibition room. He found this situation most interesting, he said, and asked her to tell him again what items she had been photographing.

'Yes, quite interesting,' she heard, and 'doing her best to impress you' and 'desperate for the money' and 'speak with your staff tomorrow' and other things that drifted past her about Giorgio Lanzani.

Then, Urbino said gently, 'It's time for us to go, Barbara.'

She understood this well enough and was relieved to hear it.

The cold night air and the wind blowing from the lagoon revived her. As they went past the Basilica, gleaming darkly and silently above them, she clung to Urbino's arm, more in affection than for support. City workers were cleaning the front steps and the pavement in front of the Basilica with a hose and brooms. Fog, like billows of a bridal veil, was slowly advancing from the water, brushing the wedding cake of the Doges' Palace and curling around the twin pillars. Above them gulls were flying mysteriously in and out of the fog.

They did not speak about Mina or Olimpia or anything related to the murder at the Palazzo Pindar. Urbino mentioned that Eugene would be arriving tomorrow.

'He should be a diversion for you,' she said.

'And for you. You're not going to escape him, Barbara dear.'

'I don't want to. I find him charming. And he brings a welcome air of spontaneity with him – as fresh as this air.'

'If by that you mean he usually doesn't think before he speaks, you're absolutely right.'

'You're just afraid he's going to keep revealing secrets about you. You've managed to keep quite a few corners dark.'

'That's because my house has many, many rooms.' He gave her shoulder an affectionate squeeze. He looked up at the sky above the Bacino. 'I hope we get some more snow while Eugene is here. It would be nice for him to see Venice in the snow.'

'And I hear the child in you speaking, too.'

No denial came from her friend, but instead a boyish smile as he guided her across the stones of the Molo, which were slippery from the water washed in from the Bacino.

They made their way to where the contessa's motorboat was moored, rocking from the passage of the boats in the Bacino.

At most other times when the contessa and Urbino went out together in the motorboat, they would part after she got into the boat and he would walk back to the Palazzo Uccello. But tonight her gentlemanly escort rode all the way home with her and delivered her safely into the hands of Vitale.

Within less than an hour of being home, the contessa was lying in her drowsy bed with Zouzou pressed against her side. A long bath had soothed her and dispersed some of the wine fumes smoking through her head.

When she was lying in her bed at night, she felt cloistered, protected. The closed, double-paned windows, reinforced by heavy shutters, kept out all sounds, even at the height of the summer season. No boat's horn, peals of laughter, or barking dogs penetrated her boudoir tonight or on any night.

She had lit candles and placed them on the nightstand next to the silver-framed photograph of the conte. The candles were a nighttime votive to her dead husband, extinguished before she fell asleep. They were also the light by which she liked to read in bed.

She gazed at Alvise's sharp-featured, good-looking face. The photograph had been taken a few years after their marriage. Other photographs of him were placed throughout the room. She let her eye run over them. She found it strange that Apollonia seldom, if ever, mentioned her dead husband, and from what the contessa could tell, there were no photographs of him in her *salotto*. Maybe she kept them for more private viewing, in her bedroom, like these photographs of Alvise, although the contessa had others scattered through the house.

For that matter, neither did Eufrosina ever mention her dead husband. The contessa had known both men. They had been kind, generous souls, and Apollonia had wielded a strong influence over both of them — husband and son-in-law.

The contessa picked up da Ponte's memoirs, but she closed it after a few minutes. She would rather think of the future before she fell asleep than immerse herself in someone's past, no matter how fascinating it was.

She picked up another book from the nightstand. A gift from Urbino, it was about treasure hunts that had been organized in country houses and gardens in England and Europe. Someday soon, God willing, the contessa planned to organize a treasure hunt at the Ca' da Capo-Zendrini or the Villa La Muta in Asolo.

As she leafed through the book and looked at the illustrations, with her fingers caressing Zouzou, she allowed her mind to drift to that future happy time.

And to another future happy time, when Mina would be free.

She patted Zouzou's head, and then bent down to whisper in her ear, 'Don't worry. Mina will soon be back with us.'

The contessa reached out and extinguished the candles. Every night Mina would come into her bedroom to be sure the contessa had extinguished them. Soon she would be doing it again. Yes, soon.

Eight

The next morning, when Urbino went to the Ca' da Capo-Zendrini, he wasn't surprised that the contessa had only a vague remembrance of what he had said last night about speaking with her staff. She looked a little weary and said she had a headache. For all the time he had known her, she had never overindulged in any kind of alcohol, and he couldn't even imagine applying the word 'drunk' to her, even if, to a less loving and sympathetic eye, she might technically have been so.

Last night she had been in a celebratory mood because of what she had accomplished that day. Urbino was pleased with what she had learned and not surprised by the ingenuity of his Nora, although unlike her namesake she did not have a high tolerance for alcohol. And her stress over Mina had made her even more susceptible to it than usual.

'You can speak with them in the *salotto blu*.'

Fifteen minutes later, after the contessa had informed her staff that Urbino wanted to ask them a few questions about Mina, he spoke with them one by one. With each of them he made it clear at once that the point of speaking with them was to try to help Mina. He doubted if there was any contact between the contessa's staff and the residents of the Palazzo Pindar, except for Eufrosina's visits, and she had said she wouldn't be back at the Ca' da Capo-Zendrini until a few weeks had gone by.

But even if the Pindars learned that he was on a mission to try to clear Mina, it would probably only confirm what they already suspected and it could work to his advantage. They might start behaving differently with him, and he would be quick to detect it.

Urbino hoped that none of the staff would let their loyalty to the contessa prevent them from revealing something about Mina that might not look, on the surface at least, helpful to her situation. He was pleased, therefore, when some of them made little effort to conceal their resentment and envy for a favored colleague. Luisa, the cook, even referred to Mina as the contessa's *cocco*, her pet, but did it with a twinkle in her eye and added, 'It's only what the sweet girl deserves.' Vitale, more careful in his words, said that in his opinion Mina had never done anything to indicate that she did not deserve 'the contessa's kind preference.' Giovanna, the contessa's former housekeeper and now semi-retired in the comfort of her own suite of rooms in the staff quarters, expressed a great deal of affection for Mina but said she wished the girl had not kept quite as much to herself.

However, no one — and he spoke, in addition to Vitale, Luisa and Giovanna, with the present housekeeper, the maids, the kitchen staff, the gardener, and Pasquale — no one had anything negative to say about Mina. Neither did any of them say they had noticed any strange behavior by Mina, except for Vitale who mentioned how upset the girl had been when she had learned that Olimpia had been to visit the contessa, and had rushed out of the house.

No one claimed to have seen her in the company of any member of the Pindar family except Olimpia, and that had been on very few occasions, since Mina and Olimpia had tended to meet at the Palazzo Pindar and seldom had gone out together in public. As far as any of them knew, she had never received a visitor.

He also asked Vitale and the housekeeper, since they were the most vigilant members of the staff, whether they had ever noticed Eufrosina anywhere near Mina's room or in any part of the staff's quarters. They had not.

The overall picture was of a hard-working, dedicated — if somewhat indulged — girl who was, in the words of almost everyone, '*molto simpatica*.'

'Mina is unimpeachable in their eyes as she is in ours,' Urbino said to the contessa afterward. 'You can be relieved that none of them is likely to pass on anything negative about her.'

'Because there is nothing negative.'

'Yes. And she appears to have kept very much to herself. Her life centered on the Ca' da Capo and the Palazzo Pindar. It only strengthens my belief even more that the solution to this case lies in the Palazzo Pindar or its collection.'

Rain, heavy at times, descended on the city that afternoon, scourging the windowpanes of the Palazzo Uccello. Urbino put on his Inverness cape and boots and grabbed a large umbrella before he set out to meet Eugene at the train station.

Ten minutes after leaving the house, he stepped inside the fifteenth-century Church of San Gabriele. Cold, rainy January days like these always seemed to guide his steps to the church. It had been at this time of the year that San Gabriele had played a big role in his first case of sleuthing. He had been set down his unexpected path by the church's relic of a Sicilian martyr, Santa Teodora.

He peered down into a crystal coffin that enshrined the body of the little saint, miraculously preserved according to the Vatican and popular belief. Her face was covered in a silver mask, her feet shod in tiny scarlet slippers. Because of his efforts, the saint had been restored to her proper place – that is, if you could say that the public display of a centuries-old dead body was a proper place.

As he took one last lingering look at the masked Santa Teodora, Urbino vowed to himself that he would restore Mina to her proper place as well. But the next moment, the irony of his fervent promise struck him, and despite the Gothic atmosphere of the chapel and the seriousness of his newest case, he smiled.

Restore Mina to her proper place indeed! By this, he had meant, quite simply, service to the Contessa da Capo-Zendrini. What had become of him!

Urbino cut through the Ghetto. As he walked over the iron bridge and into the Campo di Ghetto Nuovo on its own island, his mood darkened. The Ghetto, with its five synagogues and tall buildings, had this effect on him even on the brightest and balmiest of days. There was no way of escaping it or escaping the sense that the ghosts of the men, women and children who used to be confined within its small area at night surrounded him. The ghosts were no less sad and bleak because they wore the colorful hats that marked them out from the other Venetians.

He stood in front of a plaque commemorating the Holocaust in grim but inspiring words, focusing on the last line: 'Our memories are your only grave.'

The phrase kept echoing through his mind as he made his way out of the Ghetto.

'Our memories are your only grave . . .'

Because his thoughts were filled with the Pindars, the words, with some revision, became detached from their inexpungable historical context and associated with the more mundane tragedy across the Grand Canal in the Palazzo Pindar. In some of Urbino's darker moments, when the religion that had been drilled into him as a child faltered and came close to failing, he believed that the only immortality was in the memories of those one left behind.

Olimpia would only have twelve years' rest on San Michele – unless Gaby and Ercule paid for a perpetual resting place or the contessa intervened. But surely Mina, if she could be proven innocent and could inherit what Olimpia had willed her, would do it. She would keep Olimpia's memory alive.

But after a succession of many deaths, the memories died, too.

The Pindar line seemed on the point of extinction, unless Gaby, Ercule, or Alessandro married and had a child. The only member of the younger generation who had married was Eufrosina, but she had no children.

Urbino had to know more about Achille and Nedda. They were two of the 'holes' that the contessa and he had mentioned in the morning room when she was telling him what she knew about the Pindars.

When he reached the steps of the Ponte delle Puglie over the Cannaregio Canal, he checked his watch. He still had plenty of time to get to Santa Lucia to meet Eugene's train. He went into a nearby café and ordered an espresso 'corrected' with anisette, tossing it down quickly at the counter as he had become accustomed to doing after his years in Italy.

When he left the café, the rain had let up slightly. Small companies of tourists, far fewer than the stream that would pour through the city in a few weeks for carnival, were walking down the Lista di Spagna, for this was the main route to the Piazza San Marco.

Urbino's heart sank when he saw, at the foot of the Ponte dei Scalzi, a young man in a red-and-black harlequin hat with neon lights that flashed on and off. From his shouts at the passers-by, Urbino could tell that he was not even a tourist but a Venetian.

Carnevale, unfortunately, had already arrived, in a fashion. Urbino couldn't escape it completely.

'There you are, Urbino boy!' came a loud voice as Urbino was hurrying through the concourse toward the trains.

His ex-brother-in-law was striding toward him. Behind him, a porter was pushing a trolley laden with suitcases.

Eugene Hennepin was a stout man in his mid-fifties who had made millions of dollars in sugar cane by the time he was thirty. Five years ago his father, the so-called 'Sugar Cane King', had died, tripling his fortune and making him and his sister Evangeline – Urbino's ex-wife – even richer than they had been before.

'Good God!' he exclaimed, taking in Urbino's cape, 'where's the trombone? You look like you've run away from a marchin' band!' He was dressed in a tan trench coat and held a Borsalino hat in his hand.

A middle-aged couple – a man with Asian features and a blond, blue-eyed woman – came to a halt beside Eugene with their less burdened trolley.

'This here is Frank and Betty Chin. Met 'em on the train. Americans – even Frank. Born there like you and me, Frank was, even his father. They're goin' to a cookin' school in Venice. This is Urbino, my brother-in-law that used to be. I told you all about him.'

Urbino welcomed the Chins.

'Pleased to meet you, Mr Macintyre,' Frank Chin said. 'It's an interesting coincidence. Before coming here I read your book on Proust and Venice. I teach French literature at Bayside University in San Francisco. I enjoyed it very much.'

'Thank you.'

'I told Frank and Betty that you could help them find their hotel. It's near that big bridge with the shops.'

'I'd be pleased.'

'Do you have the Countess Barbara's motorboat or are we goin' in your gondola? Can't wait to take a ride in it. The one I bought here got tossed around on those rocks in the lake behind the house. No one's been able to repair it like it should be. I may have to pack it up and ship it back here.'

'We'll take a water taxi,' Urbino said. 'We'll go out in the gondola one of these days, and you'll be most welcome, too,' he said to the Chins.

'That would be nice,' Betty said with a sweet smile.

Urbino guided everyone out to the stairs that led down to the water, offering the Chins the umbrella, for the rain had started to come down again heavily. Betty oohed and aahed at the sight of the Grand Canal and the buildings across the way. Frank observed that it looked just like a Canaletto. Urbino told him that there was, in fact, a Canaletto at the National Gallery in London that showed part of the same scene but from a different angle.

The four of them were soon proceeding down the Grand Canal in a water taxi through the driving rain. Frank unfolded a map of the city. Urbino indicated on the map where they were and where the Rialto Bridge was, as well as the Piazza San Marco, to help the newly arrived couple with their bearings. Then he drew his companions' attention to the peculiar shape of the city. 'Like two fish biting each other or two lobster claws.' Keeping up the culinary comparison, since the Chins were taking the cooking course, he added, 'Boris Pasternak said that it looks like a swollen croissant.'

Urbino left it to Frank to explain to Eugene who Pasternak was.

Urbino pointed out some of the buildings. The scene was particularly lovely this afternoon because of the weather. The façades of the palaces glistened with the wet, and the rain-splashed windows muted and blended the colors. It was like a series of watery, misty impressionist paintings.

The Chins were astute and appreciative observers, noticing details and identifying architectural styles. They admired buildings as different as the Palazzo Giovanelli, the Fondaco dei Turchi, and the Ca' da Capo-Zendrini.

The Chins saved their greatest enthusiasm, however, for the Ca' d'Oro.

'Absolutely exquisite,' Frank said.

'It looks just like lace,' his wife cried.

'Very nice,' Eugene observed. 'But you said it's called "House of Gold", Urbino. I don't see any gold.'

'That was a long time ago.' Frank said. 'You have to imagine it, Eugene. It was covered in gold leaf, wasn't it, Urbino? I remember reading it in my guidebook.'

'Yes, gold leaf — and vermilion and ultramarine.'

A yellow and orange ambulance came racing up the Canal and pulled into the Santa Sofia traghetto stop. Three men in bright orange jumpsuits hurried out with a stretcher and rushed across the square. Betty seemed mesmerized.

'Do boats do everything here?' she asked.

'Yes,' Urbino said. 'We have garbage boats and delivery boats and fire-boats and police boats — and floating hearses. You name it.'

'Fascinating.'

A few minutes later, the water taxi arrived at the Chins' hotel on the embankment by the Rialto Bridge. Urbino oversaw the transfer of their bags to the hotel porter, and he and Eugene went inside with them for a few minutes to see that everything was in order. The small group parted with the hope that they would see each other soon.

Urbino waited for Eugene in the Dandolo bar of the Danieli. Eugene had gone up to his suite to see to the disposition of his bags and to telephone his wife May-Foy back in New Orleans.

When Eugene came down, surrounded by the scent of freshly applied cologne and his face looking even redder than usual as if from a vigorous scrubbing, they ordered a bottle of champagne and two plates of small sandwiches.

'I've got two balconies this time, you devil! Thank you. I have a view of the whole bay, though you can't see too much today with the rain. Everything looks gray.'

The waiter opened the champagne and poured out glasses for them. Eugene held up his glass. 'To old times and new times! To friends and family!'

He drank down his champagne quickly, and then poured himself another glass before the waiter could come over. 'Poor May-Foy. Wish she was here with us. Don't know why that gal always wants to stick in the house. She'd love it here. All this pink marble and stained glass – and look at those glass chandeliers! She's missin' out on things as usual. That's why I have to bring as much back for her as I can.'

Eugene had been relentless in his buying on his previous trip to Italy, but most of what he had bought had been with May-Foy in mind.

Eugene wolfed down most of his *tramezzini,* washing them down with champagne. 'So, where do we start, partner?' He reached into the pocket of his corduroy sports jacket and took out a piece of paper. 'I've written down everything we did last time, though I bet I missed a lot of things. Got out a guide book to jog my memory.'

Ten years ago, Urbino had gladly braved the heat and crowds of an August to show Eugene all the major sights.

'I want to see everything all over again, plus some new things. I want to hit the casino this time around. And I keep thinkin' of that church that was dark enough for bats. I guess there's no chance it's goin' to be anything but darker this time of year. What's it called? The one plastered all over with mosaics. I want to see the horses up close this time.'

'The Basilica San Marco.'

'Are you sure? Thought it had a different name. And then there's that place that's got the biggest paintin' in the world. Called "Paradise", right? And I want to go to that palace with its top chopped off, the one with all the weird pictures. Some rich American lady owned it. Where we saw that drowned girl. No way is either of us goin' to forget her. You were playin' detective that summer, the way you like to do.' He gave Urbino a sharp look and seemed about to ask him something, but decided against it.

'The Palazzo Guggenheim.'

'That's it. I wrote down on the list "the place with the naughty statue."'

By this, Eugene meant the Marino Marini metal sculpture of a horse and rider that was on the terrace. The rider sported an erect penis.

Eugene drained his champagne glass and stood up. 'Let's get goin'. Where do we go first?'

Two hours later, when they stood under umbrellas and looked at the Bridge of Sighs as the rain fell down furiously around them, Eugene grabbed Urbino's arm. 'Have you noticed something? I've been here for three solid hours and I haven't mentioned Evie once.'

'Yes, I did notice.'

'Let me tell you something. I'm lettin' it all go, lettin' the idea of you and Evie ever bein' together again go. She's fine the way she is. And do I know you're set in *your* ways! You can go in your different directions.'

Urbino was happy to hear this, since he and Evangeline had been divorced for almost twenty-five years. Eugene had continued to try to get them back together again. His efforts had reached a peak during his previous visit to Venice, which had been shortly after Evangeline's second marriage had failed.

'It wasn't meant to be,' Urbino said. 'I hope she's well.'

'Very well. She sends you her hugs, but she didn't mention any kisses. And that's just about the last you're gonna hear about her from me.'

'There's no need to avoid mentioning her.' Urbino slapped Eugene on the shoulder. 'Come on. Let's get to the Piazza. If we hurry, we'll be able to see the statues strike the hour.'

During the next several days Urbino fell – first reluctantly and then with increasing enjoyment – into the role of Eugene's *cicerone*, although his thoughts were never far away from the investigation. He often had been able to make important leaps forward in a case when he was occupied with something else.

Being with Eugene, someone from his past life, from before he had decided to live in Venice, re-quickened some of the currents in him that had become dangerously still. He was too often wrapped up in his own thoughts and his own world.

Urbino and Eugene managed to re-visit most of the items on Eugene's list and add a few new sights. Eugene was giving him the opportunity to experience some of the city's treasures that he had neglected for longer than he should have. If he was not seeing the city's treasures with new eyes, it was with renewed ones.

Urbino did not mind being dragged into one shop after another to find special items for May-Foy, and he even enjoyed their hours at the casino. Eugene seemed to bring him luck. Urbino was not the gambling type, and he began to gamble grudgingly, hesitantly, but by the end of the evening at Chemin de Fer, he had doubled the small amount of money he had set aside to lose. 'Beginner's luck,' Eugene called it, and this was how Urbino thought it best to think of it. He had heard terrible tales of those who had gone from being gambling cynics to gambling addicts in little more than one evening like this at the tables.

During the first three days of Eugene's visit, the weather did not clear up for long. When it did, it was mainly after midnight, but the rain began again at eight or nine, first with a thin penetrating drizzle and then more heavily, and continued during the day. Urbino knew this did not bode well for the city, even if there were many long interludes without any rain. The Piazza San Marco and the Molo, as well as other areas, were slightly flooded, sending Urbino, Eugene, and everyone else to walk the wooden planks raised above the water. Eugene got into the spirit of things, considering it almost as a form of entertainment, although being from New Orleans, he had a respect for and fear of flooding. But it somewhat consoled him to know that 'only' the monuments of the city were at risk and not its inhabitants.

Urbino did not see the contessa while he was entertaining Eugene, but they spoke on the telephone. She was trying to enlist more help, in addition to that of Corrado Scarpa, in order to secure permission to visit Mina. The day after Eugene's arrival, she had gone to La Muta to see if everything was in order, just in case Eugene expressed an interest in seeing the villa again. He had spent an enjoyable period with the contessa in Asolo ten years ago. Urbino suspected that she also wanted to get away, even if only briefly, from the Ca' da Capo-Zendrini, with its memories of Mina.

By the evening of the third day, despite the fact that Eugene was turning out to be a more enjoyable diversion than Urbino had anticipated, he was pleased to hear that he would be spending the next day with the Chins. Urbino would be able to take full advantage of the day to return to his investigation. Time was slipping by all too quickly.

At nine o'clock the next morning Urbino was sheltering from the rain under the *sottoportico* of the building Nedda Bari was renting from Apollonia Ballarin. It was the first time he had been to Bari's residence. It was situated on a small canal in the easternmost extremity of the Cannaregio, between the Fondamenta Nuove and the Rialto. The building, in a poor state of repair and with few distinguishing features, had little to recommend it except its location and the *sottoportico* that ran beside it.

He had met Bari half a dozen years ago through Natalia. Bari had asked him if he would be interested in hiring an honest and able young man to help around the Palazzo Uccello. This had been before Gildo had started working for him. Urbino agreed and he had been pleased with the young man's work. He had regretted it when he had secured a full-time position in Mestre.

Nedda, whose husband had left her with more than enough money to keep her comfortable, had dedicated herself to helping the less fortunate. She had received a degree in social work after her husband's death, but she didn't work for any organization and she didn't have any business quarters. Instead, she held court and dispensed her services liberally from her home. Urbino found her to be an affable person, who was as loquacious as she was zealous.

A thin, elderly woman answered the bell. Laughter and loud voices sounded behind her. Urbino introduced himself and asked if he could see Nedda Bari. He closed his umbrella and shook off the water. The woman led him to the doorway of a large room that looked out on to the *sotto-portico*. He hesitated to enter. He was dripping water from his boots and his cape on to the tile floor of the hallway.

Nedda, wearing a red-and-green striped robe-like dress, was sitting on a small sofa. She was a heavy-set, attractive woman in her mid-fifties with large, expressive eyes. On her lap sat a girl of about four or five, with curly red hair. The child was drinking a glass of milk. Perched behind them on the back of the sofa was a tortoise-shell cat. Another little girl, also redheaded, who looked as if she could be the other child's twin, was standing behind the sofa and petting the cat.

A small group of men and women kept Nedda company. Some were sitting on chairs and sofas, others were walking around or were clustered in conversational groups at the windows and in corners, and one was sprawled out on the faded carpet. This was a very thin man, who was tying up newspapers and magazines with twine. Everyone was talking at the same time. The aroma of popped corn was in the air.

A few sentences detached themselves from the convivial hubbub. 'I'll never go back to him' and 'I applied for the job yesterday' and 'Nedda gave me the down payment.'

Nedda looked up from the little girl, whose face she was wiping with a handkerchief.

'Signor Macintyre! What a nice surprise.' Her black, graying hair, cut very short, was sticking up in places as if from electricity. 'We were just going to have hot chocolate and coffee. Please join us.'

'Thank you. An espresso would be fine.'

'Maria, would you get Signor Macintyre an espresso,' she said to the elderly woman. 'The hot chocolate for me. Is everyone else all right?' she threw out to the room at large.

Despite all the commotion, the several conversations, and all the activity, her appeal was somehow heard. Two women, sitting across from each other on rickety chairs, said they would have hot chocolate. A stout man, who was pacing the room and reading aloud from a sheet of paper, called out for an espresso.

'Why don't you sweet little angels help Maria,' she said to the twins, who immediately scampered off.

Urbino was still hesitating in the doorway. A small pool of water was collecting around his feet.

'Don't just stand there, Signor Macintyre. Sit next to me. And please take off that marvellous cape of yours. Put it on one of the hooks. No, no, you don't have to take off your boots.' She gave a high, infectious laugh. 'Wipe them on the rug beside the door. That's it. If I worried about people getting the floor dirty, I'd have to close up shop.'

Urbino seated himself beside Nedda, not without some difficulty, given the smallness of the sofa and Nedda's size.

One of the twins came back, crying that the floor in the kitchen was getting flooded.

'Don't worry about it, sweetheart. Take the broom by the back door and sweep it out. You don't mind, do you? Then be sure the piece of wood and the cloths are pushed tight against the door. That's a good girl. No, Vittorio, don't put that magazine with the others,' Nedda said to the man lying on the carpet. 'Evelina wants it, don't you, Evelina?'

A young woman, who was standing in a corner examining a calendar on the wall, turned around. Urbino recognized the thin woman who had accompanied Nedda to Olimpia's funeral. She went over to retrieve the magazine.

'So what can I do for you, Signor Macintyre? I think you might need some more help. I'm sure I can find someone more than suitable for you.'

Before Urbino could respond, Maria, helped by one of the twins, distributed the coffee and the chocolate. On the tray was a plate with three *pignoleti* biscuits. Maria placed it on the table in front of the sofa.

'But what is this?' Nedda cried. 'Three *pignoleti*?'

'We don't have any more.'

'Susanna.' Nedda addressed a woman in her sixties who resembled Evelina and was now speaking with her by the windows as Evelina looked through the magazine. 'Would you mind getting a kilo of *pignoleti*, and while you're at the shop, get a kilo of *buranelli*, too. I hate for you to go out in this rain, but we'll need them later, too, for the children who are coming. You know where the jar of money is. Yes, yes, just take my poncho.' She turned back to Urbino. 'I'm sorry, Signor Macintyre.'

'I see that it's a busy time for you,' Urbino said in a louder voice than he was accustomed to use.

'It's almost always like this. But I can fit you in. Yes, squeeze you in,'

she said in English. She gave a loud laugh. 'I can squeeze you in the way
I have squeezed you in on this sofa!' she continued in English, before
lapsing back into Italian. 'You're thin enough.' She turned away from
him again: 'If you're going out with your mother, Evelina, be sure to
come back. You have to pick up Lucia from school. It's your job this
week. And Vittorio, you look as if you are about to collapse from worrying
– and worrying about nothing. Why don't you go upstairs? Lie down
and rest.'

It appeared that Nedda ran a nursery, a counseling office, a boarding
house, and a general shelter as well as any number of other services. If
Urbino wanted to get any information from her, he was going to have to
be concentrated and quick.

When Nedda asked him again what she could do for him, Urbino seized
the opportunity. The woman was so accustomed to doing things for others
that she assumed he had come for help of some kind. She was making it
easier for him.

'Actually, it's not about getting someone to help out at the house,
even though Carlo was an excellent worker. I am managing fine with
Gildo. I don't know if you know it, but I'm writing a book on Mariano
Fortuny.'

'Apollonia told me when I gave her the January rent.'

Urbino wondered how much of a conversation the two women had
had on that occasion. From what Urbino understood, relations between
them were not good. Although Apollonia was more than eager to take
Nedda's money, she disapproved of the kind of help she was providing
and the kind of undesirable people – in Apollonia's opinion – who came
to the house.

'I'm trying to get as much information about Fortuny as possible,' Urbino
went on. 'I was wondering if you've heard any anecdotes about him that
you could pass on. Perhaps from Efigenia, Apollonia's aunt. I believe you
knew her, and I hear she never lost an opportunity to talk about Fortuny.
I'm going through the letters Fortuny wrote her.'

Nedda nodded. This, too, she seemed to know, apparently from
Apollonia.

The man pacing the room with the piece of paper said something to
her that Urbino did not catch.

'I've told you over and over again, Silvestro,' she responded. 'I'll see
that your application will be filed this afternoon. I'll bring it myself.
No matter if we have a flood like the one back in sixty-seven. No,' she
said, turning back to Urbino, 'I'm afraid I can't help you. Efigenia and I
were not close. I knew she had been friends with Fortuny. But anecdotes?

No. Anyway, it is Apollonia you should be asking, but I don't think she's in the mood for that these days. Her health isn't very good, as I'm sure you've noticed. Poor Apollonia.' There seemed little real sympathy in her voice. 'But I have no idea what she might know about Fortuny. In fact, the only time she has mentioned his name was when she told me you were reading the letters and that the Contessa da Capo-Zendrini is putting together an exhibition of his clothes. I never see her except when I bring over the rent. She likes it handed to her personally.'

'Eufrosina is photographing some of the exhibits for a catalogue.'

Nedda gave a little frown.

'Eufrosina and her photographs.' There was no mistaking the cold sarcasm in her voice. 'You'd think she'd find something more productive to do with her time. Oh, but excuse me, Signor Macintyre. I don't mean to criticize the contessa's exhibition or your own work.' She gave a laugh in which Urbino could hear the release of nervousness. 'It's just that when you get buried in the kind of things I try to do you lose perspective. There's a place for almost everyone and everything in this world of ours.'

Nedda, it seemed, was not on the best terms with Apollonia or Eufrosina. Urbino was put on the alert, concerned as he was to understand the Pindars and their apparently limited dealings with the world. Had Nedda's relationship to the family deteriorated over the years since her engagement to Achille, or perhaps only recently? Olimpia's rebuff in front of the Palazzo Pindar a few days before she was murdered suggested a recent source of friction.

'I realized there was very little chance of your having anything to tell me,' Urbino said, 'but I have to pursue all possibilities. Much of my research leads up a dead end. I suppose you heard nothing from Regina Pindar either?' Regina was the mother of Gaby, Ercule, Olimpia, and Achille. 'Regina knew Fortuny.'

'She never spoke about him. She probably didn't think I was the kind of girl who was interested in such things. And I wasn't! Look at the kind of clothes I wear.' She indicated her tent like dress. 'I have never had any interest in clothes, even back then when I was slim – yes, slim, believe it or not.'

A reminiscent smile played across her large, attractive features. The expression in her eyes became softer.

'I guess you mentioned Regina because you know I was engaged to Achille. She was a good, kind woman, but we were different from each other, as I said. And Achille – well, Achille was different, too, different from his brother and his sisters. Everything might have been different if he hadn't died. Who knows, maybe Mina Longo would not have killed Olimpia.'

'What do you mean?' Urbino asked in a low, composed voice.

'Don't you know that if we change something in the past it changes so much else?' She looked around the noisy, crowded room. 'If Achille and I had married, I might not be helping people the way I do. Not that he would have prevented me. He was a sensible man, the best of them all. What I mean is the past, Signor Macintyre, the past! Change the past, you change the future.'

Urbino could not disagree with this. He sipped his espresso.

Nedda seemed to have forgotten about everything going on around her, which was not an easy feat. 'Ah, the past! We can't change it. You know that Achille drowned with Regina and his father off the Lido. I was supposed to go out with them. But we had an argument, Achille and I. About something silly, I'm sure. I don't remember what it was about. I refused to go out with them, even though it was a glorious day. In my memory the sky was the bluest I've ever seen. But you see, don't you? If we hadn't argued, I would have died too. I would be dead now.'

She looked down at her lap where she clasped and unclasped her hands. She and Urbino were a small island of silence in all the turmoil of the room.

Then she shifted her position on the sofa, sighed, and looked around the room with her earlier sharpness and interest.

Urbino finished his espresso and stood up. 'Thank you very much for your time. And the coffee.'

'You're welcome. But you didn't have even one of the *pignoleti.*'

'By the way, that young woman Evelina. She was with you at Olimpia's funeral.'

'Yes. I – I did not want to go alone.' Nedda turned her attention to the man on the floor. He had finished tying up the newspapers and was working on the magazines. 'No need to bring them today, Vittorio. Wait for the weather to clear. Give me that application, Silvestro,' she said to the pacing man. 'Caterina, would you go into the kitchen and see what's happening with the water?'

Urbino took his leave.

After leaving Nedda Bari, Urbino walked to an area of the Castello near the Arsenale. A man named Marcello Buono lived on the top floor of a building whose lower floors were occupied by a pensione. He was in his late nineties and the owners of the hotel let him stay on for a small rent.

Marcello had sometimes been helpful to Urbino, because the man had been saving every edition of *Il Gazzettino* since the flood in 1967. His apartment was overwhelmed with them, leaving only a small living space. But the copies were neatly stacked and ordered. It took Marcello only five minutes to locate the pile from the summer twenty-five years ago when Achille Pindar and his parents Platone and Regina had drowned off the Lido.

'Here you are, Signor Urbino. Be careful with them.'

Sitting on the sagging sofa, Urbino, with a little effort, located six pertinent articles.

One, the first chronologically, described how the boating party had never returned to the Lido on a July afternoon twenty-five years before, after taking their sailboat out into the Adriatic, where a violent storm had suddenly blown up. It mentioned the prominence of the Pindar family. Another, which appeared the second day, was about the ongoing search for the sailboat or for the recovery of their bodies. The third article, dated a week after the fateful outing, reported how their bodies had been found, washed up on shore near Chioggia. It also reviewed the events of the past week and provided a brief history of the Pindar family and biographies of Regina, Platone, and Achille. There were also individual obituaries for the three family members.

Urbino replaced the copies as neatly as he could in the stack and helped Marcello return everything to their proper place. Although the old man protested at first, Urbino gave him a generous sum of money. The man lived on a very fixed income.

As Urbino walked to the Palazzo Uccello, he went over what he had learned from the articles. Not very much, unfortunately, but there was no suggestion that what had happened had been anything but an accident. Although he now had more details about the tragedy, there was nothing in what he had learned that seemed to be relevant to Olimpia's murder two weeks ago. But perhaps there was something in the details that held a clue if he looked at it in the right way.

Or it might not be any of the details that could bring him closer to Olimpia's murderer, but the fact that Gaby's withdrawal from the world had begun shortly afterward. The deaths of both parents and her oldest brother could certainly explain it, but had there been another reason, one related to their deaths but not the deaths themselves? And there had been another change in the behavior of a Pindar, although not for about three or four years after the drownings: Apollonia's fervent, even fanatical, embrace of religion.

These were some of the many things to consider in a case that was proving to be as wrapped in layers as the cat mummy in the Pindar collection.

Urbino found Natalia in the kitchen. She had just brought Gildo a portion of *ambroyno*, the spiced chicken dish with nuts and raisins that was one of the gondolier's favorites.

'It smells delicious,' Urbino said.

And it tasted delicious, too. After Urbino had finished lunch, he brought some of the plates out to the kitchen, which was as spotless as Natalia always kept it. The only dirty dishes were the ones that Urbino placed in the sink.

'I stopped by to see Nedda Bari this morning.'

'And how is she? I didn't get a chance to talk to her at the funeral.'

'She's busy, as ever. I thought she might be able to help me with my new book. She knew some of the people who were friends with the man I'm writing about.'

'She knows a lot of people – and helps at least half of them.'

'I saw that for myself this morning. Olimpia's death seems to have put her in a reflective mood. About Achille.'

'I don't think she ever got over that. That's when I met her. Right after he drowned with his mother and father. She started coming to church more. San Gabriele. She lived in the Cannaregio in those days.'

'I never knew her husband.'

'Giorgio Bari. He owned restaurants in Venice and Mestre. He was a good man. But she didn't take it as hard when he died as she did when Achille did.'

'What did he die of?'

'Diabetes. Lost a leg near the end.'

'She said she could have gone out on the sailboat that day. But she had an argument with Achille.'

Natalia nodded. 'I know. That was probably the only fight the two of them ever had from what I've heard. Well, it was fate, wasn't it?'

'I suppose you could call it that. When did she meet Giorgio Bari?'

'About five years later. I thought she might marry the other brother. Ercule.'

'Ercule?' Urbino saw no need to conceal his surprise.

'Yes. She mentioned that they were secretly engaged. They didn't want anyone in the family to know. Of course, everyone would know eventually, if they decided to go through with the marriage, but time would have passed. The deaths of Ercule's parents and brother wouldn't be so fresh. I promised not to say anything, but I don't think it makes any difference after so many years.'

They must have kept it a good secret, for whatever reason. The contessa would have mentioned it if she had known.

'Do you know why they didn't marry?'

'What she said to me was that Ercule was nothing like his brother. She was right, there. I guess she realized what it would be like to be married to someone whose head is always in the clouds.'

Later that afternoon, Urbino telephoned the contessa.

'I had no idea,' she said when he mentioned Nedda Bari's secret engagement to Ercule. 'But is it so strange that I didn't know? Maybe the two of them wanted to keep it a secret for as long as they could because they wanted to avoid scandal. People were sure to talk. Nedda had been engaged to marry one brother and then, right after his death, she was planning to marry another brother.'

'Yes, there's a logical explanation."

'I can imagine what Apollonia would have made of it, even though the two of them weren't related even by marriage. She might have thought the relationship was too close. Who knows what strange ideas she has?'

'But those were the days before her great conversion, weren't they?' Urbino observed. 'She wasn't so religious or moralistic then, not until a few years later.'

'The seeds must have been there. It was not as if she was suddenly converted on the road to Damascus. It must have been growing and developing.'

'And maybe somehow the drownings – or Ercule's secret relationship with Nedda afterward, if Apollonia found out about it – encouraged it.'

'God works in mysterious ways, as she said to me the other day. But it's disturbing, *caro*, isn't it? What other things are there that we don't know?'

'I read the articles about the drownings in *Il Gazzettino*. At Marcello Buono's. To see if there might be anything in the public record about the drownings that we didn't know.'

'But there was nothing, right? Whatever you read we already knew.'

'Yes. Nothing indicates that it was anything but an accident, but it may have been the start of a series of events that somehow led to Olimpia's murder. In what way, I have no idea.'

Before ringing off, Urbino told her that the young woman they had seen with Nedda at Olimpia's funeral was named Evelina and asked her if she was sure she had never seen her before the funeral, as she had said then.

'I'm sure. Never.'

*   *   *

The rains continued most of the evening, although they did not prevent Urbino from going on one of his walks. He went to the Piazza San Marco, where he stopped in at Florian's. In the great square, the water falling from the skies was joining the water bubbling up through the paving stones. Already a sheet of water extended from the front of the Basilica to the Molo. Deep puddles were scattered at other points in the Piazza. Urbino was able to wade through the water in his high boots, but others – and there were few of them out tonight even in the Piazza – took to the wooden planks.

Urbino's thoughts during his walk were about the Pindar drownings and Nedda's secret engagement to Ercule. Had their engagement been as close as Ercule had ever ventured in the direction of marriage? And what had motivated him? What had made him choose Nedda? Had it been some family tradition that encouraged a brother to marry the fiancée of his deceased brother? Urbino had read of such things. Perhaps Ercule had also read about it in one of his travel accounts and had been inspired to emulate it. It would be in character.

And had Nedda broken off the engagement because Ercule was, as Natalia had said, 'nothing like his brother'? This was certainly true, at least from what Urbino knew about the resourceful, pragmatic Achille, but had there been something more specific than this, something Ercule had done or said, that had ended the engagement?

But had Nedda even been the one to break things off? Or had Ercule done it, for some personal reasons? Or because of something about Nedda he might have learned, something she had concealed from him? It might have been one of his sisters or his cousins who had discovered her secret, if she had one, and passed it on to him.

From this thought, it was only a short distance for Urbino to move to re-examine blackmail as a possible motive for Olimpia's death – blackmail in which she was either the blackmailer or the blackmailer's victim.

Questions surrounding the Pindars were continuing to proliferate the more he learned about the family. So many of them wouldn't be answered. So many, if answered, would lead him nowhere. But just one of those he was running through his mind tonight, or one of the ones he had been contemplating for the past few weeks, could provide the key to open the door.

For the first hours after getting into bed, Urbino could not sleep, as his mind formulated new questions, reviewed the old ones, and tried, unsuccessfully, to reach some tentative answers. Imprinted on his inner eyelids was a vision of the blue doors of the locked rooms. Even if blue had not been the color of the imagination, he would have still lain restlessly in his bed, imagining what lay behind the doors. For Urbino, at an impressionable age, had read stories, as had the contessa, of the darkness and evil that was contained behind locked doors and was just waiting to be released by the curious.

With all these thoughts streaming through his mind, it was not unusual that he was fully awake when the sirens shrilled, warning the city's residents of *acqua alta*.

Nine

'I feel real guilty about it,' Eugene said to Urbino the next morning. 'But I'm enjoyin' myself.'

The two men were walking on the wooden planks set up beneath the Basilica. All around them – and at other points in the Piazza San Marco, the Piazzetta, and the Molo – there was water, in some places almost a foot high, much higher than it had been last night.

The rains had ended earlier in the morning. The sky was dark gray, but Urbino didn't think the rain would return, not for a while yet. He suspected that some very cold weather would soon be setting in. But the rains had already done their damage to the city, as had been evidenced by his walk last night and the one this morning to the Danieli.

'I heard sirens last night,' Eugene said as he and Urbino drew closer to the edge of the plank to let a young woman going in the opposite direction pass. 'Were they blarin' because of the flood?'

'I'm afraid so.'

'Thought it was a fire.'

They stepped down from the planks to the dry ground beneath the Clock Tower and entered the Mercerie. Most of the fashionable shops were empty of customers. Eugene stopped to look in their windows for something that he might get for May-Foy – or something more he might get her. When Urbino had gone up to Eugene's suite, all the things Eugene had managed to buy in the short time he had been in Venice had surprised him. When Urbino had been showing him the sights, he had bought quite a few things, but it was obvious he had gone foraging for things when Urbino had left him on his own and when he had been with the Chins yesterday.

By the time they reached the Campo San Luca he had bought a silk scarf, a necklace of glass beads, and a feathered half-mask.

'So tell me more about this Fortune fellow,' Eugene said as they walked toward the Campo Manin, stepping aside as a clerk swept water out of the door of her shop. They had already been obliged a few times to retrace their steps because of deep puddles.

'Fortuny.' Urbino had decided to take Eugene to the Fortuny Museum. He would be killing two birds with one stone. Eugene would be seeing something he had not seen before – something not on his list – and Urbino would have another opportunity to surround himself with Fortuny's spirit.

Most of his biographical subjects had not left many physical traces of themselves in the city. But the House of the Magician, as Fortuny's palazzo had been known during his lifetime, had been carefully preserved in the San Beneto area near the Grand Canal. It held his workshop, library, and living quarters, and was furnished with many of his designs and creations.

'Did you know him?' Eugene asked.

'He died in 1949.'

Urbino tried to provide Eugene with an accurate picture of the Spaniard without overwhelming him with too many details. It was also a good exercise for Urbino to isolate the essential features of the man. One of the dangers for biographers was obscuring the essence of their subject beneath too many layers of circumstantial details, which were among the things that Urbino found most fascinating.

Therefore, Urbino emphasized Fortuny as a clothing and textile designer. As for all the other things that could be said about the man's accomplishments, Urbino could always provide more information when they were at the Palazzo Fortuny, depending on what caught Eugene's attention.

'You'll be able to see an excellent selection of the clothes he designed at Barbara's,' Urbino said as they came to a stop by the wellhead of a small square. 'She's putting together an exhibition at the Ca' da Capo-Zendrini.'

The Palazzo Fortuny, which managed to be elegant despite its large size, occupied one entire side of the square. Like the Palazzo Pindar, it consisted of two stories above the ground level, with an attic story at the top. The building, in the Venetian Gothic style, had a magnificent façade, with seven mullioned windows in two tiers, balconies ornamented with arabesques, floral details on the cornices, and large, weathered wooden doors. The Palazzo Fortuny was also known as the Ca' Pesaro degli Orfei, carrying associations with both the Pesaro family who were the original owners, and the philharmonic academy that established its headquarters in the building in the late eighteenth century.

'We'll enter through the side entrance,' Urbino said. 'I prefer to go in that way. And there's an exhibition on the ground floor that we don't need to see. It doesn't have anything to do with Fortuny.'

Urbino had been a frequent visitor to the Palazzo Fortuny even before he had decided to commit himself to his new project. He would go there to be carried back to a different time, the first decades of the twentieth century – just as he like to wander through the Ca' Rezzonico and be taken back to the eighteenth century.

Urbino and Eugene went to the left of the building to a *calle* where there was an entrance into a small courtyard. An attendant, who was sitting muffled against the cold in a corner in the courtyard and who was there to prevent anyone from entering the building from this point, recognized Urbino from previous visits. Urbino paid admission for himself and Eugene, and the attendant said he would get receipts from the front and give them to Urbino and Eugene when they left, along with all of Eugene's packages.

Urbino and Eugene went up the partly roofed outer staircase to the loggia on the first floor. They passed into the *portego* of the building.

'Good morning, Signor Macintyre.' The middle-aged attendant gave them both a smile. She handed them charts to the objects in the room.

Urbino thought it best to let Eugene wander on his own through the two floors, while he remained only a short distance away in case he had any questions.

The *portego*, like the salon above it, extended the length of the building and was proportionately long for its width. It had an old wood beamed ceiling and marble floor, with long, low sofas piled with cushions at both ends. The sofas and the cushions were covered in Fortuny fabric, and the walls were draped in it. Gold framed oil paintings by Fortuny were arranged above each sofa. There was a Wagnerian cycle, copies of works by Italian masters, and two self-portraits of Fortuny, one of him in his youth, the other in late middle age.

Gilded mirrors, easel paintings, small work tables, screens, ceramic jars with dried flowers and paintbrushes, lamps, heavy leather armchairs, old chests, folding chairs, reading desks, and sculptures graced the large room. Fortuny's lamps were everywhere. There were silk ceiling lamps, metal table lamps, miniscule reading lamps, and metal floor lamps. Everything showed either the taste or the inventive hand and mind of the magician of the house. For Urbino the room was a dream. It was a perfect space for living and working.

'Look at it,' Eugene said, indicating one of the lamps. 'Looks like an upside down umbrella!' He started to consult his chart.

'It's called a Scheherazade lamp. Scheherazade is a character in *The Arabian Nights*. Fortuny loved Arab designs and architecture.'

Eugene walked around the room, taking in the different objects. He spent several minutes staring at a large projector. Urbino explained that it was used to illuminate ceilings, paintings, and wall decorations.

'Never saw a painting like this one before.' He indicated a painting over one of the sofas that depicted the back of a woman's head, her neck, shoulders, and naked back. 'And who is that?' He pointed to a small portrait of a distinguished-looking man with a well-trimmed white beard and moustache.

'Fortuny.'

'Well, Mr Fortuny,' Eugene said, addressing the portrait, 'you have quite a place. Wish May-Foy was here. She could get some ideas for the big house. All these drapes and stuff are real nice. I'd like to bring some back home.'

'You can get some fabric in his authentic designs at the Fortuny factory in Venice. They make the fabric just the way it was always done. And there's a shop that sells cushions and lamps and other things done in his style.'

'And the dresses you were tellin' me about? Can I get one for May-Foy?'

'They're hard to come by. And when you can find them, they can be forty or fifty thousand dollars.'

Eugene gave a low whistle and raised his eyebrows.

'I guess Fortuny knew what he was doin', didn't he? I'll take a look at them at Countess Barbara's. Maybe if there's one I like, she can sell it to me.'

'She would never sell hers, and the others are on temporary loan. But we might be able to find one for you.' Urbino was thinking of Apollonia's Fortuny. From what the contessa had said, it did not seem that she was sentimental about passing the Fortuny on to Eufrosina the way her aunt had passed it on to her.

Urbino and Eugene went up to the second-floor salon by way of the inner staircase. The upstairs attendant, who was speaking with an elderly man carrying a guidebook, smiled and nodded.

The room had a similar beamed ceiling, but its walls were painted plaster and it did not have the separate areas and the artistic domestic clutter of the room below it. This space, along with the atelier above it, as Urbino explained to Eugene, was where Fortuny and his large group of skilled workers had produced his fabrics.

Urbino guided Eugene to the small library in a corner of the room. It was usually locked to visitors, who had to be content with viewing its contents through a large glass window. But the attendant unlocked it for him, Eugene, and the elderly man.

While the attendant stood by the door, the three of them stepped inside the small space crowded with objects. It was as if Fortuny had just finished working in the room and would soon return.

The eye rapidly moved from object to object, trying to take in as many as possible: a desk, wooden shelves with Arabic script on the panels of their sliding doors, copies of classical busts, books, catalogues, photographs, unwashed paintbrushes, tubes of paint, bottles of ink and dye, an old easel, a wooden frame waiting for its picture, a printing press, transformers, coils, lenses, drill bits, a wicker-wood chaise longue, a silk lamp, and numerous implements and contraptions that Fortuny had used in his work.

The three men walked around the room slowly, carefully. There was little space to turn around in.

Fifteen minutes later Urbino and Eugene were outside again under the gray sky, walking toward the San Silvestro boat station and avoiding the deep puddles. When Urbino saw a woman resembling Eufrosina coming out of a shop, his mind started to wander to the case. He pulled his attention back to Eugene.

'He's a very interestin' man, that Fortuny,' Eugene observed as they stepped off a flood plank. 'Sort of reminds me of that strange Guggenheim gal, collectin' all those modern paintings I couldn't make head or tail out of. She wasn't Venetian either. Guess there's something about this place that draws people like that in. They probably flock here, don't they? I suppose you fit into the category. Birds of a feather and all that. Evie always says – oh, but I promised I wouldn't talk about her, didn't I? Sorry about that.'

They continued in silence until they reached the Riva del Carbon that bordered the Grand Canal. The Rialto Bridge loomed ahead of them.

Eugene stopped suddenly, letting Urbino walk a few steps beyond him until he, too, came to a halt and turned around. Eugene stared at him with a big smile on his face.

'You're tryin' to hide it,' Eugene said. 'But I can tell sure as anything that you've got your nose in another one of those investigations. Is the old boy right?'

'The old boy is right, Eugene. And it's something I have to get to the bottom of before we leave. But if you don't mind, I'll wait until dinner tonight to tell you. It's a long story.'

'Just wish you'd be careful. One of these days . . .' He trailed off and his face went a little grim.

Urbino did not want Eugene to know anything about Olimpia's murder and how it involved the contessa until after they had visited the Palazzo Pindar, where they were now going. Urbino had decided to visit the palazzo with Eugene as a kind of camouflage, as the contessa had suggested – as if his only reason for being there today was to have his ex-brother-in-law see the collection.

'Here comes our boat.' Urbino pointed to the vaporetto that was approaching the landing.

The two men quickened their steps.

'So what are we going to see now?'

'A small private collection. A family related to Barbara owns it. You didn't see it when you were here before.'

'Good. Another thing not on my list. You're treatin' me real fine.'

*   *   *

Gaby was thrilled that Urbino had come with a visitor, and not just any visitor but a paying one as well. Eugene gave her a generous amount, far more than the cost of two admissions. She stuffed the notes into the pocket of her ocelot coat, tugged her little red cap, and smiled brightly at Eugene.

'You put all those packages right there by the entrance, Mr Eugene,' she said. She indicated a spot beside an empty wooden clothes rack. The *androne* was chilly as usual, but Urbino and Eugene removed their outerwear and put them on the rack.

'I'll show you around personally, Mr Eugene,' Gaby said as she took Eugene's arm. 'It will be my distinct pleasure.'

'Thank you, ma'am. Your English is excellent.'

'And thank *you*. Please call me Gaby. I hope you won't find me gabby though. Hah, hah! My, you have a fine sturdy figure, Eugene. A very American male figure, I would say.' She looked at Urbino, who suddenly felt puny rather than fit. 'Right through this door here. It will just be you and me, Eugene. Urbino has seen my things many times. He can go upstairs and see my brother.' She smiled at Urbino. 'Ercule is always happy to have you visit him.'

Urbino had never seen Gaby behaving so buoyant and flirtatious, but he had seldom seen her in the presence of anyone but himself, her own family, the contessa, and occasional visitors to the museum. Her long, angular face even seemed to become, at least momentarily, as round and smooth as that of a schoolgirl. She had sized Eugene up and put him into a special category, one that did not include Urbino. His presence wasn't needed for a time. Urbino far from minded. In fact, it suited his purposes.

'The first thing I'm going to show you, Eugene, is a suit of armor that went all the way to the Holy Land and back centuries and centuries ago. By the way, Eugene, you have such a strong name, and it's a good one. It's Greek. Did you know that? One part of our family line has Greek connections. Your name means "wellborn". Isn't that appropriate? I can tell you're wellborn, and they say that all Americans are natural aristocrats.'

'Don't know about that, but you're very kind, Miss Gaby. That's a pretty hat you're wearin'. Is it part of the museum?'

'You're such a joker, Eugene. No, it's not part of the collection but it is very old. It belonged to my mother. Just like my coat.'

'It's one of the nicest leopard coats I've seen.'

'Ocelot, Eugene. It's ocelot.'

'Whatever it is, you better not wear it in America. Someone might fling a pot of red paint at you.'

'Oh, that wouldn't be very nice at all!'

Gaby took Eugene's arm. She leaned lightly into him as they went into the museum. A few moments later Gaby's voice, lowered to a warm, intimate level, was describing the suit of armor.

Urbino, still very much under the influence of his restless thoughts of late last night before the sirens sounded, went to the opposite side of the vestibule. The two rooms, with their faded blue doors, were locked, as they always were when Urbino was there. Keys appeared to have been inserted in their rusted locks, recently enough so that scratches were still fresh.

No sound came from the rooms, but seeping from them was a vague sour odor.

A few minutes later Urbino knocked at Ercule's closed door. The *portego* was silent and deserted. He was about to knock a second time, when the door was opened slowly.

'Urbino!' Ercule said. He was dressed in the same two kaftans of red cotton and green velvet brocade. His head was bare of the red and orange Doge's bonnet, but the white cotton *camauro*, which accentuated the roundness of his face, was in place, tied under his chin, and on his feet were the brown kid slippers. He gave his Turkish greeting. 'Please come in. This is a pleasant surprise. I didn't expect another visit so soon.'

A fire blazed in the fireplace. At the foot of one of the divans was a litter of newspapers and magazines with holes in them. A pair of scissors lay on top of a large worn leather scrapbook.

Ercule saw the direction of Urbino's glance. 'A hobby of mine. I cut out anything that has to do with Turkey and Istanbul – anything that interests me, I should say. I have a whole shelf of scrapbooks.'

Urbino nodded. 'I came here with an old family friend,' he said, seizing on one of the most convenient ways of describing Eugene. 'He's visiting me. Gaby wants to give him the full tour. How are you?'

'Fine. But Apollonia is doing poorly. Alessandro, Eufrosina, and Dr Santo are with her. But sit down, Urbino.' He cleared away books from an armchair across from the divan and placed them on the floor near the single-pipe nargileh with its green glass vase.

'Barbara told me that Apollonia had seemed to have taken a turn for the worse a few days ago. We're concerned about her. When I saw Nedda Bari yesterday, she was worried about your aunt, too.' Urbino hoped that Nedda would forgive him for attributing more sympathy to her than she actually had seemed to feel.

The only reaction he got from Ercule was a small frown and the comment, 'She's probably afraid she'll be kicked out of the building if anything happens to Apollonia. Let's have some *raki*.'

'That would be nice.' Urbino was willing to endure more of the drink as a lubricant for their conversation.

Ercule poured them two glasses. He seated himself on the divan across from Urbino, being careful not to disturb the mandolin lying against the cushions. He picked up the silver and velvet hose of the nargileh. 'Would you like to have some puffs?' he asked, offering the mouthpiece to Urbino.

'No, thank you.'

Ercule drew on the pipe, which made a pleasant gurgling sound, and blew out a plume of sweet, apple-scented smoke.

'So where are you today, Ercule?' Urbino asked, reversing the question on the man.

'Aren't you the clever one! To answer you truthfully, I've been walking through the streets of Istanbul and taking in the views of the Bosphorus.'

'There must be places in Venice you enjoy being, other than this great Turkish parlor of yours.'

Ercule took another draw on his nargileh, this one longer and, it seemed, meditative. 'Oh, not many places. I like to go to the Basilica and just sit there, looking around and thinking. And there's a café in San Polo that's owned by a Turkish man. He's married to a Venetian woman who went to Istanbul on vacation. But as I've said, most of my enjoyment comes from just traveling to Istanbul in my mind.'

'I hope you'll get there again soon, and do it the way you want to. By boat.'

'I shall, I assure you. Dreams and memories can't feed a person forever.'

Urbino sipped the *raki*. Ercule drank most of his down – how he did it Urbino had no idea – and closed his eyes, savoring the flavor. He held the mouthpiece in his arms as if in an embrace. The fire crackled.

Letting his eye wander approvingly over the appointments of Ercule's parlor, Urbino waited until the silence between them became even more companionable before saying, 'I was thinking of something that might help you, Ercule. Help you with making your dreams reality.'

Ercule's eyes brightened with interest behind his spectacles.

'You have a lot of wasted space in this building,' Urbino started to explain. 'Almost your whole *androne* is empty. You use only the two rooms for the collection. You have the rest of it at your disposal – and the two rooms across from the collection.'

'Yes?' A cautious note had come into Ercule's voice. He took a draw on the nargileh.

'Private organizations and even the municipality are always looking for space to mount exhibitions. You and Gaby could realize a good, steady rental income. You could make enough to take your trip to Istanbul and stay a while. It's something to think about.'

Ercule emitted another stream of apple-scented smoke. 'Yes, it is.'

'Barbara and I might be able to help you find someone.'

'That would be kind of you both. But it isn't only me that has to agree. There's Gaby.' He paused. With his fingers lightly clasped, he revolved his thumbs slowly round each other. 'Well, we'd have to do something with what's in the rooms. Gaby and I. That would be a little difficult.'

'Gaby might be more open to the idea than you think. It would not mean she would have to go out of the house. It would mean bringing people into it, and the collection would have much more exposure than it has now. By the way, what is in the rooms? More objects for the collection?' Maybe the Pindars rotated their collection the way museums did, although he had never seen any variation in the items. Then he corrected himself. Alessandro's little theater and his carved wooden figures had been added recently.

'I suppose some of the things in the rooms could be put in the collection. They're clothes.'

'Clothes?'

'Clothes and shoes and hats. That's where I got my kaftans. Olimpia used to go through the things. They gave her ideas. Sometimes she used the material from the old clothes to make new ones, though Gaby hated that and did all she could to prevent her. We Pindars have been putting clothes in those rooms since the eighteenth century. I think Olimpia said there are clothes there even older than that. She would have known. She knew a lot about clothes, more than Gaby.'

'All those old clothes. Fascinating.'

'And not just old ones, but recent ones – or more recent than hundreds of years ago.' He placed the mouthpiece carefully on the small shelf of the nargileh. 'Like my mother's and father's clothes and my brother Achille's. Maybe Olimpia's will end up there, except for the ocelot coat and some other things Gaby is interested in,' he added, giving no indication that he knew Olimpia had willed the coat to the contessa. 'It's up to me and Gaby to break the tradition. If you want to look, ask Gaby. She keeps the keys.'

'There might be a Fortuny gown or something else by him.'

'Olimpia would have scooped up anything like that. But you never know. I have no idea of everything there is in there. It would take forever to do an inventory.'

Ercule picked up the mandolin and started to strum it. He soon was playing a sweet, melancholy melody that provided an accompaniment to Urbino's far less sweet and much more melancholy – even dark – thoughts.

After leaving Ercule, Urbino ascended the staircase past the closed door to Apollonia's apartment. Muffled voices came from within.

Stepping quietly, he continued up to the attic story. He went to the closed door of Olimpia's atelier. He kept himself still and listened. He could hear nothing coming from within. He turned the metal handle. The door opened easily and, fortunately, without a sound. It struck him how inconsistent Gaby and Ercule were. They kept their front door unlocked during the daytime, and Olimpia's atelier was not locked, yet the two blue rooms were.

He stepped into the room, keeping the door open behind him.

He found himself in a vast space that extended the length of the palazzo, without any partitions or smaller rooms on either side. Eight round-arched windows, smaller than the windows on the two lower floors, let in the winter light on both long walls.

Like attics almost everywhere else in the world, including the one at the Palazzo Uccello, this one had once been the building's storehouse, crammed with objects the family could not part with. In setting up her atelier, Olimpia must have cleared the space and persuaded Gaby to let her sell some of the objects. Other objects had probably been distributed throughout the house. Much of whatever clothing there had been in the attic must have found its way to the blue rooms.

He stared down at the spot, where Mina had knelt over Olimpia's body, with the scissors in her hand. None of the chaos the contessa had described was evident, and the floor had been swept clean. What had become of the money scattered on the floor? Did the police have possession of it? Or had Gaby or Ercule taken it?

He walked around the room, eerily accompanied by the faint music of Ercule's mandolin.

Tables of various sizes were placed throughout the room. Their surfaces held measuring-tape, cutting scissors, button boxes, reels of sewing silk, pincushions, clothes brushes, steam irons, remnants, and bolts of material. A black mantilla was draped over the back of a chair. Behind the chair was a hat stand with cloche hats, old-fashioned bonnets, and a pink Pashmina shawl. Two modern sewing machines and a much older model were placed at workstations.

Dresses hung on movable clothes racks and were arranged on dressmaker's dummies. Most of the dresses were contemporary styles, although many of them were made from what was clearly old silk, satin, and velvet. The dresses were not hung neatly. Two of them had slipped partly off their hangers, and several of them had been put on the rack backwards, with the hooks of the hangers facing the opposite direction of all the others. The pocket of one dress was pulled inside out.

One particular dress drew his attention. It was in the Rococo style and made from pale green damask that had been embellished with embroidery. Foams of lace adorned the sleeves. In the back, a pleated piece of material, also in pale green damask, dropped from the shoulders and made an impressive train. Urbino examined it more closely and determined, as best he could, that the stitching had been done recently and by one of the modern machines. The dress was not an antique, but a recreation of an old style. Urbino assumed he was looking at the costume the director of the theatrical company had mentioned to the contessa – the one that Olimpia had been close to completing for the Goldoni production. It belonged to the company now, as the director had told the contessa.

As he approached a table near the triple mirror, the doorbell sounded faintly from below. It seemed that Eugene was not going to be Gaby's only visitor this morning.

On the table lay a man's knee-length coat in an eighteenth-century style. It was plain black broadcloth and was cut closely, with narrow shoulders and sleeves. It was faded and worn in various spots. Urbino could tell that it dated back to the eighteenth century and was not a copy like the green damask dress. Olimpia had probably taken it from one of the blue rooms or had found it in the attic when she had taken over the space. The collar had been carefully detached and was lying beside the coat. Perhaps Olimpia had been in the process of altering the style or had been planning to use the collar on another garment.

In a corner was an elegant toilet escritoire, with gilt-brass mounts and marquetry of various woods. He pulled opened the cover and found the inside empty except for several wooden pencils, and a manual pencil sharpener. He was about to close the cover when his eye noticed a small piece of paper in the back. He retrieved it. It was crumpled. He straightened it out. It was a cash register receipt for several spools of sewing thread from a sewing shop in the Castello. A number code, followed by the color of the thread, was listed on the receipt. Each spool was a different shade of blue. The receipt was dated a week before Olimpia's murder. He put it back in the escritoire and closed the cover.

Taking one last look around the scene of the murder, Urbino was about to leave when he heard footsteps hurrying up the staircase. He wished he had not left the door open. He prepared himself for discovery, when the footsteps stopped on Apollonia's landing. He heard a door open, low voices, then silence.

'Gun, gene, gee, gun – but I already said gun,' came Gaby's voice from the second room of the museum as Urbino approached it. 'That's all I can come up with. Your name has all those "e"'s and only two consonants. "E" and "e" and "e,"' she emphasized. 'How do you spell your last name?'

'H–e–n–n–e–p–i–n.'

'My! Three "n"'s. I will see what I can do. Hen, that's obvious, pen, pin, pine – oh, Urbino!' she said when he stopped in the doorway. 'I hope you found Ercule.'

'Yes, we had a little chat – and some *raki*.'

'That nasty stuff, and at this hour! Eugene and I have been keeping sober but that doesn't mean we haven't been enjoying ourselves, does it, Eugene?'

'Not at all, Miss Gaby. She's a real walkin' encyclopedia, Urbino. I was tryin' to find her out about the littlest thing in this place, but she always had plenty to say.'

'It's my life, Eugene. I love old things with histories, even things that did not belong to my family. But I'm sure you could show me around a sugar cane museum and never stop talking. Hah, hah!'

'Maybe I could if I had one. You've put an idea in this head of mine. I tell you what, though, Miss Gaby. You'd be a handy person to have around town. It would get Urbino off the hook and give him more time for his writin' and whatever else he gets himself up to. You can pick the place and the time. And then we'll go somewhere for a tasty meal. How's that?'

Gaby's brightness had been gradually fading as Eugene spoke.

'I must stick close to the house, Eugene. There's no one else who can show visitors around.'

'Every place of business, Miss Gaby, takes a day off. And didn't the good Lord do the same when he was creatin' everything? You're goin' to wear your poor little self out. But no one else has come to the museum while you've been showin' me around. It's a quiet time of year, not like summer. This city was heavin' like an ant hill when I was here then. But I've never been one to press the ladies. You think about it, Miss Gaby, and you get back to me. I'm staying at the Danieli for another two weeks.'

'I'll think about it.' Gaby gave Urbino a nervous glance.

'Disappointed there's nothing for sale, Miss Gaby. I've seen some things I'd like to bring back home with me.'

'Which ones?' Urbino asked out of genuine curiosity.

'Those small daggers with the triangular blades. I'd like one or two. What did you call 'em, Miss Gaby?'

'"Ox-tongues."'

'If you say so. And I'd buy one of those medals they used as money.'

'*Oselle*.'

'And something big.' His bright eye moved around the room. 'The globe of the world over there. Better than the one I have, even if it doesn't have all the countries.'

'It's kind of you to appreciate my things, Eugene, but nothing is for sale.

Not one piece. I could not part with anything. Everything must stay just where it is, exactly as it is.'

'You're very organized, Miss Gaby. You can have a job at Hennepin Sugar any time you want. Just say the word to Urbino and we'll have you on the next plane to Louisiana.' Eugene clapped his arm around Urbino's shoulders. 'So tell me, Urbino. What do you think of yourself?'

'Excuse me?'

A broad smile wreathed Eugene's face. 'What do you think of *yourself*? Your statue.' He went over to Alessandro's little theater. 'May I?' he asked Gaby. She nodded. He reached for one of two figures, which, unlike the others, were not on the stage but were facing it.

'Lookie here, Urbino. So tell me, what do you think? Miss Gaby says you haven't seen this one yet – or the other one.'

Urbino took the figure. He recognized himself from the figure's sharp features, short brown hair, and black cape. It was disconcerting to see himself miniaturized and carved in wood. He was about to hand the figure back to Eugene when something else about it caught his attention. Wasn't the length of the nose exaggerated? Urbino did not exactly have a button nose, but he did not have the protrusive one that Alessandro had bestowed on him.

'A good likeness.' Urbino gave the figure back to Eugene. Before Eugene might comment on the figure's slightly elongated nose, Urbino asked what the other new figure was.

Eugene replaced the Urbino figure and picked up the other one. 'Countess Barbara.' He handed it to Urbino.

It was indeed the contessa. Wearing Alessandro's rendition of her iridescent mauve and purple Fortuny, she sat in a throne-like chair. A gold tiara crowned her head. The contessa was elegant even in wood.

Urbino returned the figure to the stage next to the one of himself.

'He's a talented fellow, your nephew,' Eugene said.

'My cousin.' Gaby turned to Urbino. 'Alessandro finished his own statue.'

Urbino now noticed that it had joined the row of other figures. He did not examine it closely. But it seemed to be a simple likeness. In Alessandro's hand was a small knife.

A low, shuffling sound came from the first room of the museum. A few moments later Ercule appeared in the doorway, still in full regalia.

'My, my,' Eugene exclaimed. 'I thought Mardi Gras was weeks away. That's a mighty fine costume, sir. What kind of mask goes with it?'

'It's not a costume, Eugene,' Gaby said. 'It's my brother's stay-at-home clothes.' She made an introduction. 'His name means Hercules.' As Eugene continued to stare at Ercule, she shifted the figures of Urbino and the contessa a fraction of an inch.

'Well, Hercules, your clothes look pretty comfortable, and that contraption of a hat must keep the chill off your head. I knew an old lady who used to strut around in public dressed in her great-granddaddy's Confederate uniform, saber, boots, and all. Never did any harm and no business of mine.'

'I'm pleased to meet you,' Ercule said. 'I hope you're enjoying our museum.'

'Certainly am, thanks to this tiger of a sister of yours. Sorry, Miss Gaby, not a tiger. What's your coat again?'

'Ocelot.'

'Bet you could make a passel of words from that one.'

But Gaby did not make the effort.

Ercule gave Urbino a little smile. Urbino sensed that he was about to mention the blue rooms to Gaby, but before he might have done so a bald-headed man dressed in a dark blue suit and a maroon bow tie appeared in the doorway. He had a somber expression on his thin, dark face. It was Dr Savio Santo, Apollonia's physician and the physician of all the other Pindar family members.

'It's Apollonia,' he said quietly, looking at Ercule and Gaby. 'She's going. You should come upstairs. Quickly.'

This was followed by a muted wail and the word 'Mamma!' Urbino recognized Alessandro's voice.

Ercule and Gaby, followed by Dr Santo, hurried from the museum.

Part Three

The Blue Rooms

Ten

The contessa was chilled to the bone. The short distance from the motor-boat to the entrance gate of the Fortuny textile factory made her feel as if she had been dipped in ice. The *bora*, snapping the flags of Italy, Venice, and Spain above the entrance, blew against her and Urbino as they waited for the guard to open the gate. The rains had stopped and the flooding had receded, but now, the day after Apollonia's death, the city was enduring this different assault.

They hurried into the small showroom, where the heat came as a welcome relief. The woman at the desk gave them a smile and greeted the contessa by name. A young woman was turning the display rack while her companion examined swatches. Bolts of patterned silk and velvet were arranged on a long wooden table, and Fortuny umbrellas and lamps accented the room. The factory made Fortuny's fabric on his original machines and according to a process that remained a well-kept secret.

The contessa and Urbino seated themselves in chairs covered in rose Fortuny fabric near the desk. The contessa knew that what she was doing this morning – choosing a fabric for the damaged armchair in the morning room – was trivial considering Mina's imprisonment, Olimpia's murder, and Apollonia's death.

However, she had convinced herself, through some kind of perverse logic, that she was doing something for Mina by replacing the fabric Zouzou had ripped. Mina had been much more upset by it than the contessa had been. It made her feel good to think that the armchair would be repaired by the time Mina was released.

When Mina was released. . . The sooner the contessa reupholstered the sofa, the sooner Mina would be out.

Another reason she had come to the Fortuny factory was that she felt closer to Mina in another way. A few hundred feet behind the showroom on the other side of a canal was the Women's Penitentiary. The contessa could have walked to it in fewer than ten minutes. She would have gladly done so, even in this horrendous cold, if the door would be open for her to visit the girl. But that still had not materialized – not yet. She was not giving up hope. Thank God, she was able to get messages back and forth to Mina, who, she suspected, in a kind of reversing of roles, was trying to soothe her by telling her that she was doing fine and that she was being treated very well.

With Urbino's help, the contessa looked through the books of swatches. Usually she would have taken a long time and enjoyed it, but this morning she made a decision after only five minutes.

'I'll take this one,' she said to Urbino. 'What do you think?'

It was the Caravaggio pattern in plum, peacock blue, and beige.

'Nice,' Urbino said. 'It's good to make a change from what you have now.'

The contessa gave the measurements to the woman and paid for the fabric. She joined Urbino, who was examining two photographs on the wall near the entrance. One was a small gold-framed, sepia-toned photograph of Fortuny. The other was a black-and-white one of his widow Henriette. The attractive, intelligent-looking woman wore a simple black dress, a small brooch, and triple strands of pearls high on her throat. She was surrounded by a sea of Fortuny fabric.

'Mina says I resemble her,' the contessa said, hoping Urbino did not think she was being vain. She wanted to evoke a pleasant memory of Mina and bring her into their presence for a few moments. 'Silly girl!' The contessa's eyes watered. 'She saw the photograph when we came to get an umbrella.'

'Mina is observant. There's always a family resemblance among the elegant. And Henriette was Mariano's muse – and you, dear Barbara, are mine.'

The contessa gave his hand a gentle, appreciative squeeze. '*And* your Nora. I'm not going to let you forget that.'

Ten minutes later, they were seated in a small quayside restaurant near the Fortuny factory. Their table gave them a splendid view across the Giudecca Canal.

They lingered over martinis, which Urbino had insisted on since it was Nick and Nora's preferred drink. And then they made their slow way through their risottos and salads as they talked, occasionally looking out at the lagoon barges, vaporetti, and other boats in the gray choppy waters of the canal.

On the way to the Giudecca with Urbino, the contessa had not been able to let the topic of Apollonia's death rest, and she returned to it now.

'Poor Apollonia.' The contessa stopped herself from adding, 'She was young to go,' realizing the illogic of the comment. It had been something her mother used to say in her advanced years when a friend her age or older died. It had struck the contessa as amusing back then, but not any more.

'A natural death, it seems,' Urbino said.

'What are you implying? That her death *wasn't* natural?'

'I always try to keep an open mind as well as an open heart. Don't you think we should be suspicious of another death in the house coming so quickly after Olimpia's murder? Even if Apollonia had been ill; even considering her age?'

This had occurred to her, too, but she had done her best to push it aside. If Apollonia had not been allowed to live all her full natural years – no matter how few more there might have been – it put much of what they had been thinking about in a completely different light.

'And if she didn't die a natural death,' Urbino was saying, 'how could it be separated from Olimpia's murder? Two unrelated murders under the same roof? No.' He shook his head. 'And with her gone, however she went, a door has been closed on whatever she might have known that could have helped us. But she was a difficult woman. Who's to say that she would have been forthcoming with any information?'

'You're right. Apollonia hadn't shown any interest in talking about the past ever since her conversion.' The contessa took a sip of wine. She was limiting herself to only one glass today after her overindulgence last week. 'It seems that Eufrosina and Alessandro are trying to make up for the haste Olimpia was buried in. I was surprised when he told me the funeral wouldn't be for five days. Seems a long time.'

'It is strange. And they're having a wake. I don't think I've ever been to one in Venice or anywhere in the north.'

'I didn't have one for Alvise – and I wouldn't have had one even if it were the custom in Venice. I hate them.'

'Maybe they want it to seem as if they can't bear to say goodbye. But of course if they do have anything to hide about Apollonia's death, they would have her buried as quickly as possible.'

'You say "they", but I don't believe Eufrosina has much to say in the matter. From what I understood when I was there yesterday, it's Alessandro's idea. He had come to it quickly, considering she had been dead for only a few hours.'

'It's something he could have planned much earlier. And to be fair, it may have been Apollonia's wish.'

For the next few minutes, they gave their attention to the risotto, which was perfect to have on a cold day like this.

'I wonder if Eufrosina and Alessandro will move back to their house,' the contessa observed when she had finished her portion. 'Or sell it.'

'Nedda has her center of operations there. She may not want to leave. You know how difficult it is to get a tenant out here.'

'Nedda is giving them an excellent rent. They would have that consolation.'

'They'll both be getting a lot of money, even if they don't sell the building.'

'Their great expectations, as you called them, have been realized.'

Urbino nodded. 'Money. So many of our questions involve money. There's the money that was scattered on the floor of Olimpia's atelier. And the money that could be got from the sale of the house and the collection. And we have no idea about Apollonia's will. That could have some bearing on the whole picture. I'm not counting anything out.'

After the waiter poured Urbino another glass of wine, he told her that he had learned from Ercule what was in the blue rooms. The contessa had not expected something as mundane as clothes.

'So no dead women hanging on hooks,' she said. 'We should be grateful for that.'

'You're barely concealing your disappointment,' Urbino joked. He then described how he had looked through Olimpia's atelier.

'It seems that what you found there were the kind of things you would expect – sewing implements and clothes. As for the receipt, all of the spools listed on it were blue thread? Blue thread, blue doors.' The contessa realized she was stretching things, but wasn't that what Urbino often did, and with good results? 'Does it mean anything?'

'I don't think so. But what it does mean is that someone seems to have gone through her things. Not just the clothes on the rack but her desk. It was empty except for that receipt.'

'We already know that Gaby took the ocelot coat. She's probably the one who went through the atelier. It isn't unusual to go through a dead relative's belongings. You have to, painful as it is.'

The contessa's mind started to wander as she thought about how difficult it had been for her to go through Alvise's things. Urbino pulled her out of her thoughts when it registered that he was asking her when she was seeing Eugene today.

'After lunch. I'll pick him up at the Danieli. I don't know what we'll do.'

'There are a few sights on his list that he hasn't done yet. Murano, Burano, Torcello.'

'We should save them for a day when we can start out early. We can do all three. And on a nicer day than this.'

'Why not take him back to the house? Show him the exhibition – or what has been set up of it. He enjoyed the Palazzo Fortuny. He said he would like a gown for May-Foy. Maybe you can help him find one to bring back.'

'There's Apollonia's. But it's not the time to bring up a topic like that with Eufrosina and Alessandro. Oriana's friend Amelia from Bologna has one. She might be interested in selling it.'

Urbino described some of the things he had been doing with Eugene. The contessa felt a pang as she was reminded, yet again, of Urbino's looming departure. Was he going to be able to save Mina before then? She had confidence in him, and he functioned well under pressure, but nonetheless she was fearful.

'Has it occurred to you that Eugene might help you with the blue rooms?' she threw out, interrupting his account of his success at Chemin de Fer. Had there been irritation in her voice? She felt embarrassed. She knew she didn't have to keep him on track in these investigations. In a softer tone, she said, 'He could ask Gaby to unlock them and show you both what is inside – since they got along so well.'

'They didn't just get along well – Gaby was also in one of the happiest moods I've ever seen her. She was girlish and seemed smitten with him. Sad, though, isn't it? Starved for romantic attention.'

'Starved not just to receive it but also to give it,' the contessa amended. 'Sometimes that can be more of a need. Gaby seized on Eugene, and as I've said before, he can be charming in his own way. Have you told him about Olimpia's murder?'

'Last night over dinner. But I don't think that would influence him not to help me. It could help. And he knows that the clock is ticking, so to speak. He was adamant, though, about Gaby being innocent of anything but being a little strange. He trusts me to uncover the truth, and he might feel that it could only help her.'

Their plates were cleared away and they each ordered a *torta cioccolata*.

'So, *caro*, I have a crown on my head and I'm sitting down?'

'Not just sitting down, but enthroned. Very regal and impressive.'

'And our Geppetto transformed you into Pinocchio.' The contessa tried to suppress a smile. 'You do tell lies – all in a good service, of course. And from the privileged point of view of someone who knows you well, you *do* seem to want to be a boy. But on the more serious side, it's clear that he's drawing attention to your snooping. If he had anything to hide, though, he wouldn't put you on your guard like that, would he?'

'He could be using that way of trying to mislead us, similar to what he might be doing by waiting so long for his mother's wake and funeral. Another one of the Pindar games.' Half an hour later, as they were hurrying to the contessa's motorboat, Urbino said, 'I'm going to see Oriana. She came back from Cortina.'

'I know. I poured my heart out to her over the phone last night. We can drop you off.' Oriana lived on the other end of the Giudecca.

'I'd like to walk.'

'As you wish, but if you catch pneumonia, you'll be of no use to anyone, Pinocchio. And be sure to keep that nose of yours out of the cold.'

The contessa was enjoying Eugene's company as her motorboat carried them up the Grand Canal to the Ca' da Capo-Zendrini.

His observations about her and Urbino's adopted city cut through a lot of nonsense, and what they might lack in refinement – an over-valued quality, even she would admit – they more than made up for in common sense, a quality she highly valued.

'All these old houses are beautiful, but look at that one with the circles on it.' It was the Palazzo Dario. 'It's leanin' to one side, practically ready to collapse if it didn't have the other house to lean against. And that building with the museum that Urbino took me to. It's all faded and fallin' apart in places. But I have to say that Venice looks a lot better in the winter than in the summer. The bright light makes the old lady look more her age, don't you think?'

'Winter does give Venice a special quality,' the contessa responded, not wanting to pursue the implications of his question. 'But I don't like the cold, not what we have today.'

'It's invigoratin', Countess Barbara. Oh, there's the place where Urbino and I saw the drowned girl.' Eugene nodded his head toward the water terrace of the Palazzo Guggenheim. A pang of sadness pierced the contessa as she was reminded of the dead girl, so beautiful, so tormented, and so threatening to her peace of mind.

'And Urbino tells me that he's pokin' around in something that has a connection to you again,' Eugene went on as they approached the Accademia Bridge. 'Seems everybody thinks your maid killed the sister of that Miss Gaby.'

'Not everybody,' the contessa gently corrected.

'Of course not everybody! Not you or Urbino. And I'm sure you're both right. Urbino is a clever fellow, the most clever person I'll ever meet. I'm sure of that. He'll figure things out before it's too late. He knows what's what even if he isn't always as clear as water. And you've got a good head on your shoulders, too, Countess Barbara.'

'Thank you. I have a lot of faith that Urbino will get at the truth.'

'Sure he will! And that poor maid of yours will soon be dustin' the house and washin' the floors and whatever else it is she does in that big house of yours. I've known plenty of ladies like your dead cousin who had special friends and not one of the friends was the least bit violent. I've told Urbino he should be lookin' into that fellow who makes those little voodoo dolls. Haven't met him, and don't think I'd like to.'

'I'm sure Urbino is considering all possibilities. He's good at figuring things out.'

'Always *has* been, the little devil! You should have seen the puzzles he worked on when he was only nine or ten! Hour after hour at a little table set up on the porch, sittin' all by himself, dressed up by his momma as if he was goin' callin' and with her bringin' him out lemonade and cookies. He knew where a piece fit just by sniffin' at it.'

The contessa smiled at this picture of Urbino. It was another one of the reasons she liked Eugene. He drew the curtain away from parts of Urbino's life. 'The child is father of the man, they say,' she said.

'That's it. Urbino's just gotten bigger. Hasn't changed much at all. Except for his name. Rayfie in those days, Raphael bein' his middle name, as you probably know. He didn't start usin' Urbino until he went to high school. Took us all a while to get used to the moniker but it made him and his momma happy.' Eugene turned to the contessa and gave her arm a hearty pat. 'So don't you go worryin' yourself, Countess Barbara. You'll have your maid back lickety-split. He'll put together all the little pieces. There'll be a big celebration before we say goodbye to you. Here. This'll make you feel better.'

He withdrew a small, brightly wrapped package from his coat pocket. 'A little gift from Louisiana.'

She unwrapped it. Inside was a sterling silver spoon. On the handle was engraved "Louisiana". The top of the handle had a pelican sitting on top of a nest of baby birds.

'Brilliant, Eugene. Thank you.'

'Didn't think it was goin' be so appropriate. If you look, you can see the word "Confidence" under the pelicans. "Union Justice" is above the pelicans but you can forget about that. "Union justice and confidence" is our state motto, you see. You gotta have confidence, Countess Barbara, confidence that you'll have your little chick back in the nest before you know it.'

They didn't return to the topic of Mina or the murder for the rest of the trip to the Ca' da Capo-Zendrini. Eugene started to talk about his new friends the Chins and how Betty the wife was interested in the different boats she was seeing on the Grand Canal. The contessa mentioned a picture book of Venetian boats that Betty might consider buying and said she would write the name down later.

She gave Eugene a tour of the galleries and salons of the house. Zouzou, who had taken a liking to Eugene that was mutual, followed them. They ended in the *salotto blu,* which held some of her most treasured furniture, art, and bibelots and was dominated by the Veronese over the fireplace. It was an allegory of love and showed an ample golden-haired Venus being admired beneath a lush tree by two dark-haired, handsome men. When she told Eugene that it was a wedding gift from her husband, he looked at her in transparent amazement.

'Pardon me for saying so, Countess Barbara, but that's a strange kind of gift. An almost naked lady sprawlin' like that with two gentleman callers. But I know they do things different here in Italy.'

Eugene's criticism of the painting as a wedding gift from a husband to a wife was far from the first one the contessa had heard.

'I understand what you mean, but my husband and I shared a deep love for the painter. I like to think that the woman is about to choose between the two men and that it's the right choice. It will change her life for the better, as happened to me. Would you like a drink?'

'I could go for some of that powerful stuff they sell on the bridge by your villa.'

'Grappa. We'll have drinks while we're looking at the Fortuny exhibition downstairs. But I won't join you in the grappa. It's too strong for me. I'll have sherry.'

'Just like Urbino. Never understood why the two of you haven't got hitched by now. You got a whole lot in common.'

The contessa took advantage of pouring out the drinks to screen her embarrassment. 'Urbino and I are content with the way things are. And, of course, there's a bit of difference in our ages.'

'As if that's stopped any older man from marryin' a young gal! My May-Foy is fifteen years younger. You aren't very old. Don't be puttin' yourself down like that.'

'Besides, think of Urbino,' Eugene pursued. 'What he needs is an older woman, plain as day. Maybe that's why he and Evie never worked out.'

Eugene mercifully dropped the topic. Ten minutes later, they were in the exhibition room, Eugene with his generous portion of Nardini grappa and the contessa with her sherry.

The items that Eufrosina had been photographing outside their cases had not been reinstalled yet. Eugene gave only quick glances at the purses, scarves, and pillows, but he inspected the Fortuny gowns with much more interest, especially Apollonia's.

The contessa had received another dress a few days ago. It was still in its tan box. She took it out and unwrapped it from its tissue. It was a pale green silk tea dress. She untwisted it and held it up. Like the other dresses in the collection it was in excellent condition, showing not even the slightest of tears at the edges of the pleats.

'You see. No wrinkles even though it has been in the box. It's the secret of Fortuny's pleats.'

She handed the dress to him. For such a large man, he held it gently and ran one hand softly against the fabric. 'It's so soft. And look at the way the color changes, all different kinds of green.'

The contessa rewrapped the dress in the tissue paper and returned it to the box. Eugene had returned to look at Apollonia's Fortuny gown.

'A real beauty. It would make a fine birthday gift for May-Foy. The red and the gold would look great on her. She has just the colorin' for it. And she's a little bitty thing, May-Foy is. She wouldn't have any trouble squeezin' into it.'

'The dresses are designed to fit most women.'

'Wasn't he a sharp fellow! Do you think this one here might be for sale?'

'I don't know. Even if it were, it wouldn't be available until after May. And it belonged to the woman who died the day you were visiting the museum.'

'The mother of that voodoo guy? Do you think you could ask him? Not now with the funeral and all. I'm not in a big rush. May-Foy's birthday's not comin' up until August. And price is no object.'

'I'll see what I can do. There's also a daughter involved. But if I can't get this one, I can try to locate another.'

'Thank you, but unless you can find one exactly like this one here, I'd rather have none at all. Only that one will do. I'm a very particular man.'

'I can see that, Eugene.'

After Eugene left for the Danieli in the motorboat, the contessa took her own solitary tour of the house, with Zouzou either at her heels or in her arms.

It was a large house, large enough to embrace many people, large enough to seem sadly empty at a dead time of the year like this. The contessa periodically filled it with guests, taking advantage of as many anniversaries and holidays and festivals as she could and even generating ones of her own. This Fortuny exhibition was, among other things, one of the latter. She would have family and friends from as far away as Argentina and New Zealand staying with her in May. Before then, there would be several people passing through town who would settle into the Ca' da Capo-Zendrini for days, even weeks. And carnival would soon be coming. Over the years she had made her peace with the raucous holiday and saw it as a good opportunity to get together with people in her own restrained, but festive way.

She went to the *salotto blu* to retrieve da Ponte's memoirs, which she had been reading before she had gone out with Urbino. She looked at the Veronese with more attention than she usually gave it. It had become such a familiar object among all her other possessions that she did not see it any more, not the way she used to. That was one of the dangers of being surrounded by so much. You stopped seeing things – even the most obvious and beautiful of them. That was why someone like Eugene was to be welcomed – welcomed for his uncluttered eye and his direct gaze.

Seeing things as others saw them . . . Urbino was better at this than she was. The case he was involved in now – the case they were *both* involved in, she corrected herself – required this kind of vision. Maybe the Pindar clan, as Urbino called her relatives, had become too familiar to her eye and mind – and her heart.

Her steps carried her up the tall winding staircase to the Caravaggio Room, which she had not shown Eugene. When she went inside, her eyes went to the painting that gave the room its name. It was a portrait of a round-faced, feminine-looking young man caressing a mandolin. With a mocking smile on his full lips, he wore lipstick and rouge, and his thick, auburn hair was adorned with a large white flower. His green robe, which had slipped provocatively off one shoulder, gave him even more of an epicene look.

Zouzou was sniffing around in a corner. The contessa seldom went into this room, although it was no longer locked as it had been for many decades. Unlocking it several years ago, hard though it had been for her to do, had been the key to solving a murder that had taken place in the Ca' da Capo-Zendrini back in the thirties – but not before another murder had taken place in it.

Urbino had solved the deadly mysteries associated with the Caravaggio Room. Surely it must be on his mind these days because of the locked blue rooms at the Palazzo Pindar. She hoped he would consider her suggestion that he enlist Eugene's help.

'Come, Zouzou. Let's go upstairs to Mina's room.'

The cocker spaniel gave a few last sniffs. The contessa closed the door on the Caravaggio portrait.

She took the back staircase up to the staff's quarters. Giovanna, who had been with her for almost three decades, greeted her from the entrance to the staff hall. She did not ask if the contessa wanted anything. Giovanna clearly must know that she was upstairs to go into Mina's room. It had become her habit since Mina had been arrested.

Zouzou jumped on Mina's bed, her white fur standing out against the turquoise blue of the chenille spread. The faint scent of Mina's perfume hung in the air.

Mina's room looked over the garden and was similar to the other bedrooms on the floor. In addition to the bed, it had a large chest of drawers, a small sink, an armoire, a table and a chair, a small sofa, several area rugs, and velvet drapes. The walls were painted terracotta red.

When she had married the conte, all the staff bedrooms – as well as their dining hall and parlor and the housekeeper's parlor – had been repainted and refurnished, making them much more comfortable and far less severe than they had been. The contessa had given the rooms many of the good pieces of furniture from the storeroom. Over the years she had made additional improvements and had had them repainted several times.

After Mina had arrived, the contessa had been tempted to add a few special touches to her chamber, but she had limited herself only to hanging one of her Pietro Longhi paintings on the wall beside the window. It was a delicate little scene of a mother and a child playing with a terrier. The mother, with her small, round face and dark expressive eyes, resembled Mina. The fact that Mina's last name was Longo made the choice of the Longhi even more appropriate in the contessa's mind.

The contessa looked around the room to be sure that everything was the way it had been when Mina had left it. She would keep the room waiting for her, and it would be hers to use even if she left the contessa's employ. She filled a ceramic pitcher with water at the sink and poured it on the lush fern in the corner of the room.

The contessa knew that she should not be doing it, but she was already planning the future for Mina. She would encourage her to continue her education. The girl had many interests, many abilities.

The contessa was about to leave when she noticed a photograph lying on the bedside table next to the lamp. She had seen it before. It showed a smiling Olimpia and Mina with the Bridge of Sighs behind them. It was the classic memento for lovers. She was tempted to ask Giorgio Lanzani to take it to Mina, but the photograph might create problems for her at the prison. She would have to give it more consideration.

With Zouzou in her arms, the contessa descended the staircase to the exhibition room. She spent several minutes looking at Apollonia's silk gown.

Efigenia's gown. Apollonia's gown. Both women gone, and the dress had survived them. Now, it was most likely Eufrosina's. But the contessa cautioned herself. It was possible that Apollonia, for whatever reason, might have arranged for it to go to someone other than her daughter, just as Olimpia had bypassed her sister and willed the contessa the ocelot coat.

Perhaps the gown would soon grace the figure of May-Foy Hennepin, thousands of miles away in a different world, a woman who belonged to a different family. Although the contessa was a fervent believer in tradition and continuity, she hoped the gown would make the journey and that it would get a new life in America.

It was not healthy to cling too much to things of the past. The Pindar family needed to make some changes. They had to break free. For them the past was not only unhealthy, it even might be deadly.

Eufrosina and Alessandro had been freed by their mother's death from her demands and vigilance.

Ercule wanted to break free, and the contessa hoped that he would have the chance. Maybe he had been the one to break off the secret engagement with Nedda – in order to keep himself available for what he really wanted to do. The contessa could not imagine him having any place in Nedda's life of social service, although if they had married, Nedda would have been leading a different life than the one she was leading now. As Nedda had said to Urbino, if you change the past, you change the future. Achille's death and the end of her engagement to Ercule, as well as her husband's death, had freed her to have the life she now did. Ercule, during the twenty-five years since Achille's death and his ruptured engagement, had been waiting, preparing to be free.

Gaby's situation was a much darker one. The contessa had less hope for her unless she got the professional attention she needed.

But a cloud was over them all – Eufrosina, Alessandro, Ercule, and Gaby – and even over Nedda because of her links to the extended Pindar family. Until Olimpia's murderer was exposed – a murderer who was hiding among them, of this Urbino had sadly convinced her – the cloud over the others would remain and they could not be truly free. In fact, some of them might be in danger.

A great deal was at stake. A great deal depended on Urbino – and on her, for whatever help she could continue to give him. It was a grim business, and poor Mina was right in the middle of it all, bravely enduring her long days on the Giudecca.

Following this disturbing train of thought, the contessa said aloud a few minutes later, 'Nick and Nora did it for the fun of it. I wish we were.'

One of the advantages of having a dog or a cat near you at moments like these was that people could think you were speaking to it when you were talking to yourself.

To reinforce her deception of the darkening shadows in the room and any unseen, unknown ears, the contessa added, 'Do you know what I mean, Zouzou?'

The cocker spaniel waved her white plume of a tail as if she had understood and were giving her mistress a comforting agreement, and not just responding to her name, spoken so lovingly.

Half an hour later, as the contessa was unsuccessfully trying to calm her thoughts with da Ponte's memoirs so that she could have a nap before teatime, the telephone rang.

It was Corrado Scarpa. She could not have been less prepared for what he had to say, although she had been hoping to hear the words during every waking hour since Mina's arrest.

'It's all arranged, contessa. You can see Mina Longo tomorrow morning.'

Eleven

As Urbino walked along the embankment of the Giudecca after parting from the contessa that afternoon, the *bora* buffeted him. It made him feel good to think of the wind blowing all the way from the steppes of Russia and St Petersburg, or so he imagined it. And there would be another snowstorm soon. He could feel it coming.

He was tempted to take a short detour and walk past the Women's Penitentiary. But it was a dismal building on even the sunniest of days, and there was no chance he could visit Mina. He did not need to see the building to feel it lowering over him and the contessa, with its reminder of how he had to set Mina free within – what was it? – little more than a week.

Urbino was hoping that Oriana Borelli could play her role. In every social set, there is usually one person who is the repository, if not also the conscientious collector, of personal information about other members of the group. Oriana not only fit into this category but also embraced it. Over the years she had provided pieces of information that had been invaluable to Urbino in solving his cases. For this reason, he was now appealing to her.

Encouraged by the thought of how she might be able to help him and the contessa, Urbino quickened his step past the warehouses and workshops, with seabirds wheeling and mewing above him, to reach the other end of the narrow island.

The austerity of the Borelli apartment, so at odds with Oriana's flamboyant appearance and manner, was something that Urbino had never become accustomed to. There was only one item in the whole room that had no utilitarian purpose – a Barovier-Toso vase filled with dried brown flowers. But the view from the living room's wide, ceiling-high windows of the distant Riva degli Schiavoni, the Doges' Palace, the Campanile, and the domes of the Basilica was more than compensation for the room's drawbacks.

Urbino took in the scene for a few minutes after entering the apartment. This was by preference and by Oriana's request.

'Keep looking at the view, Urbino dear, not at me, if you don't mind – not until I've sat down,' she said in English in her cigarette-hoarse voice. 'I don't want you to see me hobble.'

Oriana had answered the door on crutches. Her leg, broken on the slopes of Cortina d'Ampezzo, was in a cast. An attractive woman in her fifties, she was dressed in a crimson silk kimono with a pattern of cranes and flowers. A pair of over-sized sunglasses, which she wore both inside and outside and in all kinds of weather, concealed a third of her face.

Urbino did as he was told. When he turned from the windows, Oriana was installed on the neo-Biedemeier sofa. He seated himself, with some difficulty, in a chair shaped like a slingshot.

'And don't stare at my cast!'

'How's Filippo?'

'Hale, hearty, and happy. No broken legs or other members. Coffee while it's still warm?' Without waiting for an answer, she poured each of them a cup from the coffee maker on the glass table. Urbino was happy to see that there was also an open bottle of red wine. 'I told him there was no need for him to come back with me. He is having too good a time. And so was I before this happened.'

The Borellis had an unconventional marriage, characterized by mutual infidelity, tolerance, an apparent lack of jealousy, and – in some strange way – devotion to each other. Her accident had interrupted an affair Oriana had been having up in Cortina, but neither of them saw the need to have it interrupt the one Filippo was enjoying.

Oriana fixed a cigarette in her holder and leaned forward for Urbino to light it. She blew the smoke away from him in the direction of one of the skeletal halogen lamps.

'So how can we help our dear Barbara? She's in a terrible state, but she's probably revealed more about how she feels to me. Woman to woman. If you can't get to the bottom of this whole sordid affair, I am afraid for her. And I do not mean sordid because of Mina's relationship with Olimpia. I hope you know me better than that! It is dirty and ugly because Mina is in danger of being sacrificed by someone in that house. Barbara filled me in. I was sceptical at first but she convinced me, just as you did her. You see what an influence you have.'

'And I've come here to have you exert *your* influence. I'm hoping that you might be able to fill in some gaps to help us. Barbara's told me what she knows, but there's a lot that she doesn't.'

'Of course there would be. She isn't Venetian, not even Italian, any more than you are. Information about people here is not going to come her way as easily as it does to me. And she doesn't make much of an effort of gathering it as I do, even when I think there might not be any need for it. She should have a healthier attitude to gossip.' Oriana inhaled on her cigarette. 'And there's something else. She's related to the Pindars. People are not going to tell her things about them for that reason, too. And when she might notice that something is off, she might put the best interpretation on it.'

Oriana had a good assessment of the situation.

'So shall we begin with the dead?' she asked. 'Olimpia and Apollonia?'

'And Achille, too.' Urbino drained his coffee. 'Do you mind?' he asked, picking up the bottle of wine.

'Pour me a glass, too.' She took a long drag on her cigarette and exhaled the smoke slowly. 'I didn't know Olimpia well. I had her make some dresses for me a few years ago. She did a good job. I still wear one of them. I was going to have her make another dress for me when I returned from Cortina. It was more to give her the business than anything else, but as I said, she did very good work.'

'She had financial problems?'

'My neighbor knows a woman who worked for her, Teresa Sorbi. Olimpia couldn't give her all of her November salary, or the other worker either. It was the first time it had happened.'

'She could have been short on money because someone was blackmailing her.'

They discussed the possibility that her sexual orientation had been the target of blackmail but they dismissed it, as had Urbino and the contessa, for the same reasons. Olimpia had been open about it.

'Maybe she stole someone's designs and passed them off as her own,' Oriana said with a smile to show that she did not take the possibility too seriously.

'Not all that far-fetched. I can understand why someone could have been blackmailing her for that, but why kill her? Blackmailers are the ones who end up dead. Which brings us to the question, was *she* blackmailing someone? It makes more sense. She discovered someone's secret and charged a high price for keeping it. Barbara and I have gone through it. We haven't come to any conclusions. But Bianchi said that Olimpia had come into some money over the past few months.'

'Barbara mentioned Olimpia's commission from the theater company. The money could be from that.'

'All of it or maybe only some of it.' Urbino wished there were some way of finding out how much Olimpia had been given by the theater company, but he doubted if he could get that information. 'And we could be dealing with two unrelated crimes. Olimpia could have been blackmailing someone – and not necessarily someone in the house. And someone could have murdered her for a completely different reason. But whenever I consider her murderer's identity I always see the face of someone in that house.'

Oriana stared at him in surprise. 'You do? Which one of them?'

He saw the misunderstanding. 'No. I don't mean I see *one* face. I mean the face of the murderer is the face of one of the Pindars. It could even be Apollonia's face.'

'Apollonia!'

'We can't put her out of the picture. By the way, do you think you could get Teresa Sorbi's phone number and address from your neighbor?'

Oriana nodded. There was an abstracted look on her face. She was thinking of what he had said about Apollonia. When Oriana broke the silence between them, however, it was not to mention Apollonia.

'A few years ago, I saw Olimpia and Nedda Bari on the other side of the Campiello Widman.' This was near Bari's house. 'They seemed to be arguing. Olimpia was shouting. I couldn't make out what it was about.' Oriana shrugged. 'Nedda was calmer than Olimpia and kept shaking her head. It was obvious she was holding herself in. I continued on my way. I don't think they noticed me.'

Urbino poured more wine in their glasses. He turned Oriana's attention to Apollonia.

'Our paths used to cross in the old days,' she said. 'Until she put on black and withdrew into herself – or into religion. When she was younger, she was the life of the party, though it is hard for you to imagine it. By the time you met her, the change had already come. She had already started out-poping the Pope. I thought she would sign herself into a convent one of these days.'

'What do you think was behind it?'

'One thing I know for sure is that she started talking about some Savonarola at San Giacomo dell'Orio. An old eccentric who wanted to convert a few more souls before he died. It was after her husband died. Of a heart attack almost right in front of her eyes. Maybe it made her think more of mortality. It was as if a button had been pushed. She put away her Fortuny and her other stylish clothes and started draping herself in black dresses, veils, scarves, and gloves. That's the Apollonia you knew.'

Oriana paused to drink some wine before going on.

'Once she went through her great conversion, there was hardly anything you could talk to her about unless it was related to religion or about how bad other people were. She herself was beyond reproach. She had repented. She didn't believe in anyone else's repentance.'

'Were sexual affairs something that she repented?' If anyone would know the answer to this, it would be Oriana.

'That's not something I think she was ever guilty of. If we can speak of guilt in such matters.' She gave a short laugh. 'But maybe it's the ones you hear the least about who have the most to conceal. And if there *was* some deep dark secret and someone found it out, I don't think she would have been very happy about it. Some people like to talk about how bad they were before they found religion, but Apollonia was definitely not that type. She would have been devastated. Thank God, my life has always been an open book. No one would ever be able to have that power over me.'

'The new Apollonia must have been hard on Eufrosina and Alessandro.'

'Hard isn't the word for it! But they toed the line – or made sure they covered their tracks well. They knew all that money was waiting for them. It has ruined Alessandro. He's never made anything of himself, knowing that a lot of money was eventually going to come to him. We'll see what he does with it now. And what Eufrosina does. They both have probably spent it all in their heads years ago. You know how it is.'

'What kind of man was Eufrosina married to?'

'A good man. He died of leukemia a few years after they married. Diagnosed in June, dead before the new year had come. Apollonia approved of him. But Eufrosina didn't love him. It was obvious. I always felt that some other man had broken her heart, and she never recovered. That's how I think of Gaby, too. She was going to escape into the night with her lover. She waited for him to come, with her bags packed, and he never did – and she's never left the house since. Or maybe he did come,' she amended, 'and told her it was all over. She killed him on the spot and has him buried somewhere in that palazzo.'

This latter comment, though Oriana had thrown it out in so evidently a jocular manner, gave Urbino a brief pause, as his mind ran over again the question of what had triggered Gaby's agoraphobia. Had it been a delayed reaction to the death of her parents and her brother, who had left the house one day together, never to return, freezing her with fear of the world outside the Palazzo Pindar? Or had there been a hidden event in her life that she was still managing to conceal with the same kind of care she gave to the collection?

'But you don't know of anyone either of them was interested in?' Urbino asked Oriana after a few moments.

'Maybe it's a matter of the principle I mentioned. Those you hear least about . . . ' she trailed off.

'What about Ercule?'

'For as long as I can remember the only romance he's ever had has been with his books and his dreams.'

Urbino got up and stood in front of the windows, taking in the scene across the stretch of water again, and then switching his attention to San Giorgio Maggiore on his right. As it always did, the island and the church made him feel calm. He told Oriana about the secret engagement between Ercule and Nedda after Achille's drowning. When he turned around, she was staring at him in disbelief.

'Nedda and Ercule! Surely you're mistaken.'

'Only if Nedda was deceiving Natalia, and I see no sense in that.'

'Now you've told *me* something! Whatever was the attraction? They're oil and water.'

'It's hard to know what attracts people. It's often a mystery.'

'A mystery, yes, that's what Nedda and Ercule being engaged is. But you say it was right after Achille drowned. It could have been a way of dealing with the loss. And Ercule also lost his parents.'

'Yes.' Urbino watched a car ferry making its way toward the Lido. 'What did you think of Achille?'

'Achille was exceptional. He could have been the savior of that whole family if he had lived. He had everything! Looks, intelligence, generosity, a great sense of humor. Don't look at me in that way! There was never anything between us. Nedda threw herself at him. But I don't think he was in love with her. I could sense it from the way he behaved when he was around her. I wouldn't be surprised to find out he had been planning to break off the engagement. Maybe because someone else was in the background. I have nothing specific to base it on. Just my instinct for these things.'

After leaving Oriana, Urbino went to the Basilica San Marco. On this late afternoon, the church's vast interior was dim. The rich amber light of the hanging lamps, similar to the one in Ercule's *salotto* but smaller, made all the gold and colored stones glow darkly. A small group of tourists was walking slowly around, most of them looking up at the mosaics that covered the vaulting and walls but only a few noting the ones underfoot. Three worshippers sat in the pews near the Madonna of Nicopeia in the left transept. Urbino went to the altar that held the tenth-century icon that was venerated because it was believed to bring victory. Like so much else in the church, it had been stolen from Constantinople.

He said a prayer, asking for a victory different than the ones that devotees used to beseech the Madonna for – not a victory of guns and swords against a martial enemy but one of wits and patience against someone who was doing everything to hide from confrontation. And a victory accomplished before not too much more time had slipped away.

Urbino spent several minutes gazing at the Pala d'Oro behind the high altar. Some of the cloisonné enamels of the golden screen, which was encrusted with precious gems, had been looted from Constantinople.

The enamel of the Empress Irene, which was the one Urbino always seemed to be drawn to rather than the religious ones, communicated some of its serenity to him.

Urbino could understand why Ercule was drawn to the Basilica. It was not hard to imagine that you were in Byzantine or Ottoman Constantinople. Ercule had said that he would get to Istanbul 'by hook or by crook.' Perhaps, the Basilica's history of thefts – starting from the seventh century when St. Mark's relics had been stolen from Alexandria – emboldened the strange little man. How far would he go to achieve his dream of leaving Venice and getting to Istanbul? As far as theft? Or even farther?

When Urbino returned to the front of the altar, he described Ercule to the attendant, a middle-aged man in a blue suit. 'I wanted to meet him here this afternoon.'

'You are too late, signor. He comes in the morning and leaves before noon.'

'I didn't have a meeting set up. But I know he comes here often.'

'Four, even five times a week.'

Urbino got the impression that the attendant did not know Ercule by name, even though he was a familiar figure to him.

'But always early in the day, as I said. Quiet as a mouse, and always by himself. Sits just staring around. Sometimes I think he has fallen asleep, but he doesn't, as far as I have seen. Sometimes he scribbles in a book. He likes to look at the Pala d'Oro and go in the Treasury. I don't have him pay.'

Urbino's eye went to the entrance to the Treasury beneath a curving Moorish arch. He was sure that all its Byzantine gold and silver work contributed to Ercule's dreams – as well as his determination to get to Istanbul at all costs, since its precious objects had been plundered from Constantinople.

Twenty minutes later, after making inquiries in San Polo, Urbino located the Turkish café that Ercule frequented. It was tucked away in a narrow *calle* behind the Campo San Polo. It was hardly larger than Ercule's parlor, which it slightly resembled with its divans, cushions, prints of Istanbul, and nargilehs. A young man in a corner seemed half asleep as he smoked a water pipe.

Urbino ordered a cup of Turkish coffee and a small plate of baklava. He described Ercule to the owner, a thin, dark-haired man with a quick smile who was sitting behind the cash register.

'You mean Signor Ercule. He comes two times, three times a week,' he said in heavily accented Italian. 'He was here an hour ago. A very nice man, Signor Ercule, isn't he, Rosella?' he said to the blond woman who had served Urbino.

'Very nice. He loves Istanbul.'

'Like you, my dear. But he doesn't talk as much as you do,' the owner added with an affectionate smile. He turned back to Urbino. 'He just likes to rest and sip his coffee. Sometimes he has a glass of *raki*. He is always alone, but he does not seem to mind. Would you like some *raki*, signor?'

Urbino politely declined but asked for another cup of coffee and some baklava to take home with him for Natalia and Gildo.

When he returned to the Palazzo Uccello, the contessa telephoned to tell him that everything had been cleared for her to visit Mina tomorrow morning. Her voice thrilled with excitement and anticipation. He hoped that nothing would happen tomorrow to disappoint her.

The next morning, Urbino left the Palazzo Uccello early. He needed to talk to some people. First on his list was Teresa Sorbi, one of the seamstresses who had worked for Olimpia. Oriana had telephoned him the previous night with her address in the Santa Marta district.

Urbino walked to Santa Marta by way of the Ponte dei Scalzi. Even though the *bora* had ended, it was as if the city were now emitting, in damp icy waves, the Siberian chill it had absorbed yesterday. The feeble winter sunshine could do nothing to warm it.

Santa Marta, which never found its image perpetuated on a postcard, was one of the most cheerless areas of the city. Cranes, warehouses, and cars encroached upon its dreary housing estate of low, uniform tenements. It always came as a shock to tourists who wandered there. If they used their cameras, it was to record how sadly different the quarter was compared to most others of the city, where even dilapidation was romantic and picturesque.

But it had some claim to Urbino's heart, because in one of the dismal apartments had lived an old woman, an invalid now long since dead, who had provided Urbino with an important clue in solving the murder that had taken place in the summer of Eugene's other visit.

Teresa Sorbi's building, sorely in need of a new coat of paint, was in the middle of one of the rows of tenements. A line of frozen washing swayed back and forth in the wind.

Teresa Sorbi, a plump, brown-haired woman in her fifties, answered the bell on the first ring. Urbino recognized her from Olimpia's funeral. He was about to introduce himself when it became clear from the expression on her face that she recognized him. She broke out in a big smile. 'Signor Macintyre! Come in out of this terrible cold. I have some hot coffee.'

Teresa's small living room was clean and bright. Urbino seated himself in an armchair after the seamstress had removed a pile of neatly folded garments that gave off a fresh scent.

She eased her rounded figure down on to a small sofa. So great was the power of association that Urbino, knowing her profession, was reminded of a pincushion. In fact, it was not hard to imagine her with rows of common pins in her mouth as she pinned a hem.

'You've come about Olimpia, God rest her soul, and about that poor creature Mina Longo. I know that you like to find out the truth about things.' She mentioned the old woman, her former neighbor in the next row of tenements, who had helped Urbino in his previous case. 'She was proud that she was able to help you. She said you were very kind.'

'She was a good woman.' He paused. 'You're right. I've come to see you about Olimpia and Mina Longo.'

'Let me tell you right away that I don't think that girl killed Olimpia. I told the police that, and so did Rosa.'

'Rosa?'

'Rosa Custodi. We were at the funeral together. We both worked for Olimpia. We both could tell what kind of girl Mina is. Sweet and gentle. Nothing could have riled her up to kill Olimpia like that. Olimpia was like a mother to her.' She averted her eyes. 'Well, almost like a mother, Mina being so young and all. I told the police that Olimpia had been robbed – robbed and murdered. Look at the way they keep their front door open! Olimpia would have done anything to protect her money. She had money troubles.' Teresa gave Urbino an embarrassed smile. 'And that meant that Rosa and I had money troubles. To do her justice, she always paid us everything in the end. I don't know what will happen now. We both have money coming to us.'

'I'm sure she kept records.'

'Oh, she kept very careful ones, always at her desk scribbling in a book and collecting receipts.'

'You'll get your money, but it may take a while. Did her business bring in a lot?'

'Not that I could see. She didn't have many customers even though she did good work. You could show her a picture of a dress from a magazine, and she could make a pattern without any trouble. And she made original designs. I think her luck was changing with the work she was doing for the theater people. She was excited about it. We had a little party in the workshop when she signed the contract. Mina was there.'

'Did you ever see Olimpia arguing with her sister or her brother? Or maybe Apollonia Ballarin and her children?'

Teresa nodded.

'Both Rosa and me did. It was with the son of Signora Ballarin. About six or seven months ago – I am not sure exactly when but it was the summer – he came up to the workshop. Olimpia took him out on the staircase and closed the door. But just the same we heard what they were saying. Olimpia said that he was making a fool of her. She warned him to stop. He just laughed and said that she was too sensitive. As for the other people in the house, I hardly ever heard a peep out of them.'

'Did you notice anything different about her on the day of the murder?'

'She seemed nervous. But she also seemed excited. Maybe it was more excitement than nervousness, I don't know. When Rosa and I left to go home for lunch – it must have been about one fifteen, because the two of us were finishing up some work – she wished us a good appetite and said she would see us later.'

'Did she usually stay in the workshop during lunch?'

'I can't say. She never left before we did, and she was always there when we got back.'

Teresa started to cry, weeping large, thick tears that slid down her cheeks. She dabbed them away with the sleeve of her dress.

When she had recovered her composure, they spent several minutes talking about Olimpia's business affairs. Teresa gave him the names of two women who had been regular customers of Olimpia. 'They both live in the Campo San Polo. They're neighbors.'

Urbino wrote the women's names down in his pocket notebook.

'She had others, but I don't know their names. Most of her customers were old enough to be her mother. I think they were being faithful to her family.'

Teresa didn't have the addresses of Olimpia's other customers, but she had Rosa Custodi's.

'She lives on Sant' Elena.' Sant' Elena was a quarter in the far eastern section of the city. 'Let me see.' Teresa searched around in the drawer of a cabinet. 'Ah, here it is.' She took a small piece of paper from the drawer and read off the address.

Urbino took a water taxi from the Zattere to Sant' Elena. Rosa Custodi's apartment was on the second floor of a modern block of flats.

'Yes, yes, Signor Macintyre. I know who you are,' Rosa said in a raspy voice after Urbino had introduced himself. 'Teresa telephoned me.'

Rosa, who appeared to be in her late fifties, was as tall and thin as Teresa was short and plump, with long silvery gray hair that accentuated her sharp features. Her living room was barely heated and sparsely furnished, with not much more than a sagging sofa, two wooden chairs, a round chrome table, and a small cabinet that held a television set.

She confirmed what Teresa had told him – that Olimpia had had financial problems, that Mina was a gentle soul, and that the two women had never argued in her presence. She provided almost the same account of the argument between Olimpia and Alessandro and seconded Teresa's impression that Olimpia had looked nervous on the day of her murder.

'And not only that day,' Rosa clarified, 'but also a few days before, too. You can't help noticing each other's moods when you work closely together. But she never confided anything in us. Maybe she thought we wouldn't understand the kind of problems a woman like her had. But Teresa and I had no bad feelings against her. Live and let live.'

'Did you ever hear any argument between Olimpia and someone else in the family other than Alessandro Ballarin? Or with anyone else?'

Rosa nodded. 'Last July, around the same time as her argument with him. Teresa was sick. Her feet swell up in hot weather. When I was coming up the stairs after lunch, I heard shouting. A woman's voice – not Olimpia's – was saying over and over again that she was sorry. Olimpia said in a louder voice, "I can't believe you're doing this to me after everything I've done for you," or something like that. She started to sob. I was shocked. Olimpia never showed much emotion. I was too embarrassed to go into the workroom and I didn't want them to find me standing on the stairs as if I was snooping. I wasn't! I could not help it if I was there when they were arguing, could I?'

She paused. It was clear that it had not been a rhetorical question.

'No,' Urbino said.

'I respect other people's privacy. I continued up the staircase, but I sneezed. My allergy was bothering me then. Olimpia knew. When I went into the workshop, Olimpia was standing with another woman by the doors that went out to the veranda. She was younger than Olimpia, but not as young as Mina. Maybe thirty-five, but no more than that. The woman was wearing a green dress that Olimpia had made a few weeks before. I went over to my table and pretended I was sorting through my work. The woman left a few minutes later after the two of them whispered together. I never saw the woman again.'

'What did she look like?'

'Blond, pretty, but she didn't look healthy. She was pale and she had dark circles under her eyes. She was at Olimpia's funeral. Sitting next to a woman who was wearing a purple poncho. I didn't think that was very respectful. I could tell it was a lover's quarrel. Things are even harder on those people than they are on us. I kept sneaking looks at Olimpia the rest of the afternoon. She had no more tears but she sighed once or twice. I never told anyone else about the whole thing, not even Teresa. It was because I felt so sorry for Olimpia.'

*   *   *

After leaving Rosa Custodi, Urbino took the waterbus to the San Zaccaria stop. It was a few minutes past noon. He might have time to make one more visit before the lunch hour and the siesta.

What Teresa had said about the argument last summer between Olimpia and Alessandro had been tugging at the edges of his mind. Olimpia had accused him of humiliating her and had threatened that if he did not stop his behavior – whatever it had been – she would take some action against him.

Alessandro was one of the people in the Palazzo Pindar he knew the least about. This was not saying much, considering that each of them seemed to exist behind a veil that provided only indistinct glimpses and understanding. Although the veils were different in each case, what they shared in common was that they were made from the same eccentric Pindar material. If Urbino could only see some of the Pindars more clearly, it would expose someone else in the family as well. For Urbino was convinced more than ever that Olimpia's murder was a family affair. Because of the Pindars' relatively limited contacts with the world outside the house, there were few leads to follow beyond the family. He kept being thrown back on their relationships with each other.

If he could find out more about Alessandro, it would be a help, if only to remove some of the layers that were obscuring him – and could be obscuring another family member along with him.

The main things – almost the only things – he knew about Alessandro were his apparent devotion to his mother and his woodcarving.

Urbino had no idea whether Alessandro had worked with a master woodcarver or whether he was self-taught. There were several wood craftsmen in Venice who sold their sculptures in their own shops. One of the shops wasn't far away, near the Campo Sant' Angelo, in the general area of the Palazzo Fortuny.

But when he got there, the shutters were down. The owner had closed earlier than the other shops around it.

He took the ferry across the Grand Canal to San Silvestro, where he hurried toward the Campo San Polo. A shop off the square, not far from the Turkish café, sold carved wooden objects and other curiosities. He got there just as a stout middle-aged man was raising the metal pole to pull down the shutters.

'Excuse me, signore. I'll come back after you re-open if you have what I'm looking for.'

'And what is that?' The man, who had a genial-looking face, stopped pulling down the shutters.

'I'm looking for small carved wooden figures. About this high.' He measured off eight inches on his fingers. 'They're lifelike and painted,

sometimes with slightly exaggerated features and details. A friend from
Rome showed me some she bought in Venice a few months ago, but she
couldn't remember where the shop was.'

'Finally!' the man said with a little laugh. 'Your friend didn't buy them
from my shop. That is, if I have what you are talking about. I haven't sold
one in the seven months I've had them in the shop. Are those the kind
you're looking for?'

The man pointed to five identical figures clustered closely together on
a top shelf in the window. They were carved wooden figures of a woman
in a coat that had been painted with black dots against a yellow background.
The figure's face resembled Olimpia's. In her arms, she was cradling a
figure in a maternal way, whose face was pressed against her breast. This
smaller figure looked less like a child than it did a miniature adult. The
effect reminded Urbino of medieval paintings of the Madonna in which the
infant in her arms had the proportions of an adult.

'Yes, they're what I'm looking for.'

'Come inside.'

'As long as I'm not keeping you.'

Urbino said he would buy all five figures. As the owner was wrapping
them up, Urbino asked him who had made them.

'A man named Alessandro Ballarin. I have his address and telephone
number. He lives in Venice. A Venetian. I felt sorry for him. He seemed so
desperate to have me take them. He said he was self-taught. That's another
reason why I decided to stock them.' The man shrugged his shoulders.
'What can I say? I am not the best of businessmen. But I know what it is
like trying to get started. I gave him more than I should have for them. I
promised him that I'd give any buyers his name and address in case they
were interested in more.'

He wrote down Alessandro's name and address on his business card and
slipped it into the bag.

'No one else showed an interest in them?'

'Some customers have looked at them from time to time, taken one
down from the shelf. Tourists. They asked me if the figures had anything
to do with the history of Venice. I was honest and said no. No one ever
bought one.'

After Urbino left the shop, he went to the Campo San Polo. He asked
the owner of a café on the square if he knew where the two women lived
who, according to Teresa Sorbi, had been faithful customers of Olimpia.
The owner pointed him in the direction of two buildings on the other side
of the large square.

The two elderly women had known Platone and Regina Pindar. They had lost touch with the family shortly after their drowning but they had started to give some business to Olimpia a few years ago for the sake of her parents. The women were polite, if slightly curious about his inquiries about Olimpia. But he learned nothing new from either of them, even though they both praised the quality of Olimpia's work.

He went back to the café, where he ordered *tramezzini* sandwiches and half a liter of red wine. He believed he had discovered why Olimpia had been angry with Alessandro and had threatened him. It was because of the wooden caricatures. He assumed that the baby she was holding was Alessandro's way of depicting her relationship with Mina, so many years younger than Olimpia had been. Olimpia must have been furious that her nurturing relationship with Mina was being ridiculed.

Had she seen the figures in the shop window? Possibly even in other shops if Alessandro had made more? If she had, why hadn't she bought them up the way Urbino had? But perhaps she would have felt embarrassed to do it – or to have Mina go in her stead, or anyone else she might have taken into her confidence.

Although Urbino could understand Olimpia's reaction, he was puzzled about Alessandro's motivation in making the figures. Had it been his way of expressing his moral disapproval of the relationship? Had his mother been behind it in some way? Or had some animosity toward Olimpia, which had had nothing to do with Mina, encouraged him to use his skills to take this form of revenge?

Alessandro, however, had not been the one to be murdered, but the victim of his prank had been.

Then something occurred to Urbino. He was assuming that the baby held in the Olimpia figure's arms was meant to represent Mina. Was it possible that it was Evelina? She was younger than Olimpia, although not as young as Mina. If the baby was Evelina, did this help Urbino to any clearer understanding?

Urbino didn't have very specific dates for when the shopkeeper had bought the figures from Alessandro or for when Olimpia had argued with both Evelina and Alessandro, but they were all roughly within the same time period of last summer – which was also around the time when Olimpia and Mina had started to get close.

Urbino kept mulling over various possibilities, but he reached no conclusions.

Overall, however, his morning had been fruitful. He hoped that the contessa's visit to Mina had been as successful.

Twelve

Although her appointment to see Mina at the Women's Penitentiary was not until eleven, the contessa found it difficult to stay in the house after breakfast. Rather than wander around from room to room, she decided to try to turn her nervous energy to something constructive.

But what could she do?

In reviewing the possibilities, she quickly lighted upon Bianchi. She could pay him another visit. She might be able to get some information from him.

The contessa was about to step into the motorboat when, on an impulse, she went back inside the house and up to Mina's room to get the photograph of Mina and Olimpia, with the Bridge of Sighs in the background. It would give Mina some consolation that the contessa hoped would more than offset any problems that would come her way because of it.

Pasquale dropped her off on the quay near Bianchi's offices.

'What can I do for you today, contessa?' Bianchi asked from behind his heavy writing desk, not being quite able to conceal his surprise.

The contessa seated herself in the armchair that gave her a view of the Rialto Bridge.

'I've been thinking about something you said when I was here last time.' The contessa tried to figure out when that had been. Five days ago? A week? She was losing track of time. 'You mentioned — and mentioned rightly — that my main beneficiary is someone older than I am by quite a few years. I made the will when he was much more vigorous.'

'Yes. I remember.'

'I don't want to remove him from my will, you understand, but I would like to make a provision that, if he predeceases me, his nephew Vittorio da Capo of Naples be my main beneficiary. I have been thinking, Signor Bianchi, that I might not have time or opportunity to change it. Life is unpredictable. We never know what is going to happen.'

'You are correct.' He pursed his lips and nodded in what the contessa was sure he considered a sage manner.

'We see what's happened within only a few weeks at the Palazzo Pindar.'

'Indeed. As your lawyer, I recommend that you make the change. I even urge it. I'll have my assistant add a codicil immediately.'

'That's comforting.'

'I want you to think of other changes you might want. We will make up a completely new will later. But the codicil will suffice for now.'

The change was made quickly and efficiently. When this matter was behind her — which, in fact did relieve the contessa — she brought up Apollonia. Although her words were calculated, she felt a painful knot tighten in her as she mentioned her death. 'I know she wasn't a young woman and that she had been ill, but it took me by surprise.'

'I understand how you feel. I did not expect it myself — not so soon.'

'I've long considered Apollonia to have been much more far-seeing than I am.' The contessa could say this without any twinge of conscience since Apollonia, for more than twenty years now, had had her eyes focused on the afterlife.

'You are not fair to yourself, contessa. But Apollonia was a prudent woman, God rest her.'

'And judicious.'

A smile wreathed Bianchi's plump, pink face, so different from his father's stern one, which was fixed not only in her memory but also in the large portrait behind the desk. 'Are you asking me if you are in her will?'

Bianchi's question was so unexpected and so inconceivable that she was momentarily speechless. 'No, Signor Bianchi. I — '

'I am only teasing, contessa. Even lawyers can tease. It was because of Olimpia's will and the ocelot coat that I allowed myself. But to be clear, you are not mentioned in the will. She changed it recently, just as you are doing. Since you are family, I will tell you that she left almost everything to Alessandro. She gave a modest bequest of money to Eufrosina. Also her Fortuny gown and a few other personal items.'

'I see.' The contessa tried her best to keep her voice from revealing the surprise she felt and the turmoil of thoughts racing through her head. 'I am sure she knew what she was doing. As I said, she was a judicious woman — and — and fair.'

'And prudent as well, as I said.'

As the contessa was returning to the boat, she felt pleased, confused, and disturbed by the relative ease with which Bianchi had given her information about Apollonia's will.

She was pleased to have it — and eager to pass it on to Urbino.

But she was also nonplussed. Why had Bianchi been so forthcoming? This was different from his openness about Olimpia's will, since she was personally concerned in it because of the ocelot coat. Did Bianchi want her to keep the information to herself until it became generally known? If he did want her to do so, he had given her no indication.

But perhaps he wanted her, for his own purposes or perhaps at another person's urging, to reveal it to someone. If he did, this someone was most probably Urbino, given his reputation for sleuthing.

Yes, the contessa was both pleased and puzzled – and she was distressed. Bianchi Senior had been the most discreet of souls. Nothing easily passed the thin line of his lips. But Bianchi Junior had not hesitated in the slightest in telling her about Apollonia's will.

How discreet was he about the contessa's affairs?

It was all quite vexing.

Yes, her meeting with Bianchi had given her a great deal for her and Urbino to consider.

On this cold day in late January, as the motorboat approached the embankment of the penitentiary, the mere sight of it, with its small barred windows and bank of security cameras, oppressed the contessa's spirits. Its three stories of brick, sorely in need of repair, rose above her against the dark gray sky.

The contessa had seen it only once before. Four months after her marriage, she had walked past it when she was wandering on the Giudecca. Even the mild sunshine of that long-ago May afternoon had not been able to dispel the gloom of the severe, canal-side building.

At that time it had been a curiosity for her, something that she never could have imagined would one day directly touch her life, especially not in such a manner. Her interest then had been piqued because it had formerly been a convent for women. Now, when she remembered that the convent had been called I Convertiti, she found herself briefly thinking not about Mina imprisoned inside the building but the dead Apollonia, who had placed herself among the converted and was now dead.

Even though the contessa was an observant person, from the moment she went through the entrance, so much of what was happening around her did not register. Everything and everyone was an impressionistic blur – the guards, the security search, the corridor, the room she waited in, the officials she spoke to, the man who conducted her to the visitors' area, the overheated visitors' room, the woman guard watching her.

But then everything sharpened, everything came into focus when Mina was brought into the room and sat down across from her – although it isn't even correct to say that the contessa noted everything about her, eager as she was to see her. Afterwards she could not remember whether she was wearing a prison smock or her own clothes, a blindness that the contessa saw as a failure on her part and a betrayal of Mina. It was her responsibility not to let anything slip by her. She had come to help Mina.

Yet what she didn't see or remember clearly was greatly compensated by the clarity with which she saw Mina's face, even though the memory of it would haunt her in the coming days.

It was pale and drawn, and her porcelain features had lost their shine. All the liveliness in her dark eyes and the mobility of her mouth, so quick to smile, were gone. She was subdued, but she was not broken in any way, and this filled the contessa with a surge of gratefulness.

The contessa wished she could reach out and touch Mina, could hug her, but they were separated by the glass barrier. Somehow, the contessa and Mina got through their first greetings. Tears were shed on both sides. For the third time, the contessa heard herself ask, 'How are you, Mina?'

And for the third time Mina said, though her voice sounded tired, 'I'm all right. Everyone is treating me well. Don't worry.'

'That is impossible, Mina. You know me well.'

'And you know me. You know that I do not like to see you upset. And what is the purpose?'

There was wisdom in her words far beyond her much younger years.

It had taken Mina to remind the contessa that she should not appear too anxious, that Mina should not see the extent to which she was struggling because of the poor girl's situation. She knew from other circumstances she had been through in her life – most notably from her husband's long decline – that people who were ill or in distress had an added burden when they saw the pain that their situation caused in the people they loved.

And so the contessa did her best to mask the depth of her concern, even though she knew that she was not really deceiving Mina.

'How was Olimpia's funeral?' Mina's voice was hardly more than a whisper.

Mina's question gave the contessa a little jolt. Two weeks had passed since the funeral, and during all that time Mina had been on the Giudecca, without even the consoling memory of having been among the mourners.

'It was simple,' the contessa could honestly say. 'The way she would have wanted it to be. And you were there in spirit. I could feel it. I have something for you.' The contessa took the photograph out of her purse. She had asked for permission to give it to Mina when she had arrived. The guard in the room with them had been informed, but nonetheless she paid close attention to the contessa's movements.

'I found it in your room. I could not help but notice it. It was lying on your table,' the contessa said by way of excusing herself for what Mina might think was snooping. 'I decided to bring it to you. For you to have with you. I thought it might be a comfort to you, but I hope it won't create any problems for you.'

She handed the photograph to Mina. From the way the girl started weeping when she looked at it, the contessa was at first afraid she had made a mistake.

But then Mina whispered in a tear-smothered voice, 'Thank you so much. It is very thoughtful of you. It was good for you to bring it. There will be no problem.' She kissed the photograph and looked at it in silence for a few moments. Raising her eyes to the contessa, she said in a stronger voice, 'Signor Lanzani told me that Olimpia left me money and many of her things in her will. She didn't tell me I was in her will. I never had any idea about that.'

'Of course you didn't. But it shows how much she cared about you.'

'If I ever get out of here, I won't take anything.'

'You won't?' The contessa had not been prepared for this.

'Never. I killed her.'

'Mina! You mustn't say that.' The contessa looked over at the woman guard, who had an impassive expression on her face. 'Signor Lanzani must have told you not to say that.'

'Yes, he did. But I *did* kill her. If I hadn't taken the scissors out' – Mina's voice broke – 'she might not have died. All – all her blood came rushing out. I made it happen.'

'Look at me, Mina. Look into my eyes.' The contessa gazed into Mina's troubled brown eyes that were filled with tears ready to be shed again. 'Olimpia would have died whether you took out the scissors or not. It was in the medical examiner's report.'

The contessa had no idea whether this were true or not, but if ever there was a time for what Urbino called benevolent deception, it was now.

Mina continued to stare at the contessa. She licked her lips. 'I've decided. I won't keep anything.'

The sound of women's laughter came into the room. It was happy, joyous laughter. It seemed so incongruous, but the contessa supposed that after a while life in the prison must fall into the rhythms of life led outside its walls and even have the semblance of normality. The contessa prayed that Mina would never have to try to make that long-term adjustment. Despite the brave face she was putting on things now, the contessa didn't think Mina would be up to it.

'Do you need anything, Mina?'

'Thank you, but I have everything I need. As I said, everyone is very kind to me.' She gave a weak smile. 'It isn't as bad as you think.'

'I'm glad to hear that.'

'How is everyone at the house? And Signor Urbino?'

'Everyone is fine. They all send their love.'

'Tell me. How are Olimpia's sister and brother feeling? And her cousins? They must be very sad.'

'They are doing the best they can.' The contessa had decided not to tell Mina that Apollonia had died. Given the girl's emotional state, she would probably think that Apollonia had died because of grief and shock, and feel guilty for that, too, on top of everything else.

'I hope they will forgive me.'

'There is nothing for them to forgive.'

The contessa feared that Mina was about to start proclaiming her guilt again, but when she broke the short silence, she asked, 'Signorina Gaby is still worried and afraid?'

'She told Signor Urbino that she had been feeling a premonition of the danger that was surrounding her sister.'

Mina took this in and, being the sensitive, impressionable soul she was, seemed to accept it.

'And how is Zouzou?'

'Zouzou is the good little girl she always is – good even in her mischief.' The contessa was happy to move on to this innocuous topic. 'She misses you.'

But then the contessa wondered if this was the right thing to say. She was so confused. She did not want Mina to feel worse. She was a sentimental girl – but maybe it was the contessa who was the sentimental one. She should not have mentioned Zouzou.

'Who takes her for her walks?'

'I'm doing it until you come back.' Once again, the contessa was not telling the truth, but she did not want Mina to feel that Zouzou might be transferring her affections to someone else in the house.

'I'm sure she enjoys that.' Mina glanced at the guard. The contessa was pleased to see that the stern-faced woman gave Mina a pleasant smile. 'I must tell you something. It is very important. I must not tell anyone else except you and Signor Urbino. Olimpia made me promise.'

The contessa took a quick breath. 'What are you talking about, Mina?'

'A month ago she gave me an envelope. Right before Christmas. She said she wanted me to keep it safe. There is something important inside it, she said. I was supposed to keep it until she asked me for it back. Or if something bad happened to her, I should give it to you or Signor Urbino. I hated when she said that. Her face was very serious. I told her she must not draw bad luck down on her head. And – and now something terrible *has* happened to her, because of that and because of me!'

Mina was about to burst into tears again.

'Please, Mina, you must not think like that. We must think clearly. About the envelope. Do you know what's inside?'

'Oh, no! I promised that I would never open it.'

'Is there a name on the envelope?'

Mina shook her head, tears still in her eyes, waiting to brim over. 'But it's an old envelope. It's stained with spots.'

'Where is it now? You must know that the police searched your room.'

'Signor Lanzani told me. But I didn't put it in my room. That would not be safe, Olimpia said. I am sorry, but she said anyone could come into my room and look at my things, even if it was locked because – because you have the key. Oh, please, don't be upset!' She looked down at the photograph. 'I know you would never do anything to hurt me! You are too kind!'

'Of course I wouldn't. And I'm not upset.'

'I had to keep three promises, you see. Three, like in the fairy tales. I must not open the envelope. I must not keep it in my room. And I must give it to you or Signor Urbino if something happened to her. You see! She said to give it to you. She trusted you! She just did not want anyone to see it unless – unless . . .' Mina trailed off.

'You're a faithful girl, Mina. And I am sure Olimpia had her good reasons for asking you to do what you did. But where is the envelope?'

'In the library. Inside one of the books that are on a high shelf next to the windows. You made Vittoria dust all the books on those shelves the week before. I was outside the library when you told her they were German books.' Mina paused. 'It's the encyclopedia. I know because the word on the book in German is like the one in Italian.'

'Why did you put it there?'

Mina looked away. 'Because I never saw you reading the German books. English books, Italian books, and French books. But never German ones. You told Vittoria they had belonged to the conte, may God rest his soul.'

This was true. All the German books in the library had belonged to Alvise. He had started to learn German after the war when he was helping families of German immigrants who had come to Venice. He had become interested in the language beyond the purpose it served him.

'I – I did not want you to find the envelope,' Mina went on. 'Forgive me.'

'I understand. Do not trouble yourself about it. But Signor Urbino reads German. Sometimes he has borrowed the conte's German books.'

'I was taking a small chance. But I didn't know where else to hide the envelope and I knew no one would dust the books until spring. I was going to find another place before then. It's not easy to figure out a hiding place.'

'No, it isn't.'

'I put the envelope in the last volume. Now that Olimpia is gone, I must keep my promise. You must read it. You and Signor Urbino. Olimpia said the two of you would know what to do.'

The import of the whole thing hit Mina anew. It meant that Olimpia was dead, dead, dead. Her tears fell so thickly and furiously that the guard seemed on the point of getting up. The contessa waited for the storm to run its natural course, making sympathetic sounds and comments. When it was over, the contessa fell into a rambling account about Zouzou, the exhibition, and her visit to the Fortuny factory, which she hoped would be soothing, but it was a strain on her. Mina kept looking at her with large, moist eyes. And the contessa was conflicted, for, although she wanted to be with the girl for all their allotted time, she was also eager to leave and return to the house so that she and Urbino could search for the envelope. It could bring Mina closer to being released. This was what she was desperately hoping.

When they were parting, Mina said, 'Please be careful when you go out in the cold. You could get sick.'

'And you take care of yourself, Mina. Signor Urbino and I will continue to do everything we can so that you will soon be out of here. And Olimpia is looking after you, too. You kept your promise to her. I will come back to see you again as soon as I can.'

Thirteen

As soon as the contessa returned home, she telephoned Urbino. Natalia said he had gone out early in the morning and had not returned.

'I'll tell him to call you as soon as he comes in.'

But this was not good enough for the contessa. She was more impatient than she could ever remember having been.

After she had lunch, which she was not able to finish, she rang the Palazzo Uccello four times in the next hour and a half. She could hear the barely concealed irritation in Natalia's voice when she said, each time, quietly, 'I'll tell him as soon as he comes in, contessa.'

The contessa did not want to look at the envelope until Urbino was with her. This seemed important, but she was so wrought up that she could not decide why. Surely, she should just get the envelope out of the encyclopedia and read what was inside on her own. She might even save some valuable time, depending on what was in it.

But she didn't, although her steps kept carrying her to the dark-panelled room with its rows and rows of volumes, most of them calf-bound, with gilt lettering on their spines. The rich smell of the leather reminded her of the conte, who had spent many hours every day in the library. She did not even take the volume of the encyclopedia down from the shelf. She positioned the ladder, however, so that when Urbino came they would at least not lose the few moments of time it would take him to do it.

But she found it difficult to keep her eyes away from the large dark green book, concentrating all her attention on it as if it could tell her something.

She tried to interest herself in a book, and took one after another down from the shelf and brought them over to the deep-buttoned leather sofa, only to close each after a few glazed minutes of reading. She drew the purple velvet curtains across the windows, although there was no possibility that anyone could see inside the room.

Just when she was about to give in, climb the ladder, and take down the volume, Urbino rang.

'I just got in. What's going on?'

'Oh, Urbino! Finally! You have to come here.' She explained about the envelope. 'I'll have Pasquale pick you up.'

* * *

'Here.' Urbino said from the library ladder. He handed the contessa the encyclopedia volume. 'You can have the honors. Look for it.'

She took the book to the long table by the windows that looked down on the garden. Urbino joined her.

She riffled through the pages. Placed between two of them near the end of the book was an envelope.

'Here it is. Just where she said it would be.' What might be in the envelope was, for a moment, less important to the contessa than that the envelope was there. It gratified her to have this physical proof that Mina had been telling the truth about it. 'It does look old.'

The envelope was about five by seven inches. It was slightly yellowed and had fly specks on it – or the kind of small brownish stains the contessa had once been told came from flies. Nothing was written on the front. She turned it over. Nothing was written on the back either. The flap, which was not sealed, had been tucked neatly into the back of the envelope.

'Obviously Olimpia saw no need to seal it,' Urbino said. 'We should be a little careful handling the envelope and what's inside. It might be important to know whose fingerprints are on it if it comes to that.'

'You take it.'

The contessa handed the envelope to Urbino, who took it between two widespread fingers of one hand. With the other hand, he lifted out the flap and extracted a folded sheet of white notepaper, which was only slightly yellowed around the edges. He placed the envelope down on the table and, careful to touch only the edges of the notepaper, he unfolded it.

The contessa, who realized that she had been holding her breath, moved closer to Urbino, but all she could see without her reading glasses was a blur of light blue handwriting that covered only a small part of the paper.

Urbino was frowning.

'What does it say?'

'It's not much more than a note. And it's in English.'

Urbino read it aloud in a low, deliberate voice:

My one and only A,
Because we shouldn't, it is all the more delicious. Don't you agree? I love you for all the reasons against it and for a thousand and one more. I always will.
I hope you like my gift. I looked for a long time before I found one in exactly the same shade as your eyes. It is a very special shade that is only yours.
Forever,
E

Ten minutes later the contessa and Urbino were in the *salotto blu*. The contessa needed the comfort of the small room that she spent so much of her time in, and much of it with Urbino. Since leaving the house this morning, she had felt whirled around, and now the letter had made things even worse. It had immediately set in motion a series of disturbing thoughts.

'Thank you,' she said to Urbino as he handed her a glass of sherry. Urbino settled on the sofa beside her, with Zouzou between them, asleep. The letter lay unfolded on the coffee table.

'I don't recognize the handwriting,' the contessa said, after she had read it with her reading glasses on.

'Neither do I. But I haven't seen any of the Pindars' handwriting. Have you?'

The contessa thought for a moment. 'I've got a note here and there during the years, mainly from Apollonia and Regina. I don't have them anymore. I don't remember what their handwriting was like. But why are you assuming that one of them wrote this?'

'I know it's a big assumption, but everything so far has come back to the family – or almost everything, it seems. I would even go so far as to say that we need to consider that both the writer and the recipient come from the family. The fact that we have the initials "A" and "E" alerts me, too. Think of how common those initials are in the Pindar family.'

The contessa did her best to absorb the implications of what he had said. 'But – but that would be horrid. It *is* a love letter!'

'So it seems. But it's also completely possible we're not dealing with something like that,' Urbino said, clearly in an attempt to reassure her. 'I have no doubt that either "A" or "E" is – or *was* – a Pindar. The fact that blue eyes are mentioned points us in that direction, too. "A" has blue eyes – or had them. As far as I know, all the Pindars do.' He paused. 'Something the letter says makes me think of one of your Pindar relatives in particular.'

The contessa ran her eye over the letter again. She did not understand what he meant.

'The reference to a thousand and one more reasons,' Urbino said. '*The Arabian Nights*. Ercule has two volumes of Burton's translation.'

'But it's a common enough thing to say, don't you think? I've said it many times.'

The contessa, surprised at the feeling of annoyance that had suddenly come over her, silently chastised herself. Her nerves were on edge. She forced herself to calm down as best she could. Mina was at stake in all this. Although the contessa doubted – or was it that she feared? – the implications of the love letter being exclusively a Pindar affair, she knew she had to face it directly. Yes, Urbino was right. They did have to consider the worst, and she would do whatever she could to help him arrive at what she could only think of as horrid conclusions.

'And besides,' she said, continuing her thought out loud, 'by trying to establish the worst, we could end up eliminating it.'

'Yes.' Urbino scrutinized the note. 'I can't even tell if it's a feminine script or a masculine one, if there are such things. A graphologist might be able to tell, but I think I read somewhere that there is no way of being definitive about it. What we need to do now is to give our efforts to what we can do. We have to put our heads together. "A"? "E"? Who might they be?'

'There's no "O" for Olimpia. Or "M" for Mina. That's some consolation. And the envelope and letter are old.'

'They seem to be. But they could have been made to *look* old.'

'Is that what you think? Why would someone have done that?'

'We need to keep all possibilities open. And that, dear Barbara, presents a great problem. Just about any letters other than "A" or "E" would have kept the possibilities down. Now we have many to consider. The Pindars and their penchant for names beginning with "A" and "E"!' Urbino's tone was exasperated. 'We have Alessandro, Ercule, and Eufrosina. And there is Apollonia even though she's dead. And Apollonia isn't the only dead person we have to consider.'

He stared at her as if urging to think.

'There's Achille,' she said.

'Anyone else?' Again, Urbino waited.

'Yes. Efigenia, Apollonia's and Platone's aunt,' the contessa said. 'How many does that make?'

'Six. Three "A"s and three "E"s.'

'How far back do we have to go with the Pindar names? There has been an Elettra and a Euridice, an Antigone. I think there was a Euripide. I am sure there must be others that I have never known or have forgotten. It's an entire cast from a Greek tragedy.' The contessa gave a nervous little laugh.

'Let's limit ourselves to the relatively recent past, to Pindars who had some kind of direct contact with those who are alive today and with people outside the illustrious, eccentric family!'

For the next ten minutes they arranged the names in various combinations of the "A" and "E" of the letter. The contessa's head was spinning. Then she remembered something that might help.

'I have Eufrosina's signature on the contract! The letter is signed with an "E."' She went to the study to get her copy of the contract, proud that she was able to contribute something right away to proving or disproving Urbino's theory.

They carefully compared the signature and the handwriting, keeping the note on the table and not handling it. After a few minutes of scrutinizing the two, however, they realized that there was no way of determining from the signature whether Eufrosina had written the note. Her signature was distinctive, but hardly more than an indecipherable scrawl.

'Maybe a graphologist could help us with this, too. But her signature is almost like an abstract design. Let me keep the contract and the letter, though. I'll try to find someone to look at them.'

Urbino read the letter again. The contessa stared down at it but could not focus on it. It sounded as if Urbino was mumbling something under his breath.

'I've forgotten my high school mathematics,' he said clearly and distinctly now. 'If I could remember the formula, I could tell you how many permutations there are.'

'Permutations!' the contessa said in a raised voice. Zouzou stirred in her sleep. 'I feel we're playing a version of Gaby's game.' She turned to Urbino. 'A game! Could someone want us to be playing a game?'

'Who? Olimpia? Mina? I don't think so. I think the person who wrote the letter wanted to conceal identities — because it was important to them, or at least to the writer, to do it.'

'But if the person really wanted to conceal their identities, then why didn't he — or she — not use any initials at all?'

'Ah, Barbara, if only people would be consistent, then this line of work I've taken up — that *we've* taken up — would be much easier. The initials might refer not to names but to something else, like affectionate names, terms of endearment. But Olimpia apparently knew who corresponded to the initials, and she was afraid it would cost her her life. If it did, she wanted to have a hand in revealing the identity of her murderer. And you must realize what we have to consider seriously. You don't like to think of Olimpia as a victimizer because of Mina's relationship with her. But she could have been blackmailing whoever wrote or whoever received the letter. One would think, though, that she would have had more sympathy, given her own situation.'

'The desire for money blinds and deadens people,' the contessa pointed out. 'But blackmail makes no sense if the person being blackmailed doesn't have a lot of money. And the only one in that house who has — who *had* — a lot of money was Apollonia.'

She was about to tell him what she had learned from Bianchi about Apollonia's will when Urbino said, 'But does a blackmailer have to be out for money all the time?'

'What do you mean?'

'The blackmailer could want something other than money – or something that might be converted into money, one way or another.'

The contessa took some solace in a sip of sherry. 'We have to figure that letter out!' She felt a sense of urgency not untouched with fear. "A" and "E". "A" and "E",' she repeated, as if just saying the two initials out loud would yield up their meaning.

'Sometimes these things have a way of revealing themselves when you don't try too hard.'

'But why didn't Olimpia add some explanation? Why didn't she tell us what she knew?'

Urbino carefully folded the letter and slipped it back into the envelope.

'Olimpia might have thought that she'd be putting herself in greater danger by being explicit. Of course, if it is true that she was blackmailing someone, she had already put herself in grave danger, but, as I said, people aren't consistent. What she should have done was write down what she knew and told the person that she had given the information to someone who was instructed to open it in case anything happened to her. But all we have is this.'

He indicated the envelope.

'If we're dealing with blackmail, and I emphasize *if*,' he went on, 'you can be sure that someone is desperately looking for this note and would do anything to get it – even murder again.'

He put the letter, along with Eufrosina's contract, into his pocket, and then started to pace around the room as he liked to do to calm himself and stimulate his thinking.

'If that letter is going to mean anything to us eventually – if it's going to point to a murderer – it will have to take its place in the other things we know, and that we're still learning,' he said. 'Just finding one more piece of information could make everything as clear as crystal. Or maybe all it would take is to pay more attention to something we already know, individually or together. Let me tell you what I've been doing since we saw each other yesterday.'

As Urbino continued his pacing, the contessa listened to an account of conversations he had had with Oriana, Olimpia's two seamstresses, and a woodcarver. When he finished, he knelt in front of the fireplace and poked at it with the bar, then returned to the sofa and picked up his sherry.

'At least one "E" on our list isn't a Pindar,' the contessa said. 'Evelina. But from what Olimpia's seamstress said – was it Rosa? – it seems that Olimpia was the injured party there, as she was with Alessandro. And I wonder what Olimpia and Nedda were arguing about? Olimpia seems to have had more than her share of disputes in the past six or seven months.'

'Oriana said it was very heated. And the day I was in the gondola in front of the Palazzo Pindar, Olimpia didn't acknowledge Nedda's greeting. It may have something to do with Evelina.'

Urbino asked her if there was anything that Oriana had said that she disagreed with.

'I wasn't aware that Nedda was running after Achille,' the contessa replied. 'As far as I could see, he was devoted to her. I saw no sign that he was thinking of breaking off the engagement. But, *caro*, aren't we losing sight of something? Of Gaby? This whole terrible situation goes back to her fears. Gaby was the person we were giving most of our thoughts to. Shouldn't we still be doing that?'

'We should continue to keep her in the picture, yes. She is very much on my mind. And so are the blue rooms that she's in charge of.'

The contessa ran her fingers through Zouzou's white fur.

'By the way, *caro*, I played the actress with Italo Bianchi again this morning before I went to the Giudecca.'

'You did? Good for you, Barbara.'

'Nora,' she gently insisted. 'Apollonia left almost everything to Alessandro.'

Urbino stared, complete surprise on his face. 'I wonder why?'

'Maybe the will has a version of "For reasons of which she is well aware". But considering the way Apollonia had become, maybe there are no reasons, except distorted ones that she had in her head. And you know how Alessandro was always making himself indispensable. The perfect devoted son. He could do no wrong. Poor Eufrosina! I've seen the change that came over Apollonia, almost as if she became a different person. Eufrosina and Alessandro both deserve a reward for what they had to go through after her great conversion, but only Alessandro is actually getting one.'

Urbino stood up. 'I have to be going. I'm meeting Eugene.'

'Ah, Eugene. The glimpses he gives of the Urbino who used to be are delightful. Although what he tells me sometimes makes me realize you haven't changed much at all.'

Urbino, who looked suddenly uncomfortable, showed no inclination to pursue the topic. He patted his pocket, where he had put the contract and the letter. 'I'll try to find a graphologist. As for the letter, I'll photo-copy it – very carefully – and hand it over to the Questura. They need to know about it. But I don't have any faith in Gemelli.' Gemelli was the police commissario. Over the years, Urbino had developed a strained relationship with him. 'He's not likely to take anything I say about this situation seriously and it won't help that all I have – all *we* have – is theories.'

'Gemelli *should* listen to you, considering the help you've given him. He's made fun of your theories before, but he's benefited from them in the end.'

'I'll do the best I can. And we should tell Lanzani about it. I will leave that to you. But don't let anyone else know about the letter. No one.'

It had become a habit so quickly, this wandering around the house at night. The contessa was getting as obsessive on her rounds as Urbino was in his walks through the city. She always began from her boudoir, after she had retired for the night, and found that sleep would not come.

Tonight she had lain in bed, awake for two hours, her hand on the sleeping Zouzou, her head filled with worries and the initials "A" and "E" streaming through it. And she kept going over her visit to Mina. She became upset for finding comfort in one thing Mina had said – that under no circumstances would she keep any of the inheritance she got from Olimpia. Mina might change her mind, of course. It was not as if she was thinking clearly where she was now.

But the rise in the contessa's hopes that she might have Mina back at the house was followed by a drop in her opinion of herself as she realized how selfish her hopes were.

With a sigh, she got out of bed, pulled on her robe, and started her rounds. Zouzou, after staring after her from her position on the bed, joined her reluctantly.

She went up to the staff quarters and looked around Mina's clean, neat little room. She restrained herself from opening drawers and going into her cupboard. The thought that she might find something that could help Mina briefly tempted her, but she knew she was providing an excuse for herself. Yet the temptation was a strong one. In knowing more about Mina – and when it came down to it, she knew relatively little – she would feel closer to her. No, she would not give in to the temptation.

She went down to her study. It was a small, jewel box of a room, draped in Fortuny fabric. It was here that she did all the paperwork for the house and her other concerns, and corresponded with friends and family. She straightened up items scattered across her writing table.

Before she left the room, she went over to a large, glass-sheeted frame on the wall, which held her passport photographs over the years. Urbino had suggested the idea, which she had resisted at first, because of the evidence it would give of the passage of time. But she had come to like the series of black-and-white photographs taken at the five-year intervals she preferred for each new passport.

She traced with her eye how the fresh face she had brought to Venice when she had come to study music had gradually evolved into the much older one of last year. What she concentrated on was not what had been lost and left behind, but on what had endured and what had been gained. Even tonight, with her spirits so low, the photographs under the glass encouraged her with their evidence of the person she had become, the person who was doing all she could to help Mina.

With Zouzou following her, the contessa descended the grand staircase to the *piano nobile*. The long-case clock chimed the first hour of the day. The loud dull note sounded more like the end of something than the beginning.

She stood in the large doorway of the ballroom after turning on the chandeliers. The room, with its gilded moldings, stuccoed ceiling, and sixteenth-century tapestry, brought memories of all the celebrations it had witnessed, as well as expectations of the ones to come.

But festivities, past or future, were not something she wanted to think about, not with Mina on the Giudecca.

Down in the exhibition room, the contessa stood in front of Apollonia's garnet-colored gown, thinking of Apollonia and her aunt Efigenia and her daughter Eufrosina, all connected to the Fortuny. Soon, perhaps, its relationship to the Pindar family would be broken, and Eugene would buy the gown. The contessa had little doubt that Eufrosina would be eager to part with it for the excellent price Eugene was sure to offer.

Back on the *piano nobile*, the contessa made a quick survey of the library, where the volume of the German encyclopedia still lay on the table, and then went into the morning room. Zouzou jumped on the sofa and started to settle herself on it. Sometimes the contessa would spend a restless night here or in the *salotto blu*, lying on the sofa with Zouzou beside her, waiting for the dawn.

She opened the photograph album she had been paging through with Urbino on the day of Olimpia's strange and unexpected visit that seemed so impossibly long ago. She looked through it idly – at the photographs of the beautiful Apollonia in her Fortuny dress, her aunt Efigenia, Ercule in his Turkish regalia, Gaby and Olimpia in Trafalgar Square, and Gaby in the Piazza San Marco.

How sad that Gaby's life was so diminished these days, spent within the walls of the Palazzo Pindar, tending to the collection and keeping the keys of the blue rooms. Was the light-hearted young woman, the one filled with a sense of what wonderful things life had to offer, the young woman the contessa still remembered so well — was there anything left of her? Was Gaby —?

The contessa broke off her thoughts abruptly. A few moments later, she was dialling Urbino's number.

'Hello?'

She could tell from his voice that she had awakened him. She did not apologize but started right in, 'We forgot something. Or it's more that *I* forgot, since I've known it a long time and only mentioned it to you once.'

'It must be important to ring me up at — what time is it? Almost two.'

'It's about Gaby. I just remembered. Gaby. Gabriella. She used to call herself Ella, and so did everyone else, until she entombed herself in that house. Ella. We have another Pindar "E" to add to the others.'

Fourteen

'I know Lincoln freed the slaves back home,' Eugene said. 'But wasn't there some Italian who did it here? Look at the poor fellows!'

Urbino's gondola had just pulled into the Grand Canal from its mooring near the Rialto Bridge. It was being rowed this morning by not only Gildo but also his friend Giovanni, both wearing colorful mackintoshes. The addition of this extra oar made the occasion even more special. Gildo had polished the boat that morning, and it was shining almost like silver. Bright red roses filled the vases on each side of the *felze*.

Urbino was sitting inside the shelter of the *felze* with Frank and Betty Chin, who were cozily sharing the Moroccan blanket. The purchases the Chins and Eugene had made in the Rialto shops took up the remaining available space. Urbino, aware of the gray sky that threatened either rain or more probably snow, had advised that the boxes and bags be kept inside the *felze*. Eugene, without complaint, was obliged to sit on a bench in front of the entrance to the cabin.

Urbino had arranged to meet Eugene and the Chins at the Rialto Bridge an hour and a half ago. Earlier that morning he had gone to the Questura to give the commissario the letter. But Gemelli was on official business on Murano. Urbino turned the letter over to his assistant, along with a report about where it had been found and how it was related to the Longo investigation. He was grateful that the assistant showed more interest than he knew Gemelli would have. He felt he had done what was necessary for the time being.

Shortly afterward, with the help of a friend who worked at the university, Urbino had been able to set up an appointment with a graphologist who occasionally worked with the police. He examined the contract and the letter and confirmed what Urbino had said to the contessa: it was not possible to determine whether the writer of the letter was a man or a woman or whether Eufrosina, based on only her signature, had written the letter.

Disappointed that the graphologist had been unable to shed any light on the letter, he had met Eugene and the Chins at the couple's hotel and taken them to some of his favorite shops in the Rialto area. Eugene had been remarkably restrained on this occasion, buying only two dozen multi-colored glass ashtrays of hideous design that his companions could not dissuade him from. The highlight of the Chins' shopping spree had been a shop that sold hand-carved wooden models of Venetian boats. Betty had indulged herself in seven different models and had bought a copy of an illustrated book on Venetian boats that she said the contessa had told Eugene about.

Urbino had looked around the shop to see if there were any of Alessandro's figures for sale, but there weren't any. He described them to the owner of the shop, who told him he remembered Alessandro but that he had declined to buy any of his figures because he only stocked his own designs. Urbino could tell, however, that he did not have a high regard for Alessandro's work.

'Don't you all feel cooped up inside there?' Eugene shouted as they moved away from the Rialto embankment.

'We're just fine, Eugene,' Betty said. 'You're the one losing out. It's very romantic.'

'A lot more romantic if it was just you and Frank. Urbino's a fifth wheel – or whatever you'd call it in a gondola. Those contraptions are made for lovers, aren't they?'

'That's been one of their uses,' Urbino said. 'And to conceal conspirators, too. There were a lot of them in Venice in the old days.'

'None of those huts on any of the other gondolas though.'

'They went out of fashion a long time ago.'

'Out of fashion, is it?' Eugene said. 'Are you trying to bring it back *in* fashion or are you enjoyin' bein' different?'

'Now you leave Urbino alone,' Betty said. 'He's a man of imagination and taste of a European kind. He doesn't seem American at all. Here he is giving us a wonderful experience, isn't he, Frank?'

'He certainly is. It's very kind of you, Urbino.'

The gondola, guided by the two young men, moved down the Grand Canal toward the Bacino. The murmurs of appreciation at the beauty of the scene from the Chins were gratifying to Urbino.

He kept his comments and descriptions to a minimum, and his opinion of the pleasant Chins went up several more notches when they showed no need to break the silence except to ask an occasional question and to comment on how much more impressive everything was when they were floating in a gondola. Their surrender to the scene was close to complete, and transferred itself to Eugene.

In this shared mood of appreciation, the rows of palaces slowly unrolled themselves on either side. When they reached the Salute, Betty asked Urbino if he could have the gondola stop for a little while. She wanted to savor the wide church whose dome, white and luminous, rose above them.

'It's my favorite building in Venice, and I never knew it existed before I came!' Betty enthused, further endearing herself to Urbino, whose own opinion of it, enhanced by its location, knew few limits. He could imagine the Grand Canal absent of any other building but not the Salute.

As they slid into motion again, Eugene cried out, 'Here it comes!' Being outside, he was the first to notice the snow. It was falling from the dark gray sky in huge, soft flakes. It surrounded the gondola in white swirling scrims that made the scene even more entrancing.

The resemblance that the Doges' Palace bore to a fairy palace could hardly have been more pronounced, and the moored gondolas along the Molo seemed nothing less than enchanted barks.

Looking around her in wonder from beneath the low, arching roof, Betty made the obvious but apt comparison to a souvenir globe of the city that had been shaken.

As the gondola rounded the Dogana da Mare, with its statue of Fortune perched on a golden ball on the Customs House tower, and entered the choppy waters of the Giudecca Canal, the snow fell more and more heavily.

'It's enchanting, Urbino!' Betty touched Urbino's arm. 'Thank you so much!' It was as if he were some wizard who had conjured up the snow especially for the occasion.

The four passengers in the gondola and its two gondoliers had a panoramic view of the snow, as it blew at an oblique angle above the Zattere toward the Giudecca Island and the lagoon beyond, driven by gusts of wind from the Dolomites. Behind them, at moments the Doges' Palace, the Campanile, the domes of the Basilica, and the long low line of the Riva degli Schiavoni had less the appearance of vanishing from sight than of being created by the snow's sorcery. On the Zattere embankment children were shouting, laughing, and trying to catch the flakes. Everywhere – by the water's edge, in doorways and windows, from the shelter of cafés – people were taking in the sudden spectacle of the snow.

The gondola slid into a canal in the Dorsoduro quarter, entering the network of narrow waterways that would slowly bring the party back to the Grand Canal.

Gildo and Giovanni moved the craft along with slow strokes of the oars through intricate, winding ways. Occasionally the young men cried out a warning "Oy!" or produced shrill whistles. The languid movement of the gondola through the gray-green waters increased the enjoyment of Eugene and the Chins, who could more easily survey the scene as it was being transformed by the snow. Here, the snow was accumulating quickly, already caking the windows. It seemed to possess a light of its own. The prow of the gondola soon acquired a white mantle, as did the shoulders of Eugene and the two young men.

'First a flood, now a blizzard! Well, a snowstorm, anyway,' Eugene said, brushing the snow from the shoulders of his trench coat. 'If you throw in the boilin' heat of the summer, I guess I've seen Venice in all kinds of weather.'

The gondola continued through Dorsoduro and regained the Grand Canal by the Ca' Rezzonico, the eighteenth-century palace where Robert Browning had died. Urbino drew his companions' attention to the Browning quotation on the plaque by the land entrance to the building:

> Open my heart and you will see
> Graved inside of it, "Italy".

Eugene chuckled. 'Suits you to a "T", old boy!'

From the Ca' Rezzonico the two young men rowed the gondola swiftly with the tide up the Grand Canal. For a while, the small group was seeing the same scene they had earlier, but now under the spell of the snow. By the time they passed under the Rialto Bridge, Eugene and the Chins fell, as they had earlier, into a contemplative and appreciative silence.

Urbino's thoughts, however, were far away from the scene around him. He was thinking about the letter he had turned over to the Questura, about where it might have come from, about who 'A' and 'E' might be, and what the letter might have to do with Olimpia's murder. It would appear that it had a great deal to do with it, but Urbino was cautious by nature, having regretted not often but nonetheless very keenly when he had leapt to an incorrect conclusion. Yesterday afternoon he had told the contessa about his 'big assumption' about the letter's importance, but today he was withdrawing somewhat from that position. He did not want to run the risk of having the letter prevent him from looking for and seeing what he needed to.

In any case, whether the letter was of major importance or not, he had to have more information. He hoped he might get some before the morning was over.

He was charged with anticipation as Gildo and Giovanni moved the gondola out of the Grand Canal into the Santa Croce district.

'Where are we going now, Urbino?' Betty asked, not unlike a child who wondered what new delight her parent had in store for her.

'I thought you might like to see an unusual art collection that few tourists manage to get to.'

'That sounds nice. Oh, look at that building, Frank! The roof. It has one of those terraces Urbino was talking about. It's all covered with snow. How absolutely lovely.'

While the Chins were preoccupied as they did their best to get a good view of the *altana*, Eugene leaned forward from his chair toward the *felze* and said, in a low voice, 'Do you want me to ask Miss Gaby today?'

Urbino had followed the contessa's suggestion and asked Eugene to bring up the topic of the blue rooms. Tomorrow was Apollonia's wake, when all the Pindars would be gathered together. Today might not be the best time to make this visit to the Palazzo Pindar but it was Urbino's only opportunity.

'Yes. Don't make it too obvious.'

'Oh, you can trust me for that!'

If Urbino had been worried that they might be imposing on Gaby because of the wake tomorrow, his worry would have immediately been dispelled by the reception she gave his little group.

Her long face adorned itself with a smile and her blue eyes glinted with pleasure.

'My, my,' she said, noticing the snow on their clothes. 'It's snowing outside.'

Her voice had a gentle, wistful note.

'I hope we're not keeping you in,' Betty said, her eye moving from Gaby's red cap down the length of her ocelot coat, then up again. 'It seems as if you're on your way out.'

'I'm neither coming nor going.' Gaby gave a strained laugh and pressed a slightly trembling hand against her throat. 'I'm here at your service.'

She collected their entrance fees, which she put into a pocket of the coat.

'Play your game, Miss Gaby,' Eugene urged her. 'The one with names. "Chin". What can you make of that one?'

'What is this about a game?' Betty asked, looking from Eugene to Gaby.

'This interestin' lady here can make new words out of a bunch of letters in any old word. She's very economical. Hardly wastes anything. "Chin," Miss Gaby. "C," "h," "i," "n." That's what you got to work with. Chin's a word *and* a name!'

'Eugene, you're embarrassing me. Only four letters and only one vowel. That does not give me much. But it is a — a lovely name.' She gave the Chins a quick smile. 'Let me see. There's "in" and "inch" and "hi". That seems to be the limit. I'm sorry.'

Her delivery had been far from as spirited as on other occasions.

'No need to be sorry about anything, Miss Gaby. I tell you what. Let's throw in "Betty".'

'To be honest, Eugene, I'm not in the mood for it now.'

'Why of course you're not, Miss Gaby! I wasn't thinkin' properly. How could you be in the mood? Not with your relative dyin' just the other day.'

'Oh, my.' Lines of concern crossed Betty's face. 'We are so sorry to hear of your loss.'

'Please accept our condolences,' Frank said.

'You are very kind. My aunt wasn't young, but it is still hard, especially on her son. My heart breaks for the boy.' Tears welled in her eyes. She gave a quick, almost imperceptible glance up the staircase. It was possible that Apollonia's body was already laid out upstairs, waiting for the wake. 'And we had another death in the house recently, my sister,' Gaby added, the tears now falling on her cheeks. Urbino wondered whether the tears had been hastened by the memory of Olimpia's death or whether they were still only for Alessandro and conveniently fell now as if for her sister.

'My, my!' Betty exclaimed softly. She gave Urbino an almost imperceptible frown as if she were displeased with him for having put her and her husband in an embarrassing situation. 'We can come back another day. Can't we, Frank?'

'Of course.'

'No, I insist.' Gaby wiped under each eye with the sleeve of her coat. 'Follow me. There are many things waiting for you to see them. They need to be admired, or else they will be dead, too. If you understand what I mean.'

'Yes,' Betty agreed hesitantly. 'I suppose I do.'

She and Frank followed Gaby, with Urbino and Eugene in the rear.

Gaby stopped before one item after another, giving detailed descriptions in a voice that became stronger as she spoke. Like a bazaar shopkeeper who notices his customers' glances of interest at specific articles among his wares, Gaby shifted her focus from one object to another, depending on whether Betty's or Frank's eyes strayed in its direction. She also extolled items that they ignored, for she could not bear to have any of her beloved children neglected.

The Chins lost some of their uneasiness and started to examine the items with close attention. Betty praised the Turkish tiles and a gilt settee whose seat and back were covered in needlework. Frank said their culinary teachers would find the old cooking utensils very interesting. They would tell them about the museum.

'You are so kind!' Gaby said. 'Word of mouth is the best form of advertisement. And we have no other kind for our treasures.'

Urbino joined Frank, who was now bent over a small display of shells and fossils. Frank was reading the card with the description of the objects. It was in English and Italian in a spidery handwriting. Urbino noted that it did not bear any resemblance to the handwriting on the letter. Urbino was thinking of some way to ask Gaby about the cards when Eugene did the job for him.

'Don't you think some spankin' new cards, maybe in bright colors, would help spruce things up here, Miss Gaby? Did you write these out?'

'Oh, no. It was my cousin, Alessandro. The one whose mother just died. He was kind enough to do it for me. He has such a fine hand, don't you think?'

'I reckon he does, but printin' would make it easier on the eye.'

Gaby brought the group over to the large portrait of her seventeenth-century ancestor, the severe-looking Creonte Pindar. It was apparent that the Chins did not warm to it, although Betty commented on his blue eyes and said they must run in the family. 'But yours are much warmer,' she added.

Eugene had a bored expression on his face, but he remained quiet until Gaby had come to the end of her description of Creonte's accomplishments.

'I tell you what, Miss Gaby. Why don't you show us the theater now? It's a fine piece.'

At first, the Chins showed only a polite interest in the carved wooden figures, looking at them from a distance. Eugene handed them the one of the contessa.

'I guess the crown means she's Italian royalty,' he said. 'Hope you get to meet her. There's not too much stuffy about her at all.'

The Chins' interest quickened when Eugene, under Gaby's sharp observation, picked up the one representing Urbino and handed it to Betty. The Chins looked back and forth with amusement between the figure and its flesh-and-blood version.

'He captured you quite well,' Frank said.

'My cousin Alessandro made all of them,' Gaby said. 'The same one who wrote the cards.'

'A very talented fellow,' Frank said.

'Thank you,' Gaby responded, as if Frank had paid her, not Alessandro, the compliment.

Betty was smiling. 'And you're wearing the same black cape! But you must have done that on purpose because you knew you were taking us here!'

'I hadn't thought of that at all.'

Betty was staring at the figure more closely now. She then gave Urbino's nose a quick glance.

'It's all so clever,' she said. 'The stage, the figures, the bouquet of white roses.'

Gaby took the Urbino figure from Betty and returned it to its place beside the contessa, both of them turned toward the stage where the other figures were lined up facing them. Patiently, Gaby took each of the small figures off the stage, one by one, and told them its name and its relationship to the other figures – and to her.

Urbino's eye ran over each of the figures: Ercule in his long white robe, with his round figure and exaggerated spectacles, Gaby in her small red cap and scarf, Eufrosina holding large ungloved hands palm outward, Apollonia all in black and holding purple rosary beads, Alessandro with his carving knife, and Olimpia in her cartoonishly rendered ocelot coat.

Urbino wondered how Olimpia had found out about the other carved image of her. Perhaps Alessandro had placed it in the theater at first instead of the one that was there now. Gaby, with her indulgence of Alessandro, probably would not have protested and might even have enjoyed her sister's humiliation until Olimpia had insisted it be removed.

'My dead sister, Olimpia,' Gaby was saying. 'My ocelot coat used to belong to her.'

'It looks like the coats the old movie stars used to wear,' Betty said. 'I've never seen anyone wearing one myself.'

'You're riskin' it if you do these days, as I told you, Miss Gaby, especially back home.'

'I only wear it in the house. But my mother and Olimpia always wore it outside and they never had any problem.'

'Your family has such interesting names,' Frank said. 'I believe there's a Greek influence somewhere?'

'Yes. Our family has Greek ancestors, and our family shipping company had a lot of business with Greece.'

'And Turkey,' came a man's voice from behind them.

Ercule had quietly come into the room. He was decked out in his kid leather slippers and two embroidered kaftans, a short-sleeved dark green one over a bright orange one. The Chins, who would have been forgiven if they thought they had gone to the other side of the looking glass since entering the Palazzo Pindar, stared at him.

Introductions were made.

'You look like someone out of *The Arabian Nights*,' Frank said.

'You haven't seen the whole costume,' Eugene said. 'The other time I saw him he had on a little white hat with earflaps, didn't you?'

The portly Ercule gave him a weak, strained smile.

Before the Chins might have had a chance to ask Ercule some questions about his outfit, Gaby led them over to the antique globe and started to praise its virtues. She pointed to all the places where the Pindar company used to have offices.

Eugene edged closer to Urbino and bent close to his ear. 'I'll do it now.' He straightened up and cleared his throat. 'You know, Miss Gaby,' he said in a loud voice that reverberated among the objects in the room. 'I couldn't help noticin' those two blue doors in the big room.' Eugene threw Urbino an altogether much too conspiratorial look. 'I'd like to take a gander at what's inside, if you don't mind.'

'The locked rooms?' Gaby said in a high uneven voice. She looked at Ercule.

'It can't do any harm, Gaby. Why not?'

'But there's nothing in the blue rooms that compares with the collection, Eugene.' Her reluctance to give them even visual access to the rooms couldn't have been more clear.

'The blue rooms?' Betty said.

'Yes,' Ercule said. 'The two rooms with blue doors across from the museum. Maybe you noticed them when you came in. When our relatives die, we put their clothes inside. It's a family tradition.' He stared pointedly at Gaby. A look of mulish withdrawal had come over her long, narrow face. 'I think Urbino would like to see what's inside, too.'

'Very well.' Gaby's face had set into a stern, disapproving expression. Obviously, her eagerness to show off the possessions of the family collection did not extend to the contents of the rooms. Did she feel it would be a violation of some kind? Was it a matter of care and protectiveness? Or something much more personal? It was only to be expected that Urbino briefly thought about Oriana's joke about Gaby hiding a dead body somewhere in the Palazzo Pindar.

Everyone followed Gaby across the vestibule. She walked and stood waiting at the doors until Ercule joined her. Their slow, quiet movements contributed to an air of ceremony. From her coat pocket, Gaby withdrew a metal ring with two large keys. She applied a key to the lock of each blue door, then nodded at Ercule. As Ercule started to pull open the first door, which gave a doleful groan, Urbino was seized with a brief, inexplicable flicker of fear that was just as intense as his fascination.

A sour, musty odor engulfed the group as soon as both doors were pulled open. It was composed of dead air, mold, and perspiration, overlaid by traces of perfume.

The interiors of the rooms were dim, their only illumination coming from the vestibule. All the clothing items crammed inside blocked the windows.

Piles upon piles of outer clothing crowded the first room, reaching within a few feet of the ceiling. The second room was like a slagheap of footgear, purses, neckwear, belts, hosiery, gloves, hats, head coverings, and other items that Urbino's eye either could not take in or easily identify.

Perhaps a principle of order and organization had reigned once upon a time, but it had long since been abandoned. It was as if all the Pindars from all the previous centuries had been forced to take off every last scrap of cherished garment in the cold vestibule for the waiting maws of the silent rooms. Urbino was able to make out, affixed to the walls, the edges of cupboards and the dull gleam of hooks, but they had long ago reached their limits, requiring that all future items of the dead had to be piled on top of each other.

Modern styles were, in most instances, in the front of the rooms, with older items behind and beneath them. But the pile gave evidence of having been disrupted, as if something had burrowed outward from within or dug into it from outside. And if the intention had been to preserve the objects by placing them in the dark secrecy of the rooms, it appeared, from the look of many of them, and from their accumulated offensive odor, that they were in the process of disintegrating.

The eye picked out a Renaissance girdle, all beribboned, on top of a broad-ribbed turtleneck sweater, a mate-less embroidered glove lying beside a balaclava, and high-platformed Venetian *chopines* keeping company with tennis shoes and high-button shoes. An embroidered lace bridal veil was snagged in the buttons of a waistcoat. The mouth of more than one purse was gaping.

The odor became stronger and more offensive as the moments passed, as if the rooms were taking a much too long delayed opportunity to exhale.

Betty took a step backward into the vestibule. It may have been only because of the odor, but Urbino sensed that it might also have been because of the disturbing associations generated by the sight, associations that were all too keen to him – not of people already dead but still living and stripped of their clothes before they went to another place to meet their death.

Ercule and Gaby seemed unaffected by the sight and the smell.

'Hardly any room left,' Gaby said. 'We still haven't put my sister Olimpia's things in.'

'Do – do you mean you put everything here?' Betty asked.

'Not everything!' Gaby shot her a twisted little smile. 'I didn't put this coat in, did I? And my aunt Apollonia – the one who died the other day – she hated the rooms. She made her son and daughter promise that none of her things would be put in them. They had to put them to use, give them to the poor, or burn them.'

Ercule had his arms folded across his chest. 'But we don't only put things into the rooms. Our sister Olimpia used to take things out. She had a professional interest. She was a dressmaker and when she died she was designing costumes for a play. I even think Alessandro took out some things, though I'm sure Apollonia never knew.'

Urbino remembered Alessandro's belted tweed coat that had given off a musty odor in the Chinese Salon. The coat was most likely one of the things that Alessandro had taken from the blue rooms.

The Chins were not able to take their eyes off the rooms. The odor had not yet dissipated.

'The rooms must have been a real treasure trove for her,' Urbino said.

He thought of the black broadcloth coat in eighteenth-century style, its collar detached, up in Olimpia's atelier. It must have been something she had raided from the blue rooms. He had not noticed any other old articles of clothing, but he had not given the atelier as thorough a search as he would have liked. And now that he knew that the blue rooms held not only clothes from the distant past but recent ones as well, he realized that some of the newer clothes that he had seen might very well have come from the blue rooms.

'Eufrosina might find it interesting to photograph some of these things,' Urbino added.

'Eufrosina? She hates the rooms. She calls them graveyards.'

The door to the embankment opened and Eufrosina, as if conjured up by their references to her, entered the vestibule with a whirl of snow. She looked very pale. Wisps of damp hair straggled from beneath her knit hat. Far from being dressed in mourning, she was wearing a bright red coat, although her leather gloves were black and looked like the ones Apollonia had been accustomed to wearing. She was carrying her satchel.

She came to a momentary halt as she saw the group standing in front of the blue rooms. It seemed to startle her to see the rooms open, but she regained her composure enough to give them all a cursory, collective greeting before going up the staircase.

'You see,' Gaby said in a low voice. 'She doesn't even like to look at the rooms. Like mother, like daughter.'

Fifteen minutes later, the snow was still coming down thickly when Urbino emerged from the Palazzo Pindar with Eugene and the Chins. It helped to dispel some of the gloom that the blue rooms had cast on him – and, as was quite evident to him, on the Chins. Only Eugene seemed unaffected.

Over his companions' protests, Urbino insisted that he was putting Gildo and Giovanni at their service for the next few hours.

'I have to see to some business matters. The gondola can be your floating sleigh. And you won't be out in the cold this time, Eugene.'

Before leaving them in the hands of the two gondoliers who were waiting with the gondola in front of the Palazzo Pindar, he arranged to see them when they returned in a few days from Parma and Bologna, where they were going on a restaurant tour sponsored by the cooking school.

Fifteen

After calling the contessa from the Palazzo Uccello and telling her about the blue rooms and the disturbing impression they had made on him and the others, he sat in the library, with a glass of sherry, and let his mind run freely and almost randomly over what he had learned about the Pindars and their relationships with each other during the past two weeks. Unlike any of his other cases, his investigation hadn't taken him far afield from the immediate circumstances of the murder, largely because of the strong gravitational pull of the family and his assumption that the murder had been a family affair. Although there were so many odd pieces to try to put together, almost each one was directly related to the Palazzo Pindar and the family.

He feared he might have been neglecting two pieces that had a tangential relationship to the Pindars.

One involved Nedda Bari, whose connections with the Pindars included both branches of the family living at the Palazzo Pindar and went back more than twenty-five years. The other was Evelina, who appeared to have had a particular friendship with Olimpia before Mina came on the scene and who was now part of Nedda's entourage. And Evelina's name began with 'E'.

After fifteen more minutes of pondering, Urbino was on his way to Nedda's house. The snow had completed its magical transformation of the city, softening sharp angles, accenting curves and arches, and providing a powdery frosting to the parapets of the bridges. A greater silence had fallen on the city. Urbino's boots squeaked in the snow, and he enjoyed the sharp pure sting of the air in his nostrils. He was brought back to his childhood visits to Vermont, when he used to wake up on snowy mornings and rush out into the yard, expecting the snow to have turned into sugar.

His reverie ended when he entered the Campiello Widman, where two costumed figures rushed over to him from the other side of the square and started to dance around him, gesturing in the air with their arms but without uttering a word. One was dressed in a voluminous black cloak, lace cape, three-cornered hat, and black oval mask. The other wore the costume of Columbine, with a white half-mask. They raced away toward the Grand Canal, sliding in the snow and being chased by a little boy blowing a squeaker.

Drifts of snow had collected under the *sottoportico* of Nedda's building, blown in from the canal side. The moored boats, covered with tarpaulins, seemed like soft waiting beds with clean white sheets.

Maria answered the bell. She hesitated when Urbino asked if Nedda was at home.

'Who is that, Maria?' came Nedda's voice from the front parlor.

'Signor Macintyre.'

'Show him in.'

Urbino took off his cape and did his best to stamp the snow from his boots before going into the parlor.

Nedda, who was sitting on her sofa, had a small glass of clear liquid in her hand. A half-empty bottle of anisette stood on the table in front of her. Nedda's large, attractive face was flushed and had a slack look.

The room, which had been a hub of activity on his previous visit, was silent and filled with shadows. The rest of the house was quiet.

'Sit down and have a drink.' Nedda's voice was slurred. 'Maria, bring another glass for Signor Macintyre.'

Maria complied and then left them alone.

Nedda poured anisette into Urbino's glass and more into her own.

'*Salute!*' She raised her glass and downed most of the anisette in one gulp. She gave him a quick look, in which there was a great deal of sharp awareness despite her inebriated state. 'Let's not play games. I am not the type for that. There is no need for either of us to pretend this time. You're investigating Olimpia's murder. I knew it the other day but I didn't say anything because of the others. You've come at a good time. We are alone now, and anisette always puts me in a truthful mood. I have nothing to hide.'

Urbino, who was always alerted and sceptical when anyone said this, took a sip of anisette.

'From what I read in the newspaper and what I heard,' Nedda went on, 'Mina Longo killed Olimpia.'

'Heard from whom? Ercule?'

'So you know? It must have been Natalia. But that was a long time ago. Yes, he told me how he saw Mina with the scissors and how she was screaming that she had killed Olimpia. It couldn't have been more obvious. Ercule and I bump into each other from time to time. No reason not to be civil. And he helped me rent Apollonia's building. It was good for him and good for me. He and his sisters got money from Apollonia for the apartment and I got this building. And I have no intention of leaving!'

'I'm sure something can be worked out with Alessandro and Eufrosina.'

'Let them try to get me out! They will see a different side to me, especially that Eufrosina. She's had it coming for a long time.'

'What do you mean?'

'I mean that I won't restrain myself any longer from slapping her face, and that's all I'm going to say about it!'

Nedda was making even less of an effort this afternoon to conceal her dislike for Eufrosina.

'Maybe Ercule will help you with Alessandro and Eufrosina,' Urbino suggested as a way of staying in the same general area of her relationship with Eufrosina.

'If it's to his financial benefit. Only money is going to get him his dreams. That was one reason why it never worked out between us. Even back then he had his wild dreams, and was always looking for money.' She drank down the remaining anisette in her glass. 'It would have been ridiculous, me and Ercule. What a mismatch! It was only my grief that brought us together for a while. He was Achille's brother, and he was devastated by his death. I'll say that for him.' Nedda's face clouded. 'But that was a long time ago.'

She poured herself more anisette.

'If you think the anisette is going to get me to talk about my relationship with Achille, you're wrong. That's a sacred topic. But you've also come about Evelina – Evelina Cardinale, right?'

There was no point in pretending otherwise. 'Yes. She was Olimpia's friend.'

'*More* than her friend. But it was all over a year ago.'

'How do you know her?'

'She's the daughter of one of the women I help. She started to ask for advice about her relationship with Olimpia. Olimpia was too possessive, she said. Evelina is an assistant at a veterinary clinic in Dorsoduro. Olimpia was always giving her money, telling her she should quit her job. I encouraged Evelina to break away. It wasn't that I had anything against Olimpia. I am a very accepting woman. I could not do the kind of work I do if I weren't. So I gave Evelina a place to stay. Olimpia had been paying for an apartment near the clinic. She's still living here. She's upstairs now. But don't think she had any animosity toward Olimpia. She wished her well.'

'Did helping her cause any problems between you and Olimpia?'

'It certainly did! But then Mina Longo came along. Olimpia became friendlier to me after that. We got together once in a while.'

Nedda's description of a reconciliation with Olimpia did not match what he had seen in front of the Palazzo Pindar.

'She seemed happier than she had been when she was with Evelina,' Nedda said. 'I guess everything –' She broke off. 'Can you believe I was going to say that everything worked out for the best in the end? But Longo ended up killing her.' She leaned back, not quite suppressing a sigh. 'The past. Change one thing in it and you change the future.'

The philosophy was very much on her mind these days.

She stood up, swaying slightly. 'Excuse me, but I think I'll go upstairs and lie down.'

Maria appeared from the hallway and steadied her with a firm hand under Nedda's elbow. From the way Maria did it, Urbino suspected it was something she often did for Nedda.

'If you want to speak with Evelina,' Nedda said, turning around, 'I'll see if she can come down. Neither of us has anything to hide.'

Ten minutes later, Evelina came down the staircase. On closer inspection, Urbino found that she was indeed pretty, as Rosa Custodi had said, in a delicate manner similar to Mina, with light brown eyes. But her pale face was drawn and her blond hair needed a careful application of a comb or a brush.

'Nedda said you'd like to talk with me.' Her voice was soft. She dropped her eyes before his gaze. 'About Olimpia.'

'Yes. I've been asking Signora Bari some things about her, too.'

'You don't think Mina Longo killed Olimpia, Nedda said.'

'No, I don't.'

'I don't want to believe it, but it seems to be true. To think of Olimpia being murdered by someone she cared about. It is too horrible.'

Her lips started to quiver. She went to the window and looked out at the *sottoportico* and the canal.

'I have only good things to say about Olimpia and Mina Longo,' she went on in a strained voice, her back turned to Urbino. 'They seemed to be good for each other, better than Olimpia and I were. I don't like to have any bad feelings toward anyone. I am glad Olimpia and I made peace between us before she was killed. And I'm glad I forgave her aunt Apollonia in my heart long before she died.'

'What do you mean about Apollonia Ballarin?'

Evelina turned around. She had a calm, composed expression on her face now.

'She cursed me sometimes when I was going up to Olimpia's workshop. Olimpia told me to ignore her. Her mind had been twisted by religion, she said. But I could tell it bothered Olimpia – bothered her for my sake and her own. She had to put up with a lot with Apollonia living in the same house. I am not religious, Signor Macintyre. But I believe in forgiveness. That's why I'm going to Apollonia's wake and funeral. Nedda and I will go together. And I forgive Mina Longo, too.'

Although Urbino believed in forgiveness, Evelina's quickness to reveal her forgiving spirit put him on his guard, as he had been earlier when Nedda had been so apparently open and honest with him.

'Did Olimpia ever mention the blue rooms?'

'The blue rooms?'

Urbino explained.

'Oh, those rooms. I asked her what was inside them once. She said they were storerooms for clothes and other things.'

'Were the rooms ever open when you went to see her?'

'No. Never.'

Urbino did not go directly back to the Palazzo Uccello, but he wandered through the snow-filled city to savor the rare atmosphere and to stimulate his thinking – or rather to try to sort out its various elements, for it was thick with theories and speculations.

In his abstracted state, he found his way to the Piazza San Marco, which was relatively empty. A few people stood in the white expanse as if they were in the middle of a country field, looking at the pigeons wheeling above them and pecking in the snow.

He turned into Florian's for a glass of wine. Like the other patrons, he sat at a table next to one of the windows to enjoy the scene outside. Soon, the municipality would be setting up the stage for *carnevale* across from the Basilica, and something far less serene than the snowfall would be transforming the city. But Urbino would be in America by then, escaping the madness. He was far from able to appreciate this thought since it only brought even closer to the surface the anxiety he felt over Mina and his imminent departure with Eugene.

After leaving Florian's, Urbino retraced some of his steps to the Fondamenta Nuove to stand on the bridge near the Church of the Gesuiti.

He looked across the dark gray waters of the lagoon to the cemetery island, whose brick walls and cypresses were cloaked with snow. Olimpia lay there, and soon Apollonia would – one the victim of the foulest of play, the other dead, it would seem, in the sad natural order of things.

Was it possible that a fatal connection existed between them – a connection other than the family one – that had led either directly or indirectly to Olimpia's murder? Something that had to do with the morally righteous Apollonia's animosity toward Olimpia and the forgiving Evelina – and, he assumed, toward Mina as well, who had taken Evelina's place?

He had begun his investigation into the mysteries of the Palazzo Pindar with the fear that Gaby might be about to become a victim for some unknown reason, but now she was squarely within the small company of suspects for her sister's murder. Her reluctance to open the blue rooms could mean there might be something in them that could connect her, through the past, with her sister's brutal murder.

Gaby's fears, Olimpia's murder, and now Apollonia's death. The sequence continued to intrigue him, and even more so because he could not be sure that the death of the eldest member of the Pindar clan had been natural. If it had been the result of foul play, so much of what he and the contessa had been considering – the results of all their poking and peering and peeping about – needed to be re-fashioned.

Pulling himself out of these thoughts, Urbino noticed that the waterbus was approaching the nearby dock. He hurried to catch it. He needed to get home as soon as possible now.

Back at the Palazzo Uccello, Urbino put on his smoking jacket of dull red brocade in which he had never smoked a single cigarette, cigar, or pipe. In the library, after pouring himself a snifter of brandy, he selected Smetana's *Moldau* and Shostakovich's *Symphony Number Five* and *Violin Concerto Number One* to listen to. They seldom failed to encourage his meditative moods.

He sat down at the long priory refectory table. Serena abandoned one of the maroon velvet seats of the mahogany confessional, and, after kneading for a minute, settled in his lap.

He drew a vertical line down the center of a blank sheet of paper, making two columns.

At the top of one column he wrote 'A' and at the top of the other 'E'. Beneath each letter he listed every relevant 'A' and 'E' in the case.

A	E
Achille	Efigenia
Apollonia	Ella (Gaby)
Alessandro	Ercule
	Eufrosina
	Evelina

Three in the group – Achille, Apollonia, and Efigenia – were family members who had died over the course of more than twenty-five years. Also on the list was someone who was outside the family but linked to it through Olimpia. This was Evelina, whom Urbino considered the wild card of the group. She brought with her Nedda, who, although not on the list, had to be considered as a player in the game, because of her relationships with Achille, Ercule, Apollonia and Olimpia.

He worked out various combinations of the two names, scribbling them on another piece of paper. He enjoyed playing with the combinations, seeing what he could come up with.

Sometimes the combinations were bizarre, even shocking. Other times his imagination ran away with him, but he let it run as far as it would go, even though he ended up with what seemed to be the most unlikely of scenarios.

Through it all, he assigned different values to his wild card Evelina, further complicating the picture. And he reminded himself that he needed to see beyond the initials, which risked misleading him by not encouraging him to look in other areas – for example, mainly Nedda Bari, but even Italo Bianchi.

There were so many unanswered questions – even, quite probably, unanswerable ones.

Had there been anything in Apollonia's life before her embrace of her '*vita nuova*' that might clarify her relationships with her two children and her Pindar relatives? Something that might connect her in some way with Olimpia's murder? Why had she left Alessandro the lion's share of her assets and possessions?

Was Gaby's admiration for Alessandro as transparent as it seemed? What had triggered her condition? Had it been the deaths of her parents and Achille? Had the death of one of them hit her harder than any of the others?

And what was behind Eufrosina's nervousness? Was it only something professional, because she feared the contessa would cancel the contract? Had there been some reason for removing the Fortuny items from their display cases other than, as she had told the contessa, the greater facility of photographing them?

How much had Evelina Cardinale's rejection wounded Olimpia? Had she got over it so easily? Had Nedda had an ulterior motive for facilitating their breakup?

What was at the heart of Apollonia's aversion to having any of her clothes deposited in the blue rooms? Why had Gaby abandoned using the name 'Ella'? Had her refusal to sell her share of the Palazzo Pindar played a role in her sister's death?

And what contribution might the blue rooms have made to Olimpia's murder?

Yes, so many puzzling questions – questions unanswered, questions unanswerable. And many of them he had been asking too long without reaching any even provisional answers.

During the past two weeks, Urbino had become dubious about some things that seemed perfectly normal and had been tempted to explain away the most unusual of eccentricities. Usually in his cases, he looked for peculiar, inexplicable behavior, but this time it seemed to be present almost everywhere among the Pindars. He had started to think that it was their normal behavior that might be the most suspicious – normal behavior that had nothing peculiar about it unless it was its normality.

Yes, it was a strange case, rich in ambiguities, and one that stimulated, provoked, and perplexed him from almost every angle. Everything looked so different if you just put one piece in the background or completely out of sight. It was as if he were tilting a kaleidoscope and finding new patterns in the chips of colored glass.

He read the letter over and over again, hoping he would see it in an altered light and that it would yield up some meaning he had missed on his other readings.

He did his best to gather the pieces, the names, the possibilities into some semblance of order, but more often than not, he came up with a jumble not unlike the ones in the two blue rooms.

And just as the Pindar family had discarded very few of their garments but had stuffed them into the two rooms, so was Urbino careful not to discard or ignore anything – even the smallest, most apparently inconsequential detail – that might prove to be useful to clothe his theories. He never lost sight of the possibility that Olimpia's murderer might be neither the 'A' nor the 'E' of the letter, but someone who had been set into deadly motion because of it.

Sometimes he felt as if he were trying to force a suspect into an ill-fitting garment or into one usually worn by the opposite sex.

And all the while he was doing this, echoing through his mind like a refrain were Nedda Bari's words: Change the past and you will change the future.

Except that Urbino tailored her words to fit his own search for the truth, posing the question, What in the past had brought about Olimpia's murder and was still affecting the residents of the Palazzo Pindar?

He paused to drink in the melodies of the third movement of Shostakovich's violin concerto, and then, after filling his snifter with more brandy, returned to work on his list, scratching out names and combinations, adding others, and all the while trying not to violate either the established facts or his strong impressions.

After a long process of judicious elimination, he ended up with one combination, one scenario, one train of events that he felt had most plausibly led to Olimpia's murder.

He went over it again. He could come up with nothing else that satisfied him, nothing else that gave him that pleasurable chill that signaled he had come upon the truth. It was the feeling he had had as a child, when he had picked up a piece in a complicated jigsaw puzzle, turned it around in his hands and examined it, and realized that it would not only fit a crucial part of the puzzle but would also make all the other pieces easier to put into place.

He sat at the table thinking, stroking Serena, and listening to the final movement of the concerto.

When the movement had rushed madly toward its conclusion, he got up, placed Serena back on the cushions of the confessional, and went to his study to get the copy of the letter.

Very carefully, with a pair of scissors, he cut it down to the dimensions of the original letter – which he was now certain had been found in one of the blue rooms – and then he did his best to give it a worn look.

He took out a wooden box in which he kept his photographs and looked through them for ones of Apollonia. He took out six. They were of Apollonia alone and with Eufrosina and Alessandro, with Gaby and Ercule, with Olimpia, and with the contessa. He put the doctored copy of the letter with them.

When he finished, he telephoned the contessa. He gave her the benefit of his thoughts, working it all out for her.

'It makes sense, *caro*. But are you sure that it makes more sense than any of the other possibilities?'

'I am.' He then told her what he planned for the next day.

'At Apollonia's wake?' The shocked note in her voice was sharp and clear.

'When it's a case of murder, I don't think we should consider what is appropriate or not. Only what is likely to get results. It's our opportunity. We can't miss it.'

After remaining silent for a few moments, the contessa said, 'I'll support you in whatever you do.'

'It's not only your support I'll need. There are a few things you can do – and *not* do.' He told her what these were in detail.

'Shouldn't the police be involved?'

'I'll ask them to have some men outside the Palazzo Pindar – if I can convince Gemelli it's worth his trouble. I'm going to contact him now.'

Sixteen

Urbino kept stealing glances at Apollonia's face against the white lace-covered pillow of the casket. It looked less stern in death than it had in life – that is, her more recent life, not her younger days of indulgence. Her dead lips had a slight smile.

Would she approve of what he was doing and what he hoped was about to happen?

The fact that he had such thoughts was a sign of his uneasiness. Although he had tried to brush off the contessa's misgivings last night, he was troubled that he planned to take advantage of Apollonia's wake to pursue – and hopefully to end – his investigation.

Apollonia's face was as unreadable in death as it had often been in her later days. But this did not prevent Urbino, any more than it has millions of others when confronted by a script, from interpreting it for his own convenience.

He read approval in it. He read the call for justice, stern and implacable.

Apollonia wore a simple black dress. Eufrosina had found it in the back of her mother's closet, enclosed in clear plastic, with a note that indicated she wanted to be buried in it. The dead woman's hands, ungloved for the first time in many years as far as Urbino could remember, clasped a worn Latin missal that had belonged to her mother. Her head was wrapped in a piece of black lace, as usual, but the covering looked new and fresh.

The wake was being held in the Pindar *grand portego*. The large space, with its high-backed chairs, broken chandelier, and flaking plaster, no longer had the somber air of neglect, of having long since passed the time of its utility. Quite the contrary. This evening it seemed to have come into its own.

Alessandro, after great thought and effort, and with the help of the funeral director, had organized a wake that he considered befitting a woman of his mother's reputation and interests as well as a wake that bore his particular, peculiar stamp.

He had engaged three of the funeral director's employees to admit mourners before they made even one indecorous push of the bell and to usher them up to the *portego*. A large armoire had been moved down from Apollonia's apartment and placed on the staircase outside the portego entrance for outer garments – although many of the mourners had preferred to keep them on because of the frigid temperature in the large room.

The casket, which stood at the far end in front of the windows, had been placed on a bier about four feet high that had been constructed for the purpose. Alessandro had spared no expense for his mother's last appearance before the world. The bier was draped in rich dull black satin. Through some inner arrangement of the casket which was concealed from even the most observant eye, Apollonia's body had been raised above the sides of the casket so that she could more easily be viewed in profile.

At either end of the casket, on high dark wood pedestals, were majolica turquoise urns that must have been pulled from some dark corner of the Palazzo Pindar. They were filled with lilies that rose above Apollonia's head and feet. A brass incense burner stood between the casket and the windows behind it, snaking the smoky scent of amber into the room. On either side of the incense burner, long candles in large silver candlesticks flickered their cold light on Apollonia's face. Rows of dark wood chairs, arranged in a gentle curve rather than a straight line, had been set up in front of the catafalque to accommodate the mourners.

Because the casket was raised high, the mourners who went up to the catafalque were almost on a level with Apollonia's face. Those sitting in the chairs had to look upward. A black curtain of the same material as the draping further reinforced the effect of Apollonia being on a stage. It was attached by golden rings to a wheeled frame of metal piping, painted black, which Alessandro had also had specially constructed for the occasion. The curtain had been pulled as far as it would go to one side, to give an unobstructed view of the deceased.

It was now close to ten o'clock in the evening. A small number of Apollonia's friends, most of them elderly women, had come earlier and left. Among them had been the two women from San Polo who had been Olimpia's customers. The seamstresses Teresa Sorbi and Rosa Custodi, more out of curiosity than respect, had made a brief appearance.

Oriana had put herself through the effort, despite her crutches, for old time's sake. She had been helped upstairs by the two employees of the funeral director and then down again an hour later.

Apollonia's confessor from the Church of San Giacomo dell'Orio, gaunt and white-haired, had led them in what had seemed to be interminable prayers. He had left, followed soon afterward by Dr Santo and the funeral director, who would be back in the morning with a funeral gondola to take Apollonia first to the church, then to San Michele for the burial.

At Alessandro's request, the mourners who had remained – Urbino, the contessa, Eufrosina, Gaby, Ercule, Bianchi, Nedda and Evelina – had retired to the first semi-circle of chairs in the middle of the room.

Alessandro sat beside his sister with Gaby and Ercule on his other side at one end of the row. Urbino and the contessa occupied the next two chairs. An empty chair stood between them and the next grouping of Nedda, Evelina, and Bianchi. The lawyer had been unusually silent since arriving, but his eyes had been taking in the scene and the other mourners with quick, bird-like movements.

Small tables had been placed among the chairs. On the tables were vases of white roses and framed photographs of Apollonia at different points in her life. They included childhood photographs of her playing in the sea on the Lido and eating a cone of gelato on the Zattere, a wedding photograph of her and her husband reclining in the twin seats of a gondola, and a recent one of her sitting stiffly on the sofa in her living room in the Palazzo Pindar.

Urbino and the others were passing the photos around, commenting on them, and exchanging reminiscences about the woman lying on display.

So far, everything was conspiring with Urbino's plan, even this sentimental touch of the photographs that he considered one of the more thoughtful of Alessandro's details.

Urbino reached for the wedding photograph again and gave the appearance of studying it more closely than he had before.

'I may be mistaken,' he said. 'But isn't her wedding veil the same one that's in one of the blue rooms? I saw it yesterday. It's very distinctive.'

'Absolutely not,' came Alessandro's quick reply. He tugged at his blond moustache. 'Mother never wanted anything of hers to be put in there and she never took anything out. I wouldn't violate her wishes, may God rest her soul.'

'And I wouldn't either,' Eufrosina made clear. 'None of mother's clothes will go anywhere near the blue rooms.'

'As the one in charge of everything,' Alessandro said, with a sharp glance at his sister, 'that is my responsibility. It's one of the promises I made to her the last time I saw her, just the two of us.'

Eufrosina glared at her brother. Dressed all in black but, like her mother, gloveless for the occasion, she looked weary, as if all her energy had been taken out of her. She was being forced to endure the wake and tomorrow's funeral with the knowledge of her mother's rejection. It could not be easy. Bianchi looked back and forth between Eufrosina and Alessandro, with a closed expression on his face.

Alessandro had been doing nothing to conceal an unmistakably superior air as the architect of the ceremonies and as his mother's champion in death as, apparently, he had been in life. Bianchi's revelations had obviously empowered Apollonia's son in ways that went beyond a huge bank account. Gaby was fawning over him, almost clinging to him at times. She had lost no opportunity to praise the arrangements he had made for Apollonia's wake.

'Most of mother's things,' Alessandro went on, 'will go to San Giacomo. They will be able to distribute them among the needy. Eufrosina is taking some of them and will use them in the way our mother wanted, won't you, Eufrosina?' It was not really a question and he did not wait for any response, but said, 'I assure you our mother will have nothing to do with the blue rooms in death anymore than she did in life.'

The contessa took this opportunity to say, 'Urbino was telling me about the rooms. I wish I could see them, since they represent so much of the history of the family. *Our* family. Oh, not now,' she added, as if someone had started to get up to bring her downstairs. 'I mean no disrespect,' she said to Alessandro and Eufrosina, lowering her head and her voice.

'There must be so many interesting things in the rooms,' she went on. 'And valuable ones – though I understand why dear Apollonia' – her eyes slid in the direction of the catafalque – 'felt about them the way she did. All those clothes that once saw so much life and light are buried there.'

Eufrosina nodded.

'They aren't buried,' Gaby said, with a petulant note in her voice. 'They're being preserved.'

'Of course they are,' the contessa agreed, steering a delicate course. 'And when something can be retrieved after it's been forgotten about for a long time, you could say that it's redeemed. It can have a new life.'

This philosophy did the double service of soothing Gaby and being in the spirit of the solemn occasion. Once again the contessa, this time joined by most of the little group, looked at the catafalque. There, the dead, pious Apollonia, who had already embarked on her journey to a new life, served as an excellent example of what the contessa had said.

'Olimpia once showed me some things she had retrieved from one of the blue rooms.' The contessa was addressing Gaby, but her gray eyes included the other members of the group. 'She said they belonged to her grandmother, her mother, and Achille.'

Urbino observed the other mourners as covertly as he could manage. The only one who showed any reaction was Nedda, who sat a bit straighter in her seat at the mention of Achille. When she had arrived, Urbino had noted a slight glaze in her eyes. And there was the unmistakable scent of anisette on her breath, too strong to have been left over from the previous evening.

'I always told Olimpia I didn't want her to go ripping the clothes up and sewing them into something else,' Gaby said with exasperation. 'They should stay the way they are.' She paused before adding, 'And where they are.'

'I don't know what she was doing with them.' The contessa's voice was soft and calming. 'Maybe she just used them for inspiration.'

'Inspiration, hah!' was Gaby's response. Contrary to what one might expect of a person who had recently expressed her fear of something terrible happening to her, Gaby seemed to be energized by the wake. She gave no sign – actually quite the opposite – that she was disturbed by this inescapable evidence that death not only comes to us all but also can come directly into the house she was burying herself in. It had come to Apollonia. It had come to Olimpia. And neither had had to leave the house to find it.

'Whatever Olimpia did, Gaby, I'm sure she did it with good intentions,' the contessa said.

'Apollonia had the right spirit about her things.' Urbino threw in. 'The way she wanted either the family to use them or have them donated to the needy.'

'She also said that what was left over should be burned,' Ercule pointed out, although Urbino sensed that his comment was not so much directed at him as at Alessandro. Ercule looked at his cousin, opening his blue eyes wide behind his spectacles.

Dressed in a simple dark gray suit and a plain maroon tie, Ercule appeared to be more in costume than he did when he was wearing his Turkish outfits, and he seemed to have lost a vital part of his identity.

'Burning has always been a form of purification among many religions,' Urbino observed.

'For the sinful,' Alessandro said. 'My mother wasn't sinful.'

Alessandro's defense of his mother could not help but start a brief train of thought in Urbino – and possibly in others present – about Apollonia's more profane life before her sacred conversion. Had she distributed the clothes from that epoch among the poor or had she burned them, assuming that she had indeed mentioned the virtues of consumption by fire to Ercule?

'Of course she wasn't sinful, Sandro dear.' Gaby reached out to pat his hand. But this was not enough for her to show her concern. She also leaned over and pressed her lips to his cheek. Alessandro, screwing up his face like a child receiving an unwelcome kiss, seemed to endure her attention more than find consolation in it.

'I wasn't suggesting that she was,' Urbino said. 'Your mother was a model to us all. And she would be proud of you, Alessandro. And you, too, Eufrosina. You've planned her departure from her earthly life with a great deal of love and thought.'

Eufrosina cast down her eyes at the praise, assuming a humble expression. Alessandro rearranged some of the photographs on the table beside him, smiled, and nodded.

The group fell into a long, dead silence during which a slight creak seemed to sound from the direction of the catafalque, as if the casket were settling its weight more firmly.

Nedda broke the silence. 'Achille had some lovely clothes.' Each word of this apparent non sequitur sounded as if she were forcing it out of her.

Her comment, which was a most fortuitous one from the point of view of Urbino and the contessa, did not encourage anyone to speak.

Once again Urbino watched the other mourners. Eufrosina shifted uneasily in her seat. A reminiscent expression came over Gaby's face. Ercule frowned. Evelina stared nervously at her friend. Alessandro was staring in the direction of the catafalque, his good-looking face stony. Bianchi wore a puzzled expression, which might have been because he was finding it a little difficult to follow what was being said, since everyone was speaking English.

'He had a beautiful sweater. A lovely blue.' Nedda glanced at Evelina, who continued to stare at her and seemed to want to say something. Her lips moved silently.

'Blue like the blue doors?' Ercule, whose moon-shaped face had become flushed, loosened his tie and opened the top button of his shirt, despite the chill in the room. Alessandro noticed it and glowered at him. Ercule redid the button and tightened his tie even more snugly than before.

'No,' Nedda said. 'It was like the blue of his eyes. You remember how blue his eyes were, don't you, Ercule?'

Ercule must have been thinking of something else, because he didn't seem to hear Nedda's question. Then after a few moments, the question must have registered. 'Of course I do,' he said. 'He – he was my brother. Blue eyes run in the family. I have them and so does Gaby. So did Olimpia.'

And so did Alessandro and Eufrosina, he might have added.

Nedda lifted her chin and said with quiet firmness, 'Not the same blue as his were. No, not the same. None of you. His were a very special shade of blue. I can see his eyes now as if they were right in front of me.' Her voice now sounded far away.

Evelina was looking at Nedda with increasing concern. She bent close to her and whispered something that Urbino could not hear.

'How interesting, Nedda,' the contessa said. She had been avoiding Urbino's eyes throughout the exchange and only now brushed him with a glance. 'One of Achille's things that Olimpia showed me was a blue sweater. It must have been the one you remember. A lovely blue, as you said. It's amazing, isn't it, the way we can forget so much of our life but how some things – even small ones – are so vivid after many years?' She even managed a convincing sigh as if she were contemplating some of the unforgettable little details and moments of her own rich life.

Urbino had told the contessa last night that her improvisational skills would be called upon for the wake, and she was showing how good she was at them.

Eufrosina was becoming visibly agitated. It seemed that she wanted to get up and leave the small group, but she remained in her seat. Her brother had also been undergoing a change in his manner since Nedda had started to speak. His face had fallen into an expression of disapproval. Gaby took his hand again and started to chafe it between hers as if she needed to warm him. And Apollonia's son did look in need of warming, for his whole manner had become icy. He withdrew his hand forcibly.

'Do you remember the blue sweater, Eufrosina?' A flicker of a smile passed over Nedda's face. 'He got it right before he drowned.'

'Why should I remember it? I hardly ever saw Achille, and I didn't live in the house back then.' Eufrosina's fists tightened in her lap. She gave Nedda a black look. 'What's this blue, blue, blue? Blue doors, blue rooms, blue eyes, blue sweaters! We are here to pay respects to my mother, our mother. Aren't we, Alessandro?'

She turned toward her brother. But Alessandro, wrapped in a cold cloak of disdain and disapproval of everything, including his own sister, ignored her appeal to what they had in common.

'You must think I'm stupid, Eufrosina,' Nedda said. 'I'm not. And I never have been.'

'You're drunk. Drunk at my mother's wake! Disgraceful, isn't it, Alessandro?'

But her brother continued to ignore her. He looked morose, un-approachable.

'I've always respected your mother,' Nedda said quietly. 'Always tried to protect her.'

'My mother didn't need your protection.' Alessandro said in a low voice, breathing heavily. 'I was there for that.' He stood up and strode across the room to the catafalque, trying to put as much command into his small figure as he could manage. He drew the black drapery across the front of the catafalque, obscuring Apollonia's stern profile from view. He stood in front of the drawn curtain for a few moments, his arms folded across his chest. He then rejoined the small group, but this time he took the empty chair between the contessa and Nedda, managing to keep more distance between himself and his sister and Gaby.

The contessa began a series of reminiscences about Apollonia, which gave the appearance of returning the wake to its proper spirit. Alessandro started to warm slightly and contributed to the anecdotes, but he didn't draw the curtain away from the catafalque. Urbino shared a pleasant memory of when he and Apollonia had enjoyed a bowl of traditional mulberries together on the Giudecca during the Feast of the Redeemer seven years ago.

Ercule threw himself into the spirit of things and confided how Apollonia had given him old photographs of Istanbul that she had found among her mother's possessions. 'Old black and white photographs. Lovely. It was very kind and generous of her. Have you ever seen them, Eufrosina? I'd like your professional opinion, although even if you say they're not good, I'll still cherish them.'

Eufrosina had withdrawn into herself. She stared at the drawn curtain, her eyes hardly blinking. Nedda was glowering at her.

'Have you seen them, Eufrosina?' Ercule prompted.

'No, I haven't.' Her voice was little more than a hoarse whisper.

This was the opportunity Urbino was looking for.

'Speaking of photographs,' he began, 'I have some of Apollonia. They're ones of her with the two of you.' He looked at Alessandro and Eufrosina in turn. 'And some of her with Gaby, Ercule, Olimpia, and Barbara. I brought them with me. I like what you did with the photographs of her, Alessandro. It's a very thoughtful touch. You can have mine. Maybe you can make copies of them, Eufrosina, and give the copies to me. The two of you can keep the originals.' Urbino got up. 'Let me get them before I forget.'

He went to the armoire out on the staircase landing. From his overcoat pocket, he took the photographs and the copy of the 'A' and 'E' letter, as he had come to think of it.

The focus of everyone's attention was now on the photographs in his hand.

As he handed them to Alessandro, he made sure that the copy of the letter, unfolded, which was underneath the photographs, fluttered to the floor. It settled face up. It was as if the laws of chance were eager to cooperate with Urbino and conspire against the murderer.

Urbino let it lie on the floor.

'What's that?' Alessandro asked. He got up and retrieved it. As he started to read what was written on it, his jaw clenched and his eyes slightly narrowed.

'I must have picked it up with the photographs back home. I had a lot of things on my desk.' Urbino took the letter from Alessandro's somewhat unwilling fingers and held it so that it remained in clear view. He gave the appearance of waiting for Alessandro to look through the photographs, but all the while he was paying covert attention to the others, especially one of the others.

Eufrosina's long fingers were curling and uncurling themselves. She rose and approached Urbino, who now was making a show of folding the letter. As he was about to slip it into the pocket of his suit jacket, she said sharply, 'May I see that?'

Urbino handed her the letter. Eufrosina's eyes were glittering and she was passing her tongue repeatedly over her dry lips.

Eufrosina unfolded it slowly, as if she were afraid of what she might find written inside. She became pale. She looked back and forth between the letter and Urbino. She examined the letter more closely.

'But — but this isn't the original,' she said, with an odd inflection. 'I don't understand.'

Bianchi, who was making up for having been so talkative with the contessa about Apollonia's affairs, continued to keep his silence, but he had a look of professional interest on his face as he looked in the direction of the letter in Eufrosina's hand.

Gaby came up behind Eufrosina and snatched the letter from her hands. 'What is this about?' Her eye ran down the page. She blinked with bafflement.

Alessandro was sitting quite motionless but the hand that held the photographs was trembling slightly. Eufrosina's eyes were filled with confusion and anger.

'It's something Olimpia gave me to look at a few weeks before her death,' Urbino said to Gaby. 'I never had a chance to return it to her before she was murdered. I suppose it belongs to you and Ercule now.'

Ercule, who during the past few moments had been changing color like a chameleon, went over to Gaby and squinted at the letter. She held it tightly in her hands, as if determined not to relinquish it. Evelina, who had looked startled when Urbino mentioned Olimpia's name, grabbed Nedda's hand in hers.

'It's a kind of love letter.' Gaby spoke in a flat, inflectionless voice.

Evelina, Urbino's wild card, jolted upright. 'A love letter? Olimpia gave it to you?'

'She gave it to me to read. She didn't write it to me. In fact, she didn't write the letter, but she wanted me to know what's in it. She said it came from one of the blue rooms.'

Alessandro, with a puzzled expression on his face, jerked to his feet. The photographs scattered on the floor.

'She gave *you* the letter? What else did she give you?' Gaby was now close to shouting. 'And she gave *you* the ocelot coat!' she threw out at the startled contessa. 'Did she forget she had a sister?'

Gaby, still holding the letter, dropped into her chair.

'Where's the original?' The face Eufrosina turned to Urbino was dead white.

'I gave it to the police. It's evidence, you see.'

Evelina stood up, took a quick step forward, and then came to a halt. 'Evidence of what?' Her voice was harsh and unsteady.

'Of the person who murdered Olimpia.'

Gaby gave a scream and dropped the sheet of paper on the floor as if it were on fire.

Eufrosina swooped down and grabbed the sheet of paper. She ripped it into pieces and let the scraps flutter to the floor. Sharp notes of laughter burst from her lips. Then, as if with a pair of scissors, she cut the laughter off abruptly. She muttered something indistinguishable, and then in the clearest of voices and the most even of tones, she said, 'The police know?'

'They know everything,' Urbino said, stretching the truth for the occasion.

Eufrosina reached one hand to her throat in a pathetically expressive gesture. It was unfortunate that she – or someone else – could not capture it with a camera.

A shudder ran through her body.

She dropped to the floor as if felled by a physical blow.

Epilogue
Sewing Things Up

Urbino stared out into the Piazza San Marco from the windows of Florian's. The scene was far different than it had been three weeks before, when he and the contessa had watched the snow come down on an almost deserted square and waited for Eufrosina to join them.

People sauntered and promenaded across the large open space, which had lost most of its blanket of snow. *Carnevale's* days of indulgence would not officially begin for a week, but revelers were stealing an early start on the moveable feast. They posed in costumes for photographers, sat on the edges of the temporary stage with beer and wine, and danced to the music of the Florian orchestra. Merchants walked through the crowd selling confetti, horns, masks, and hats. A snowfight had erupted among a group of children that claimed a young Japanese woman as one of its unintentional victims, but she just laughed and brushed herself off. A large chandelier was suspended above all this activity, waiting to be illuminated on the last evening of the festivities when the square would become transformed into a large, open-air ballroom.

Urbino focused his gaze on a still point in all the swirl of activity. This was a stout — and recently much stouter — snowman, with a pigeon perched on its head, which had been visibly disappearing as Urbino sat with the contessa in the Chinese Salon.

It was two days after Apollonia's funeral at the Church of San Giacomo dell' Orio and her burial on San Michele. The weather had remained bitter cold until this morning and now, in late afternoon, a persistent drizzle was falling on the city. All the beautiful transformation of the city was being washed away, but the rain had not put a damper on the spirits of the people in the square and under the arcades.

'Nothing lasts forever.' The contessa, who had been looking at the melting snowman, echoed Urbino's thoughts as she so often seemed to do. 'Neither the good nor the bad. I suppose it all balances out in the end.'

'That's the most comforting way to look at it.'

Two figures, carrying blood-red umbrellas, were prancing around the snowman. One was dressed in a parti-colored Harlequin costume and wore a white cap. His face was covered with a black half-mask with demonic features. His companion, whose face was concealed in a black feathered mask, was someone in an old-fashioned black nun's habit, complete with a wimple. A red devil's tail peaked out from the rear of the black robe. They joined hands with a couple dressed in baroque costumes, and started to dance around the melting snowman. When they stopped, the nun bent over and kissed the snowman. The watching crowd whistled and clapped.

All the tables in the Chinese Salon were busy. The room was filled with laughter and animated conversation, and wafting through the air were the aromas of coffee and of the mint, cocoa, and cherry in the small Rosolio glasses. A couple in black capes, lacy white shirts, black pants, white stockings, and high-heeled shoes occupied one table. A black *bautta* mask partly concealed the man's face, and the woman held a gold and jeweled demi-mask on a stick.

The contessa reached down to pet Zouzou. She lay asleep on the floor by the contessa's divan, with a pink-and-red-striped blanket beneath her and a small porcelain dish of water beside her.

'This will be the last time I come anywhere near the Piazza – or even leave the house, who knows? – until Ash Wednesday,' the contessa said. 'You're fortunate you're escaping it this year.' She had already anticipated the end of carnival in her choice of today's deep purple dress of simple lines, which she always wore on Ash Wednesday. Her honey-blond hair, pulled back from her face and held by a black comb that matched her onyx necklace, was in the style habitually reserved for the solemn day. 'And by then Mina will be back.'

Mina, whose release from the Giudecca had been delayed, would be returning to the Ca' da Capo-Zendrini after a visit to her family in Palermo. So far, she had been sticking to her resolution not to accept any of Olimpia's legacy except for a few personal items she would choose when she had the opportunity. She intended to turn over everything else in equal portions to Gaby and Ercule.

The contessa looked at Urbino affectionately. 'Well, you've done it again, *caro*. Order out of confusion. And in record time. You can go to America with an easy mind.'

'*We've* done it, Nora. We're a team.'

The contessa's responsive smile was touched with sadness, almost regret. 'Yes, we've helped bring Eufrosina to justice. But she's my cousin. I feel disloyal – silly and irrational as it might sound.'

Eufrosina had confessed to the police and given them the dress she had been wearing at the time of the murder, stained with Olimpia's blood. The strange hoarding instinct of the Pindars – or a perverse desire to be exposed – had prevented her from destroying it. At the wake, she had collapsed from within, after being brought to the edge by the connivance of Urbino and the contessa – and by Nedda's fortuitous but unwitting contributions. Urbino hoped they would soon have a copy of her confession to fill in some of the holes.

Urbino looked out into the arcade where photographers, much more assured in their activity than Eufrosina had ever seemed to be, were carefully posing masqueraders against the columns. Urbino wondered whether, if Eufrosina were assured in all aspects of her life, she would have escaped detection. After all, there had been only one physical piece of evidence against her – the bloody dress – and it had been something she had revealed herself. Urbino hadn't come upon it.

He had made some broad leaps across empty spaces in reaching the conclusion that Eufrosina had murdered Olimpia. It was not one big thing that had led to his exposure of her at Apollonia's wake, but a series of little pieces. Among them had been Nedda Bari's animosity toward her and the hemorrhaging of her funds, which Apollonia had attributed to extravagance but which had been the result of blackmail payments. Her fear of her mother was another important piece, as was Oriana's opinion that she had never loved her husband and that some other man had claimed her heart. And the contessa had commented on Eufrosina's emotional closeness to Achille, although she could never have imagined how close she had actually been. Even the fact that Eufrosina wore gloves all the time and that no identifiable fingerprints but Mina's had been found on the scissors had made its contribution.

As Urbino had felt when he had assembled jigsaw puzzles as a child, each easily neglected and even trivial piece had significance as long as you did not also lose sight of the much larger picture.

The contessa had a troubled look on her face. She must still be contemplating the sad and unavoidable costs of their having freed her loyal Mina.

'But Olimpia was your cousin, too, don't forget,' Urbino emphasized. 'You have loyalty to her and her memory. For your own sake and Mina's. Mina loved her. And speaking of Mina, if you hadn't been what you call disloyal to Eufrosina, Mina would still be in prison,' he said, finding it necessary to reinforce the obvious.

'But it's all taken its toll on us, hasn't it? You're looking a little weary.' Her gray eyes played softly on his face. 'Things are so mixed up in my head – or is it my heart? When I console myself that justice has been done, I see Eufrosina's face in front of me. And then when I think of poor dead Olimpia, I remember that she was a blackmailer, after all. I can all too easily imagine her taunting Eufrosina with the letter. But then I even get upset at Apollonia for having become so hardhearted and inflexible in her later years. If she had been more understanding and forgiving, Olimpia would never have been able to blackmail Eufrosina. If she hadn't been so afraid of her mother, none of this would have happened.'

'But not just afraid of her disapproval, Barbara. She was afraid of being cut out of her will.'

'As she was anyway. Do you think Apollonia knew about Eufrosina and Achille?'

'No. She would have confronted Eufrosina. It was a case of one child getting the greater influence over a parent. Alessandro wanted almost everything and now he has it. But he didn't have to make too much of an effort to turn Apollonia against Eufrosina. She seems to have kept asking her mother for money, to pay off Olimpia and to liquidate her debts. A woman like Apollonia couldn't easily abide the idea of Eufrosina throwing away her carefully conserved money, though I suspect much of it is going to slip through Alessandro's fingers quickly. He should be able to carve a whole army of figures and not have to worry about financing himself. He has some talent, I will grant him that. Who knows? He might open a shop.'

'What about Nedda Bari? She seems to have known about the affair.'

'Known or strongly suspected. She was suspicious about the blue sweater, though she doesn't seem to have known for sure that Eufrosina gave it to Achille. But she kept whatever knowledge she had to herself. She wanted to protect Apollonia, she said, and I am assuming she meant protect her from the knowledge of Eufrosina's affair with her own first cousin, someone you said was almost like a brother to her. Can you imagine Apollonia's reaction? You're shocked enough yourself, and so am I. Remember that Apollonia didn't even approve of widows remarrying. Small wonder that letter gave Olimpia so much power over Eufrosina once she figured it out.'

The contessa selected one of the petits fours on the plate.

'Eufrosina was desperate to find the letter once she had killed Olimpia. It linked her not only with Achille but also with Olimpia's murder. She had plenty of opportunities to look for it in the atelier and Olimpia's rooms in the weeks after the murder. It was obvious that someone had gone through her desk and other things.'

'And the exhibition,' the contessa exclaimed. 'She took Olimpia's purse out of the display case. She thought Olimpia might have put the letter in it.'

'And she removed the other things for cover. I thought it was suspicious when you told me about her unannounced visit to the exhibition. But she should have realized Olimpia wouldn't have put the letter in the purse. You or someone else might have found it.' Urbino took a sip of his sherry and glanced into the Piazza, where all the noise and activity struck him as some kind of ritual for the rapidly vanishing snowman. 'Do you have any idea whether Eufrosina ever went up to Mina's room, looking for the letter?'

'Surely someone would have seen her and mentioned it to me, but I suppose it's possible.' The contessa shook her head slowly. 'Can it really be only three short weeks ago that Eufrosina met us here? Three *long* weeks, I should say. I don't know which they are. Back then we were concerned with Gaby. Little did we realize…' Her voice trailed off.

'All Gaby's fears seemed to be about things outside the house, pre-cipitated by the deaths of her parents and Achille. But who knows? She might have sensed that something was wrong in the house. Many people who live alone or isolate themselves become sensitive to every little thing around them. It was visibly painful to her to have us all gaping inside the blue rooms. Probably Olimpia was afraid that if we took Gaby seriously, we might find out about the blackmail.'

'Which you – *we* – did.'

'But only after she had been murdered because of it.'

'What was it that Gaby said? "There's sin in Eufrosina"? You don't think *she* knew, do you?'

'No. If she had, she would not have just played around with it that way. She would have been more direct with me. She wouldn't have wanted her sister's murderer to go free.'

'What do you think will happen to her and Ercule now?'

'Some good things.'

The contessa's gray eyes widened with surprise. It was not what she had expected him to say.

'Yes,' Urbino emphasized. 'Eugene told me something this morning that's going to make a big change in their lives.'

A smile of pleasant expectation curved the contessa's mouth. Urbino explained how Eugene had done some thinking about the Palazzo Pindar when he had been away from Venice with the Chins. Yesterday, on his own and without consulting Urbino, he had gone to the Palazzo Pindar and spoken with Gaby and Ercule. He had told them he would like to buy the Pindar collection but that the collection would be kept in the building. Nothing would change, he said, and Gaby would be the curator for as long as she wanted.

'The only conditions are that they put up a plaque mentioning the Hennepin name and install a top-of-the-line security system. He'll pay for it. He took to Gaby. When he heard about what happened at the wake, he became determined to help her. He's offered them a lot of money. He's proud of coming up with the idea, and he has every reason to be.'

'That's absolutely wonderful, *caro*! Are they accepting?'

'It seems they are. They would be foolish not to. They get a great deal and lose nothing. And Gaby seems to have great trust in Eugene. It may be because he seemed to come from nowhere, from outside the house, and is helping solve their money problems. He may even be able to get her to agree to see a professional, who would come to the house. I'm hoping she's going to start healing, not despite what the family has just gone through, but somehow because of it. We'll urge her on our part.'

The contessa nodded.

'Eugene will set as many things in motion as he can before we leave. He's an astute businessman. He says he'll return later, maybe when I come back, so that everything can be firmed up. Bianchi is drawing up the documents. Gaby keeps the collection and her relationship to it. They both keep the house. And Ercule will have enough money from his half to go to Istanbul for a long time.'

'And the building stays in the family. But Gaby will be alone once Ercule leaves.'

'Not necessarily. Alessandro might end up staying and have Nedda continue to rent his building. Or, if he decides to move back in himself, maybe Gaby and Ercule could rent out Olimpia's atelier and the floor below it to Nedda.'

'If Nedda thinks it would be suitable for her.'

'It could work out well for everyone concerned. And it would be good for Gaby. She would have an almost constant stream of people passing through the house. When you think of it, it could all make for a good mix in the Palazzo Pindar. It would help keep up its reputation for eccentricity – a long history of it. And eccentricity – true eccentricity – is an endangered species these days.'

'It isn't hard to see why *you* would come out in defense of it.'

When Urbino could not dispute the truth of something, he remained silent, as he did now, enduring the contessa's gentle, ironic smile.

'And what about the blue rooms?' she asked. 'Do you think Ercule and Gaby will clear them out?'

Urbino thought a few moments before responding. 'I doubt it, Barbara. Neither of them is up to that. And to be honest, I believe that some doors should remain closed – even locked forever.'

'Why does that not surprise me?' The smile returned to the contessa's face. She held his gaze until he looked away.

The contessa sipped her tea.

'This case of ours, Nick, has been too much about the past. Let's think of the future. My Fortuny exhibition and your Fortuny book. The successful conclusion of your business back in America. And a happier future for my remaining Pindar relatives.'

'To the future, Nora.' Urbino raised his sherry glass. 'And long live eccentricity!'

Zouzou chose this moment to awaken. She gave a quiet little bark that sounded like one of agreement.